Joe Swift was born to play football.

And Hunter Davies, author of *The Glory Game*, was born to write about him.

Striker is the story of one footballer, but it could be the tale of any football-daft lad who rises to the top in the greatest sport in the world.

From wasteground kickabouts to the madness of Italian super-stardom, Joe Swift sees it all: the brutal attentions of the less talented on the pitch; the erotic attentions of the women for whom a famous footballer is the ultimate sex-symbol; the rapacity of the smooth operators in sheepskin car-coats for whom a supremely talented player is just another cash cow. Joe's career is a frantic rollercoaster, culminating in a hazard of Italian football that not even Gazza will have contemplated.

Like the great matches, *Striker* is full of excitement, humour and gritty reality. It is the ultimate football novel. And not a sick parrot to be seen anywhere . . .

STRIKER

HUNTER DAVIES STRIKER

BLOOMSBURY

First published 1992

Copyright © 1992 by Hunter Davies

The moral right of the author has been asserted

Bloomsbury Publishing Ltd, 2 Soho Square, London W1V 5DE

A CIP catalogue record for this book is
available from the British Library

ISBN 0 7475 1225 6

10 9 8 7 6 5 4 3 2 1

Typeset by Hewer Text Composition Services, Edinburgh
Printed in Great Britain by Clay, St. Ives plc, Bungay, Suffolk

Prologue

"I can write only from memory. I never write directly from life. The subject must pass through the sieve of my memory, so that alone what is important or typical remains as on a filter" – CHEKHOV

They're my memories, so I'm going to tell my story. Why should I let some other bugger do it? For the last thirteen years people have been trying to, ever since that twat in the *Cumberland News* did that interview when I was fourteen and I'd just got into the North of England Under-Fifteens and he quoted me as saying my ambition was to play at Wembley, meet Miss World, eat a hundred Mars Bars and buy a house for me Mam and Dad. What a load of cobblers. I'd never even met him.

It all came true. More or less. Let's see now. I must have eaten a hundred Miss Worlds or similar for breakfast, bought and sold several sweetshops, and my Dad's back garden is now bigger than Wembley. But that's not the point. He put words into my mouth, that reporter bloke, shoved thoughts into my head. At the age of fourteen my mind was vacant and I was in a trance, living only for the next game, any game, twelve-a-side in the playground or one-a-side against myself.

If I had to meet the kid I once was, walk into a time machine and be told that's him, don't you recognize him, I'd have to say no chance, that's not me, that's nothing to do with me. I look at the school photos and see a little fat shit in the front holding the ball, daring anyone

1

to take it away from him. I can remember the boots, remember my Mum putting water on my hair to make it lie down, but the person underneath the hair and inside the boots is a total stranger.

So if I can't imagine me then, and I was there, why should I wait and let some piss-artist in a flash suit who was never there tell my story? I know what would happen. He'll follow me around for three days, staggering from wine bar to wine bar, dragging behind him some tart he says is his personal assistant, till she gets down a few hours on tape, then he makes up the rest. No, that was yesterday. Got you there. I don't associate with those sort of tabloid ponces today.

I now get a different sort of creep, don't you know. The heavy press send out a poseur fresh from college, still wet behind the goolies, in horrible jeans and a sweaty t-shirt, his hands all inky with flogging the fanzine he still runs, who just loves football and has conned some half witted editor into giving him the money to do an in-depth socio-economic study of a modern hero, just to prove all the crappy theories he's already got wrapped up in his inky, stinky, long leggy, dandelion-feeted, spotty head.

They all think they know, the ponces and the poseurs, but they don't. They can't crawl out of their own skulls, far less put a foot on the park. I may not remember everything, may not recall all the feelings, but bloody hell, I was there, I used to be me. I was once that fat kid in the school photo, who grew into that flash git on all those thousands of back pages. I'm bound to have a better chance of getting near me than a jack the lad reptile or an intellectual boy wanker. Who was it did the Live Aid thingy? Geldof. I read that he didn't like the way some bloke was doing his life story, so he did it himself. That's what I'm going to do. I'm letting Tom have twenty grand, poor sod, he needs it, and he is my mate, just for the privilege of not writing about me. Last year, he was going to do it, anonymously of course, and I was getting a hundred grand for pretending I'd written it, but I've realised that's how it would turn out: anonymously. Just like all the others.

I can't remember how many bloody books there's been about me. Even my lawyer has written one. They've come out every year for the last five years. Life stories, picture books, instructional books, plus the videos, the tapes and those shitty songs I'm supposed to have written myself. All phoney. All pathetic.

2

I have the time at the moment, stuck in here, as you know, if you read the tabloids. And if you read the tabloids, then you're pathetic. Like me. Never miss them. I hate those poncy papers like the *Guardian*, shoving in the tits in their health pages, or the bare bums on the arts pages. Give me straight up and down sex. But not much point at the moment, thanks. I'm resting, if you can call it rest, in this place.

It was Fanny who first suggested I should do it myself, last time I was home. What do you think I have all those Miss Worlds for, I said. That's why I keep them on hand. Gerrit.

That's it, she said. You can't be serious for long, can you, without making some stupid, vulgar, sexist, loudmouth remark. So write it that way, showing yourself as you are, then everyone who really knows you will really know it's you. Hmm, I said, sounds like a lot of hard work. What else have you got to do, she said. Cheeky bitch.

Look, just write what you can remember, the scenes and incidents that stand out in your mind. That's what Chekhov did. Who's he play for, I said.

Right then, think about it as a letter home, which of course you never write, but this can be A Letter from Life, how it looked from the places where you happened to be sitting at the time.

Now I think about it, she's right. English was my best subject at school, plus R.E. I once got a hundred per cent in R.E., just cos the teacher fancied me, but I preferred English. Botty, who was Head of English, always said I had talent. What is writing anyway? Just a matter of putting one word in front of another, like walking is putting one foot in front of another. You don't need special training for either. I can do that.

Fanny and Tom went to university because they had no alternative in life. All Fanny was good at was being good at things, I mean school things, the sort of rubbish they want you to learn, so you can pass the stupid tests they themselves set. She did it to protect herself, show the world she was somebody, surrounding herself with qualifications. She never went forth naked into the world like me. That sounds biblical. Told you I was good at R.E.

I didn't have to be naked. I could have gone on, done the works. I was clever enough to have gone to college and clothed myself in some disguise, I dunno, PE teacher perhaps, my Mum always wanted me to

3

be a teacher, so she could show off, or a draughtsman, that's what my Dad fancied. He didn't know what it meant either, but when he was at his sec mod all the geniuses in his school became draughtsmen.

Every time you go out on the pitch you're naked. I suppose opera singers feel the same, or actors on stage, or painters when they take up a fresh canvas. It's not the same as starting from square one, having to prove yourself. It's worse than that. You have to prove the image of yourself that's gone ahead, the one which people have picked up, or had created for them. You're exposed to other people's expectations.

People hate you, without even knowing you. They feel personally furious if you let them down, when you haven't promised them anything. They want to attack you, to pull you apart, to make up for some weakness in themselves. You should see the stuff that's been written about me since I've been here. Sick, most of it, but no sicker than a lot of people in this world. Especially in the world of football. Especially people who want to own clubs. They've got to be loony.

Journalists don't understand any of this. They don't understand the pressures in being public property, from above and below, of having to perform on demand. They just want you to say you're over the moon, or sick as a parrot, which is what footballers *do* say. I've said it myself. We've all been brought up on the back pages. Just like the journalists.

Are you skipping already, huh? Tom warned me that if I did it myself then I should cut down on the homespun wisdom. Keep it simple, concentrate on the narrative, not the theories. I said piss off. I'm doing it my way. Just tell me what Chekhov said, and I'll shove it at the beginning. That'll impress Botty.

I want to try and bring back the feelings, not just the facts. You know most of the facts anyway, or think you do, all that shit in the cuttings, as told to, by the nation's highest-paid footballer, tra la, sold for the world's biggest transfer fee, blah blah. (Will it go through, now that all this has happened, don't ask me, how do I know.)

I'm more interested in the Inside Story. Inside Me. Getting it down will be better therapy than the crap they'll soon be offering when all this is over.

So that's the plot. Are you coming? Right, let's have you. No more messing around. Hands off cocks. Hands on socks. I want you out on that pitch in ten seconds. Now which bloody trainer used to say that? God, I'm forgetting even before I'm remembering.

Dear Person,

I have been commissioned to write my own book, so here I am writing it, warts and all.

It's the warts I'm writing to you about. They now tell me I can slag myself off, and my own family, as I know they won't complain, not when you think what I've done for them, and I can say what I like about any dead people (Cyril Knowles, you only had one foot) but I'll have stupid lawyers on my back unless I let certain living people read what I've written about them. You are still living, are you, at the last count? Nine, ten, not out.

Anyway, nothing to worry about, just a formality, and I know you will be over the moon when you read the mention of your good self. No, you don't have to pay for the mensh. Just write via my lawyer (address above) and tell me it's okay. I'll send you a free copy when it comes out, and I come out, signed of course. Lucky. Well, you know what a nice bloke I am really. (Just kidding, Cyril Knowles. You was brilliant.)

Yours in sport,
JOE SWIFT

1

I can't remember a time when I wasn't playing football. It was what I did when I wasn't sleeping. I got up, played football, went to bed, that was it, what else did life hold? All the other activities were marginal. I loved eating, but I often did it standing up at our back kitchen door, watching the lads in the lotties, waiting for me to return to the game, while my Mum moaned that the meal was ruined, because I'd kept her waiting so long, and now I was ruining my digestive system as well.

School was an irrelevance. Lessons were like an enforced half-time, which you were made to endure, till you got back to what really mattered, the game in the playground. Life's a match, and then you die. Who first said that? Me, I think, so don't pinch it.

And yet and yet, after all that boasting, I can't remember my first game. I can remember my first wank, which I'll tell you about later, or I might not, depends on how I feel, and my first fuck, oh yes, can't miss out that, it's what modern autobiography is all about, innit, but I can't remember my first proper game, with goalposts and real nets.

The first proper team I was picked for, as opposed to picking lads in the street who were going to play for or against me (and I was always the boss, when it came to street games, picking both sides), was the cubs. I was only seven. One Friday evening, just as we were finishing, the Akela said I was to turn out next day for our pack, St Ann's, 63rd Durham. She was a big fat woman with hairy legs and never liked me, till someone told her I was good at football, so she put me in the team to play the Palatinate pack. These were posh kids, from the middle of Durham City, with parents who were

university lecturers. We had drawn them in the first round of the
Cubs Cup.

I was dead excited, being picked, even though Fanny tried to ruin
it by saying there were only eleven kids in our pack, which wasn't quite
true. There were ten older kids, aged between ten and eleven, who
naturally all went straight in the team, being the biggest, but Akela
then had to choose one person from the younger kids to make up
the numbers. Some were pretty big, some could even kick straight,
but she chose me, the youngest in the pack. At first she said I was too
fat, but Cedric Clitherland, who was eleven and lived in our street
and was a Sixer, came forward and said no, I was really good for a
little fat lad, give him a chance.

She took us in a minivan, which really belonged to the Scouts, but
she was allowed to use it, as she was going out with Skip, a Jock
feller, though we were not supposed to know that. People in uniform
didn't do that sort of thing, not in uniform anyway, not when other
ranks might find out about it, but me and Cedric had seen them at
it in the back of the van, parked at the far end of Blucher Way one
dark winter's night, just where the street light had been vandalised.

We were coming back from the chippie, sharing one packet, when
we passed the van, realised it was the Scout van, and went to look
through the back window. It was a bit steamed up, but we got our
snotty noses to the window. They were lying together, flat on the
floor, so you would have missed them unless you got right up close.
Her mini skirt was round her waist and he had his hands on her
hairy fanny. The first fanny I ever saw. It was disgusting. Really,
it gave me a shiver. I was revolted. Cedric wanted to stay, just to
see what he did next, but I said no, I had to get back, me Mam was
waiting for me.

Perhaps that was why Akela let me in the team. She knew we'd
seen her. Cedric had made a bit of a noise, giggling, but then he
was always giggling. He flew up to the Scouts not long afterwards,
God, I'd forgotten that expression, flying up, and he became a
Queen Scout. Then he went into the Army and got killed in
the Gulf War when a gun he was loading went off by mistake.
It was in the *Durham Advertiser* last year. Someone sent me the
cutting.

I could hardly sit still in the van as she drove us into Durham for that first match, even though I felt exhausted already. I hadn't slept all night.

I can remember getting to this pitch, down by the river, seeing real goalposts, and nets, and being given a real strip to wear, red and white squares they were, more like a rugby shirt than a soccer shirt. I was completely dwarfed by mine and it came down below my fat little knees and all the big lads laughed. Wait till we get on the pitch, I'll show them, I thought to myself. But we never did. The other team never turned up. We waited and waited, then she drove us all the way back to our cubs hall again. I went home, screamed and shouted at my Mum, kicked down every door in the house, was told I was having no tea, then I went to bed, still wearing the strip.

So that would have been my first real match, if it had happened. All I can remember is it not happening, very clearly. A week or so later, I did play for the cubs one evening, in a friendly, with no strips and no goalposts. I suppose that was my first match. Pity I can't remember who it was against and what the score was.

I then went back to playing in the street, sometimes two-a-side, sometimes twenty-a-side, depending on who wanted to play. Sometimes it was just me, playing on my own in the rain, cos no one else on our estate was allowed out.

For hours, I practised taking corners and penalties against a wall, aiming at a chalk mark. I would sometimes play for a whole hour, just keeping the ball up. Then I had this trick I invented, or thought I invented, when you run over the ball, then turn, and flick it back the way you've come. A stupid trick really, as you can get no power behind the ball, but in the street, with a light plastic ball, which is all we ever used, it was a pretty neat thing to do.

I then read in 'Roy of the Rovers' that no one can call himself a true player unless he can kick equally well with either foot. That became my goal in life, goal, ha ha, no this was serious. I became obsessed, determined to be able to use my left foot, I really did. No one made me. I made myself. Is that the secret of all true talent? Glen Hoddle once told me he'd perfected all his tricks by the age of eleven. I started about seven, trying to use either foot, but was I polishing skill which was naturally already there or teaching myself? Discuss. But not now, some other time, I'm in a hurry to get on. We've a long way to go. If only those bloody bells next door would stop ringing I could get on even faster. Hurray, they've stopped.

I practised against a wall, making myself use either foot, kicking it first with the right foot, then forcing myself to hit the rebound with my left, however it came to me, whatever the angle, even if I fell over and looked really stupid. That was stage one.

Next, in a game, just in the street, I would deliberately run down the left wing and cross, till I could do it without thinking, I mean without thinking whether to use my left foot or not, till it was a natural thing to do, using the foot that was most convenient to use.

The final stage was hardest – kicking a stationary ball with my left foot. Running with the ball then striking it with the left foot is not too hard, as you are in full flow, mind and body in motion, and you eventually do it without thinking. But standing still, doing it cold, then you have a physical and mental barrier to overcome.

I would deliberately take corners with my left foot, when there was no need to, just so I would be able to, in case I ever needed to, though I couldn't think when such an occasion might arise. Your body knows if it's not your natural foot to kick with, so you can feel yourself standing awkwardly, walking forward awkwardly, striking the ball in a clumsy, unfluent manner. The rest of the kids would shout and swear at me for ruining a good chance, by slicing the ball, or putting it behind. But I kept at it. In the end, I could do it without thinking, hitting a dead ball or a moving ball, with either foot. Not penalties. I drew a line at penalties.

The theory of ambidextrousness, is there such a word, which I discovered by myself, is that you double the possibilities by kicking with either foot. Taking a corner, for example, you can make it inswinging or outswinging. You can also act much more quickly, when you can use either foot, taking a free kick when the opposition is still half asleep. As for dribbling, yes I call it dribbling, a one-footed player is always bound to go the same way, use the same trick, make for the same wing, in order to manoeuvre himself on to his best foot. What am I on about? I hate football theory. I hate people talking football theory, and even worse, writing it down.

Right, no first match, but I do have a First Day of my Football Life, a day I can see clearly, even now, a hundred years of solitude later. Literary reference there, which Fanny will get, not that she'll get this far. She'll skip anything to do with football. It's my real life she wants me to explore. That's coming up later, folks, after the break.

It was a Saturday in 1972, just another day in the universe, but naturally I put in my diary anything that really mattered. I don't have it to hand, alas, as I have nothing to hand, stuck in this place, but I would have put in what we had for tea, plus Newcastle United's score, my team, as I did every Saturday. There was no need ever to record United's score, as the public prints had it in black and white, hor hor, for all to see, whereas our tea was a private affair, whose memory departed once it was over. More important was the score in any game I played in, even if it was just a street game, plus how well I played, marks out of ten, and how many goals I got. That day I didn't play in the street. I played *three* real games. And I've kept the scores in my head ever since.

In the morning, I turned out for Blucher Primary, my school, still aged only seven, seven and three-quarters to be precise. I was in the team for the first time. I'd been sub three times, and come on twice, but this time, I'd been picked, the youngest player to make the team in the history of the universe, Blucher Primary section.

People always expected me to be slow, being a fat little lad, but I wasn't really, because I always ran my little heart out. I was weak, though, kicking a real leather ball was agony. It would never go as far as I wanted it to go. I'd take a shot at goal, seeing an opening, and it would just trickle forward a few yards, so I'd have to run after it, pretending it was a pass into space which the other idiots hadn't realised, then I'd pick it up, hold on to it, dribbling till I was almost on the goal line, then tap it in.

I was very hard to knock off the ball. Being such a little fat git. Everyone said I was dead selfish, as I hardly passed, which was true, I am selfish, always have been, in everything, but it started because I couldn't pass. I hadn't got enough strength in my little fat legs, not when I was aged seven.

We got hammered, 1-5, by St Aloysius, Catholic kids who were real brutes, and they kicked me all over the pitch, but I got our only goal and it was our best score ever against St Aloysius. Usually they stuffed us fifteen–nil.

I came home knackered, all bruised and bloody, limping up our

11

front path, still in my boots. My Dad was in bed but my Mum rushed to the front door, dead worried, saying she'd better get the doctor, and I groaned and said oh oh, no no, I'll be okay, putting on the agony, hoping for sympathy, or at least attention, as I took her through the match, especially my goal, and what cheats they had been. She took off my boots, bathed my ankles and knees, made me lie on the couch, and even let me have my mince and potatoes on the couch, which she never did, as normally we had to sit up at the table for proper meals, and without the television on.

When I'd finished eating, I jumped straight up, grabbed my boots, then went off to play for the Cubs, with my mother shouting after me that she thought I was dying.

I'd played for the Cubs about six times by then, and was really the captain, though there was a captain who didn't know I was the captain. I used to take all the free kicks, penalties, corners, throw-ins and even went in goal once, when the other side had a penalty, saying out of the way, I'll save it, which I didn't. We were a useless team, in a really useless league, but I tried just as hard for them as I did for the school, which did matter, as parents used to line the pitch and cheer us on, or have arguments with other parents. Nobody watched us with the Cubs, not when our manager was that hairy Akela. I think, looking back, she was a bit simple, though I didn't realise it at the time. We won 5–1, as the other lot were even more useless than us, but we could have won 15–1, if everyone else had tried as hard as I did.

I was taken off before the end, after I started fighting our captain. He was twice as big as me and all I did was butt him. He had handled the ball in our penalty area, for no real reason, just stupidity, and I got so mad I just ran at him with my head down. I hit him in the stomach and he collapsed in a heap, as if he was dead, just putting it on. Akela took me off.

Then after tea, I played in the lotties, oh joy, oh rapture. Lotties was short for allotments, just behind our street, and they had been allotments at one time, many years ago, till the Council decided they were going to extend our council estate, but they never did. They flattened them out, then just left them. They were immediately taken over by the Big Lads on our estate, those at secondary school, and turned into their playing field. Little kids like me, still at primary school, were not allowed on the lotties. Even when they weren't using it, some thug would come out of his house and chuck you off. Little kids played in the street, that was nature's rule, till they got to be Big Kids.

I was in the house finishing my tea when a Big Lad came for me, Stanley, aged fifteen, who lived at the end of Blucher Way. Blucher Way was going to play Rocket Road, our deadly rivals, and we were a man short. When I got out there, they were playing seventeen-a-side, so a man less would not really have mattered.

There were no goalposts, just coats on the ground, and no boundaries. You played on one side up to our back hedge and to Rocket Road on the other, or not, as the case might be. Most games I had watched ended in fistfights, with lads arguing about whether a goal was in or out of play. They were all grown men to me, though they were probably sixteen at most.

Stanley told me to play up front, right on their goal line, as we weren't playing offside. My job was to poach, hang around, not do anything flash, or show off, not let them see I could play, just wait for my opportunity.

It was almost dark before I got it, and we'd played for about two hours. The score was nine each when it was decided to play Winning Goal. In other words the next goal would decide the match. I'd done nothing much till then. Just collect the ball, on the rare occasions I got it, then pass it quickly to one of the Big Lads on our side. I'd not given the ball away, or failed to collect it, but I hadn't taken anyone on. I was scared really, in case I was tackled, i.e. flattened.

I got the ball on their penalty spot, with about four of their team between me and the goal. I decided to go backwards, holding on to it, till I could see someone in a better position. I went back almost to our penalty area, wondering what to do, while everyone jeered at me, from both sides. It was the jeering that did it. I started going forward again, beating one man, then two, moving to the right-hand goal line, then I came back, and with my left foot, angled the ball into the far corner of the goal. Not a hard shot, just beautifully positioned.

Most of the Rocket Road team shouted that it had gone over the coat, but they always did that. So did we. It hadn't. It was just inside the corner, and they knew it, because the match ended then, with both teams leaving the lotties. Our team carried me down Blucher Way. I thought if I die now, I'll die happy.

Is there life after football? Is there life apart from football? I did love it, live for it, but now, looking back, I think I was overcompensating, trying to hide from certain realities in my so called normal life I did not want to face. Ah football, the great escape.

L'HÔPITAL LE BON SAMARITAIN . . . LIMBE,
HAITI . . .

Dear Joseph,
I do apologise for the delay in answering your letter which
is due to the fact that a) I have been living in a medical
mission station in Haiti for the last fifteen years and b) I
was utterly appalled to read the reference to me in the
chapter you sent me. Your lawyer is right. I could very
well take action. I don't think for a moment that the world
at large will identify me, as thank God you do not use my
name, but doubtless there are still people in the Durham
district who will remember my time as an Akela. What
you have described is not only wrong, but obscene.

Hector, who ran the Church of Scotland Scouts, always
wore a kilt and sporran, which is what I think made your
disgusting imagination run riot. Of course I will not sue.
I do not do that sort of thing. I am just very very sad.

I have read only one chapter, so I do not know what you
are now doing, but I wish you well in whatever career you
have chosen. My good wishes to your mother and father,
should they still be alive.

                                    Yours sincerely
                                    CYNTHIA CLEGHORN (*Miss*)

2

My first happy memories are of football. If I try hard, I can think of other memories. Only I don't want to think of them. But I'll have to, so here we go, let's get it over with.

It says on my birth certificate I was born on January 7, 1965, at 28 Blucher Way, Durham. All I'm aware of is drifting into consciousness, into flesh-and-blood life, about the age of five, when I landed in our street, and found myself playing football. I might have been anywhere, or been anyone, up to then. I once hoped I hadn't been born, but was a spirit that by some awful, shitty mistake had floated into 28 Blucher Way, and would very soon float away again.

Nothing particularly wrong with 28 Blucher Way. There are lots of equally cruddy places. You see them in the TV documentaries about the deprived Northeast where they eat their babies, keep pigeons in the bath and have coal butties for breakfast. What am I saying? It was the worst council house on the worst estate in the whole of County Durham, built just after the war, with horrible windows, horrible doors all painted the same shit green. Ours was the one with the overgrown garden full of junk and broken lawn mowers and dead prams. You couldn't miss it, though people did tend to look the other way, should they per chance find themselves taking an evening stroll down Blucher Way, en route for the lovely lotties.

Old Ma Crummock, our next-door neighbour, who was a right nosy parker, would never give us my ball back, and was always complaining about the garden, and about me. She was also a terrible snob, giving herself airs and graces ever since someone told her she looked like the Queen Mum. She looked more like the Queen Mum's horse.

When I was little, all the houses on our estate appeared much the same to me. Just some had lawns and flower beds and some had, well, jungles. I quite liked our garden being a jungle, great to play in, have fights and camps and hide, but people like Ma Crummock were always complaining, getting on to the council to have us evicted, lowering the tone, bloody cheek.

It was only as I got older, and looked around, that I saw the differences and realised that on every council estate there was a subtle social hierarchy. You could tell it by the net curtains, the type of flowers, the chiming doorbells instead of the council knockers. The real aristocracy ordered greenhouses and garages from the *Radio Times* which they put up themselves, being clever buggers. Today, of course, the differences stand out a mile, now that people can buy their own council house.

The social climbers on our estate usually managed to engineer swaps and bag the best houses, the most desirable ones, such as ends of terraces, with corner gardens, or better windows. What they didn't want was outside the bus stop or the chip shop, or next to the Swifts. People really did engineer moves away from us. Rotten sods. Don't play with the Swifts, they smell. Keep out of their garden, you'll catch something.

Right, let's now step inside 28 Blucher Way. As quickly as possible. I hated it. I only have bad memories, which is why I've wiped out most things and can only vaguely remember a few domestic incidents. All of them horrible. But then it was a very bad time for the Swifts, though I didn't understand what was going on at the time.

I just thought my Dad was a selfish, lazy bastard. He seemed to lie in bed all day long, had done all my life, as far as I could remember. That was why the garden was overgrown, and the house was such a mess. He wasn't well, my Mum said, he's a bit depressed, so we had to be quiet in the house and not upset him and not get on his nerves, and that means you, Joe. What about me, I said. He's upsetting me, I used to say. I've got nerves as well, you know, look, in my bum, it's full of nerves. Don't be rude, Joe. I had a passion at the time for showing people my botty. Okay, so some things haven't changed.

My Dad seemed to have it in for me, for some reason, yes, you can't believe it, lovely me, life and soul of any gathering, but that was just it. He couldn't stand me being the life and soul, all action and excitement, all noise and nervous tension. I would come into a room and say something, thinking I was just talking normally, and he would say don't shout. He complained that I never sat still, that I ran around all the time, knocking things over. I said that was his fault, cos he wouldn't let me play football inside the house. He said I was always answering back, arguing and being bolshie, fighting people, fighting walls, fighting furniture, then having temper tantrums when I didn't win.

Worst of all I never slept, apparently, not till I was five years old. My Mum said that, so it must be true. I think they hoped that chasing a football all the time in the garden and then in the street would exhaust me and make me sleep, but it didn't. It seem to make me more excited and frenetic, if anything, so they used to fill me up with drugs, no, nothing nasty, just syrup stuff from Boots, to knock me out, calm me down. That didn't work either. I just went on as normal. Ruining their life. So they said.

I have no memory of any of this pre-five stuff. I'm just telling you what I've been told. I have to accept it. Personally, I don't believe it, but Fanny says it's true. From the moment I was born, I was a pain.

Fanny is two years older than me, my big sister, one of nature's bossy betties. I hated her as well. She never shouted. She never knocked things over. She never screamed and had temper tantrums or picked fights, and never ever moaned that she was bored. 'Always gainfully employed,' was my mother's boast about Fanny. Stupid thing to boast about, if you ask me.

Fanny was neat and tidy, polite and obedient, well-organised, good at everything, gave no trouble, gave no cheek, a total bore in other words, but very clever. Too bloody clever. She always maintains she taught me to read. Pity she didn't make a better job of it. I might have progressed from the *Sun*.

She helped my Mum with my Dad, the creep, whereas I just complained, or banged doors, or refused to do anything. She would go to the shop for him, get him cigarettes, his newspaper, turn his radio on for him, find him a play to listen to, take him drinks and even bring him his bedpan when he said he couldn't get up out of bed, which must have been horrible for her, as a girl of only eight or nine. It could explain things, about her later attitudes to men. No, I won't try and explain it now. Let's just get rid of this draggy early stuff first.

Listen, I'm hurrying. I don't like remembering it myself. For years I wiped Blucher Way from my mind. Named after one of George Stephenson's locomotives, by the way. Hence Rocket Road across the lotties. Round the corner was Locomotion Terrace. Come on, you must have done the history of railways at school, or were you not listening, like me.

My Dad came home from the pit one day and just took to his bed. That's how I saw it. On the sick, I presumed, perhaps with that lung disease with the long name. The doctor did come and gave him a chitty, but I thought it was a trick. He looked fine to me, lying in bed, listening to his stupid plays, smoking away, drinking beer and eating peanuts and crisps and being bad tempered with me. The crumbs all matted on his chest and looked disgusting, sort of fungus and mouldy, ugh.

I used to tell my Mum to run away, I'd help her pack, get her things for her, I'd go with her and look after her, but she'd smile, then sigh and look away.

One day I bought her a train ticket to Newcastle. I don't know how I got the ticket. I think I'd been to stay with Granny Fenwick and she'd brought me back on the train and I'd bought the ticket when she wasn't looking. God knows how I got the money. I was supposed to get pocket money, but I never did. Perhaps I nicked the money from her purse. Anyway, I bought her a single ticket. When my Dad was having his lunch one day, still in his bed, moaning as usual, I took her by the hand and said I had a present for her. I dragged her into the back kitchen, closed the door so HE couldn't hear, and gave her the ticket. This is for you, Mam, to go away, Mam.

'I can't go Joe,' she said. 'We're having a baby.'

Then she burst into tears and ran upstairs. Oh God. I think seeing your Mum cry is the worst thing that can happen to anyone. Worse than missing a penalty. Worse than a ref handing you a red card.

We are having a baby, so she said, which didn't make sense. I wasn't having the baby, why did she drag me into it? It's her. And *him*. The thought of them at it was horrible. I was still only about five, but I must have had some vague notion of how you did it. The very idea was revolting. And impossible. How could they have done it, when he was in bed all day long, eating his horrible peanuts in his horrible jamas.

I tried to drown Colin when he was born. No, not quite straight away, though I might have done, but when he was about one. My Mum was washing him and had to go and attend to my Dad cos he was shouting for something, so I tried to stick Colin's head under the water. He started crying, so my Mum rushed back, just in time to save him. I said it was a mistake. I was trying to teach him to swim.

I can see the bath clearly, me holding his little head down, and can almost feel the water, which is a load of cobblers. I now realise it's not my memory, but a handed-down, second-hand memory, passed on to me. Colin has even more details when he tells this story, showing off about what a sod I used to be, yet he was only a baby, so he's a bloody liar for a start. But basically, it's true. My Mum told me, and she never told lies.

Then my Mum fell poorly. Something to do with her legs, varicose veins, and she had to go into hospital. My Dad was not in bed all the time by now, but still hanging around the house, out of work, sitting and smoking, doing nothing, so Fanny was in charge of the house, doing all the cooking. I can't remember where Colin was. Perhaps he went to my Granny Fenwick, my Mum's mother, in Newcastle.

I hated Fanny looking after me. When I came in from playing football, starving and thirsty, all she made was toast. I missed my Mum's stovies. This was a dish my Gran made, sort of meat and potato-stew things. The house smelled different, looked different, felt different, all the time my Mam was away.

On the day she was due back from the hospital, I stood at the window all day long, with no clothes on. I refused to let Fanny dress me. I can still feel my little willie pressed up against the cold of the glass. Okay, I must have made that bit up, but neighbours did see me. I can remember Mrs Crummock, from next door, coming to the door and telling my Dad it ought not to be allowed, she was going to contact the Social Services, and him banging the door in her face and telling her to get stuffed.

When my Mum eventually did get home, she told me off. That was the most awful part. She came straight in, when I'd been waiting for her for hours, crying for her, and told me off. That Fanny had grabbed her first and told her all the things I'd been doing wrong, the cow. I was so furious. I said that's it, nobody wants me in the house, nobody cares about me, they've all been horrible to me, Her and Him, so I'm going.

I rushed out of the house down the street, then back into the house again. I realised I wouldn't get far, wearing no clothes. So I pulled open my drawer, threw everything on the floor and put on some clothes. Then I shoved my football boots, my Newcastle United shirt and some other clothes in an old red tablecloth and slung it over my shoulder on the end of a stick. I think I'd just finished reading *Dick Whittington*, or Fanny had just finished reading *Dick Whittington* to me. That's how he carried his stuff, when he went off to London town to seek his fortune.

I walked into Durham City, which took ages, as we lived about three miles outside, and I'd never done it before, not on my own, not on foot. I remember going down Claypath and there was this Italian ice cream shop and I was dying for an ice cream or a drink, but I had no money. I sat in the Market Square, wondering what to do next. Then I decided to go to the station, as I knew where that was, but I'd forgotten what a climb it was, getting up to it, with my bundle of stupid clothes.

I was thinking of going to Newcastle, to see my Gran, as she was always kind to me, then I was thinking no, I'll go the other way, to London, and make my fortune, just like Dick Whittington. I was still thinking when I decided to have a rest, just outside the station. I must have fallen asleep. When I woke up, there was this horrible tramp, poking me, so I jumped up, and ran all the way home.

Fanny has never let me forget all that, me running away. It still makes her laugh, the sight of my fat little angry face and my bundle of clothes. What happened before, and the cause of why I ran away, is never talked about. Looking back, I suspect my Dad did have some sort of mental breakdown, or deep depression. My over-excited presence didn't exactly help.

Blucher Way has long gone, but its image remains in our family language, for me and for Fanny. Colin was too young. When something horrible has happened, everything is chaos and a right mess, we say it's as bad as bloody Blucher Way.

I tried once to talk to my Mum about these memories, and about what was wrong with my Dad. What do you mean? You know, I said, when he was bedridden all those years. He was not, she said. What nonsense. He was unemployed for only three months, that was all, when the pit closed. What are you talking about? And you never ran away. You got to the front gate, then you rushed straight back in for your tea. That was all.

Giles Radice Sheltered Housing,
Chester-le-Street

Dear Little Joe,

I always called you that, and your father was Big Joe, my my, it all seems a long time ago. My niece has just read me some of your book and I'm now waiting for my cocoa to come so I thought I'd drop you a quick note to say thank you. I must say it makes a change from Book at Bedtime! When they do it on Radio Four, I do hope Alan Bennett is the reader. He's my favourite. If you want to put in more about me, then please do. Come and see me here, any time, I always leave the key under the black stone. You could do a book on my life story, many people have told me that. You wouldn't believe the times I was mistaken for the Queen Mother. Many people have told me that.

You were a lovely little boy, so you were, as happy as the day was long, and your mother and father were lovely, they were all lovely, perhaps a bit cheeky now and again, and I had to pretend to be cross, but I never was, bless your cotton socks.

The language, well, I was a bit shocked at first, because I never heard you swear, nor your mother and father, in fact no one swore in Blucher Way, so I don't know where you've got it from. You have to have it in books these days, I suppose. It's the fashion. I was listening to Morning Story the other day and you wouldn't believe what they were talking about. Well God bless and all the best.

HETTY CRUMMOCK (*Mrs*)

3

I always wanted to be a professional footballer, which is about as unusual as saying you want to breathe fresh air, live in a nice house, have lots of money, fuck every woman you fancy. So what else is new. The whole world and his groundsman wants to be a professional footballer. Does anybody want to be an engine driver these days? Or a policeman? Kids at Eton, or Kensington Palace, or the slums of Buenos Aires, or the back streets of Naples, lie awake at night, wishing they could become footballers.

When we lived in Durham, I used to hear stories of boys who had once lived on our estate who were now said to be in the reserves at Sunderland, or playing in the first team at Hartlepool. I never knew them, and I never heard of them again, but it proved it could be done, that normal ordinary human beings from our sort of street could become pros. Naturally, we all knew about the Charlton brothers. I've told umpteen idiot reporters that I wanted to become a footballer after I watched them on the telly, winning the World Cup in 1966. A lie of course. I was only one at the time, and we didn't have a telly.

My Dad boasts he saw Jackie Milburn and Len Shackleton play, and both of them were better than any modern player, so he says, certainly any modern player in the Northeast. He has a point there. These days, the successful ones all move away, sharpish, like Gazza and Chris Waddle and yours truly. People like Bryan Robson never even played for a Northeastern team, despite being born and brought up in County Durham. Now who did Bobby Robson first play for? Before my time.

It is interesting that so many famous English players have been Geordies, yet Tyneside is not as big in population as Merseyside, or Manchester, or Yorkshire, and nothing like London. Is it the invigorating North Sea air? Could be. It freezes your balls off so you have to run around to keep warm. Or the stimulating aroma of dead coalmines and clapped out shipyards, a warning to us all? They used to say it was the hard life miners led which made them want to get out of the pit and on to the pitch, which I always thought was stupid. People have hard lives everywhere. I feel sorry for those poor bairns in Kensington Palace. They can never grow up to be anything interesting.

Perhaps it's the Nordic influence. I once did a school project on the Norsemen, one of the few I ever finished, how they invaded us after the Romans left, raped the women, beat up the blokes, burned down the pubs, so how come they blame hooliganism on football. They were big and athletic, the Norsemen, like Big Jack. I can just see him as a Viking. I was blonde when I was little. There's a photo somewhere of me aged about four with long golden ringlets looking a right fairy which I later scribbled all over with a biro, and got belted by my dad.

Personally, I think it's the Newcastle Brown Ale. Terrible stuff. I always hated it. You have to run around like a halfwit, just to sweat it out.

I'm not really a Geordie, anyway, so bugger all the theories. On me Mam's side we're a Border family, the Fenwicks. The Forsters, the Fenwicks, they rode and they ran. You must have read *Young Lochinvar*. My Gran used to drive me mad, reciting all that rubbish. I get my football talent from her. True. She played for Newcastle Ladies before the war. I bet you didn't know there was such a thing as women's football in the olden days. They got huge crowds and the men got jealous, so my Gran says, and stopped it.

On my Dad's side, we're Scottish, from somewhere near Glasgow I think. His Dad came over the Border in the Thirties. On the run probably.

I ceased to be a Geordie when I was about eight, though people in the South always think I have a Geordie accent, but they know nowt about out. I consider myself a Cumbrian, yup, a real rural lad, with straw sticking out of my arse.

What happened was that my Dad eventually got a job across in Cumbria, so we had to move. He was taken on as an electrician in a boys' home near a village called Rigg just outside Cockermouth. He'd been an electrician in the pit, not a miner, so it was a bit easier for him to get another job, compared with the miners, though you wouldn't have thought so, from all that depression he went through.

His new job wasn't strictly as an electrician but as a craft assistant. He had to teach the basics of electrics to the lads in the home, at least that was the theory. He really got the job because he weighed about sixteen stone and could keep discipline. He thumped any kids who got stroppy.

My Mum was very pleased because she had aspirations and didn't like him coming home all filthy in his overalls and washing at the sink. She had never liked us living in a council house, certainly not Blucher Way. Now I think about it, I wonder if it was her that made him depressed that time.

She was always the clever one and had passed the Eleven Plus for Dame Allens in Newcastle, then left at sixteen, which she always regretted, to become a secretary in the council offices. That's how she met my Dad, who was then a council electrician. How he got off with her, I dunno. Must have been his looks, not his brains. He was tall and handsome in those days, before he put on weight and got miserable.

Rigg Hall was an old castle, once owned by some lord, and had amazing grounds and a baronial hall. Nice class of place, which looked great in photographs, and impressed relations when they came to see us. You could hardly believe it housed Naughty Boys. My Mum always called them that, to make my Dad sound more like a social worker than a warder. It was a prison really, a borstal for young offenders, who had done too much thieving, nicking cars, bashing up old ladies, mainly across on the Northeast.

I was shit scared of them when we first arrived. They seemed huge and frightening, especially the first day when I came across this massive lad on his own in the woods, shouting at himself and kicking trees. As I got bigger, they seemed to get smaller and I realised most of them were runts, pathetic kids really, who had done stupid things, and been stupid to get caught. They all had terrible homes, of course, and no one wanted them back, so you had to feel sorry for them. A few were a bit mental, and could be violent, but you soon knew which they were. Mostly, they were just soft lads. A lot became good friends of mine.

The Hall had a brilliant football pitch, always kept immaculate, and our house was right beside it. They'd built a little row of new houses for the staff, which looked like council houses to me, no better than Blucher Way, except they were new, but my Mum loved it. The pitch had real goalposts, which stayed up all the time, and I did shooting practice for hours, on my own.

When I was about ten I started turning out occasionally for Rigg Hall, if they were short, mainly because my Dad took the lads for football, as one of his so-called craft jobs. They didn't have many games, as local people didn't like playing against borstal boys, and they were never in a league, but we played a few friendlies. They were hell to play with. Even the kids who were quite good would wander off in the middle of the game, not running away, just bored, their attention wandering, looking for something to thieve or somewhere to have a fag.

I got in the village school team straight away, but I was never made captain, the bastards. The headmaster, who also picked the team, had it in for me. The school itself was okay, though I hated it at first. I got mocked for my Geordie accent. They thought I was a city slicker, coming from Durham, and I used to get bullied in the playground, till I got a bit older and taller, and okay, fatter and heavier.

From the village primary I went to Cockermouth Grammar School, about seven miles away. That surprised everyone, me getting in, as I'd been thought of as a daft fat git, not clever, like Fanny. I liked it from the beginning. I felt I started equal with everyone else, having lost my Geordie accent by then and speaking like the others. I didn't feel like an outsider any more.

Fanny was already there, two years ahead, which was a drag, as she was dead clever and hard-working and all the teachers went on about her, expecting me to be the same. I could have done better, no problem, but what's the point of learning all that history and geography if I'm going to be a footballer. That's what I told myself, and everyone else. They just laughed. In the wilds of Cumbria, no one had heard of anyone becoming a footballer before. In our village, you went on your dad's farm, or got a job in the shoe factory in Cockermouth.

The really adventurous ones joined the army or the merchant navy and got away, lucky buggers.

I didn't want to go to the Grammar School at first, as it was a rugby school, but my Mum insisted. The town did have a football team of sorts, and at the age of twelve I got into it, the under-13s. Not such a great achievement, it was a pretty small town, but we had a great team that year. Our captain was a tall gangling lad called Cally who was a right thicko, a real farm yacker, but he was enormous, even at thirteen, and a great clogger who kicked everyone in sight. He was a good defender though, brilliant in the air, and he used to go mental if anyone went past him.

In training, I used to dribble round him, daring him to get the ball off me, running up and down the field with him after me. I would see his eyes going funny, almost disappearing, and his jaw would jut out and his mouth would slaver. In the end, I had to let him have the ball, or he would have killed me.

We did well in some cup competition, named after someone I can't remember, and found ourselves drawn against Carlisle Boys. Alf Armstrong, our manager, took us through to Carlisle in the school minibus. It was a big day for our lads, going through to Carlisle, and we played on a pitch with real nets and corner flags and a little grandstand. We expected to get stuffed, as Carlisle was the Big City, about ten times the size of Cockermouth, so Alf told us to play a defensive game, and concede as few goals as possible for the honour of Cockermouth Boys. The last time they'd met, Carlisle had won 13–1. I thought it was stupid, and said so, as I always did when anyone tried to dictate football tactics. I said if we're gonna get stuffed, let's play our normal game, and just enjoy ourselves.

I played centre forward in those days, so I was left up front, on my own, as a lone striker. I quite liked that. The opposition always ignored me, when they saw this tubby little lad, all on his own, who looked as if he couldn't run anywhere. I used to try to keep the ball, hold up play as long as possible, give our lads a rest, and save any dribbles on goal for later, when a proper chance came along. The only trouble was that the ref, who was from Carlisle, kept on giving fouls against me, saying I was illegally holding people off with my arse and my elbows. Of course I was. When you've got five round you, and no one to pass to, that's the way you have to play.

They attacked almost non-stop, and Cally managed to cripple a few of them while our goalie played out of his skin. They began to get disheartened and the crowd of about a hundred boys and parents and officials started getting on at them. At the beginning, I'd heard one of them shouting Sheepshagger at Cally when they saw him lumber on to the pitch.

With about five minutes to go, I got the ball with only two defenders in their half, everyone else having gone up for yet another corner, so I put my head down and went for goal, beating both of them, then dribbling round their goalie. I then carried on and did a trot round the crowd, waving like Stan Bowles used to do, remember him, one of my heroes, then I gave a V sign to the bloke who had shouted Sheepshagger. The ref took my name for ungentlemanly conduct. Can you believe it. Aged twelve.

Afterwards we had to have tea with their team, and the local officials, in the little grandstand. I followed the ref round and round the room till I got him in a corner and asked him why he had given so many fouls against me. He said go away boy, don't talk to me like that. In the end, Alf had to drag me away.

I'd seen this sod arrive before the match, in an orange MGB GT sports car, and was surprised he turned out to be the referee. I went off to our minibus and in the back I found an old potato which I'd noticed on the journey coming. Country lads, you see, we carried that sort of gear, often a few dead sheep as well, recently shagged of course. I then stuck the potato into the exhaust of the ref's car, and went back to the tea.

Their manager came up and congratulated me on the goal, forcing it out, though I could see he hated me, and I said yeh, it was pretty good, but I'll be scoring a lot more in the future, you can come and watch me at Wembley. Just a joke, to put them in their place, all the Carlisle lads had thought they were it, before the match began. He didn't get the joke and obviously thought I was a right bighead.

It was brilliant getting on the coach to go home. We all pissed ourselves at the sight of the ref, trying to start his car, opening the bonnet, scratching his head, then running round and kicking it. Naturally, I told them all what I'd done. I've always found it hard to keep secrets. I look upon it as sharing, not showing off. Alf sang to himself as he drove us home. On the back row, where I was sitting with Cally and Tucky, our goalie, someone had a dirty magazine they were passing around.

The whole journey home was terrific, except for one incident, which there's no need to go into. There are some secrets perhaps I should keep. This one would certainly not be showing off. We'll move on quickly.

I expected, after that victory, which was thanks to me, that I'd get picked for the County side. I waited for the post every day, going mad when it didn't come. I even asked Alf to ring up, contact someone, see what the stupid buggers were playing at. Then I found out that the ref and their manager were both County officials. I'd obviously upset them in some way. Upset them? How could I ever upset anyone?

The next time I was picked for Cockermouth boys I refused to play, saying I was ill, which I agree was daft. They'd done me no harm. I just saw my whole dream of being a professional footballer collapse. Getting into the County side was the vital step, as real scouts watched them. They didn't come out to Cockermouth to watch us play.

On the day I should have played for Cockermouth against Working-ton Boys, which was another big match, I turned out instead for the Hall boys, against another borstal side from Scotland. That was the day I gave up being centre forward, for ever.

My Dad made me captain, even though I was by far the youngest, so I decided to come back into midfield, so I could shout at them all, organise them, stop them sloping off, and also so I could have more of the ball. When you play up front, and the game's going against you, you hardly get a touch. I can't remember the score, but I remember loving it.

It was partly through growing up, getting bigger and stronger I suppose, that I was able to compete in midfield, win the ball, and hold on to it. I'd been escaping from the physical side by playing up front, to avoid all the big lads, plus wanting to be flash. I found I could still be flash in midfield. I was now becoming one of the bigger lads myself, putting on a spurt, needing new boots all the time, getting hairs on my cock, that sort of stuff.

Okay, let's go back to that coach. Cally was laughing at these naked women in this dirty magazine, well we all were, sniggering at the pubic hair and the monster breasts, and everyone was saying ooh, I could give her one, no messing. I must have joined in, saying I could give her two. I said I'd dribble round those tits, no problem, then wow, a hole in one. Suddenly, Cally turned on me. He was huge, over six feet already, and had ginger hair on his cock since he was about ten, because he'd shown us it, at primary school, in the playground lavs. He was supposed to have had it away, with a farm girl on his dad's farm. Or a sheep. Or a cow. Or a tractor. Anyway, no one doubted he'd done it.

'You don't know what it's for, you little cunt,' he said to me.

I missed his threatening tone of voice at first. I thought I was the hero of the hour, the goalscorer, the one who'd settled that ref. Okay, I might have been showing off a bit, getting overexcited, but most of them were my mates, from our school, we all knew each other.

'Let's see if he's really got one.'

Before I could stop him, he'd grabbed my flies and pulled out my little cock. Tucker and two others held me down. It looked limp and pathetic, despite my boasts, and they could see I only had two hairs anyway, long and weedy, stray strands which I'd been trying to coax into becoming a forest.

They pulled back my foreskin, which really hurt, trying desperately to get a hard-on for me. I'd had one before, I wasn't that backward, usually to my embarrassment, such as standing in the dinner queue at school, convinced one of the serving women could see, but I hadn't known what to do about it. It took ages, and it exhausted them as well as me. From the front of the bus I could hear Alf, sipping from a beer bottle, singing some stupid song about Four and Twenty Virgins, coming down from Inverness.

They all cheered in a half-hearted way, relieved it was over. I can still see their faces, a bit alarmed by what they'd started, ashamed at having managed it, when obviously my body wasn't really advanced enough anyway for such treatment. So, that was the first time. Nothing to boast about. The next ten million times I did it were a lot more fun.

Dunbeaten, Silloth

Dear Swift,

So it was you. I naturally blamed one of my pupils, as I was the headmaster of a Carlisle secondary modern at the time and had just expelled two boys for smoking. In trying to repair it myself, I made it worse, and kicking did not help, so I was forced to get a new one. I enclose the bill for my exhaust, £39. Incidentally, it is not fair to suggest that you were not chosen for the County because of that incident, or similar. I'm afraid we considered you not good enough, nor with the right character, and we had two other boys competing for the same position whom we deemed much better. Perhaps we were wrong. So be it. Incidentally, as regards that disgusting scene at the end, I recognize the boy you refer to as 'Cally' from your earlier description. I remember him playing. I see you have shown some taste in changing his name, but if you had any decency at all you would delete the whole scene, if not the whole chapter, probably the whole book, which I have not of course read, and have certainly no intention of doing so. There are too many of these cheap confessional books on the market.

Yours,

ERIC WINSTANLEY, B.A., J.P.

4

I was fourteen when my Dad went off to college. That surprised you. Surprised everyone, especially my Mum. She had always wanted him to be more ambitious, but when the chance came up, she started having second thoughts. She didn't want to be left on her own, stuck out in the wilds of the country. She didn't want the responsibility of looking after three kids. I expect she also worried about what he might get up to, mixing with a load of young students, including young single girls. It's only now, looking back, that the possibility has come into my mind. At the time, you never think of your Dad getting his leg over with anyone, not even his wife.

I was well pleased my Dad was going. It would be more for me to eat. He'd stopped moaning about my voice, or he'd got used to it, and now he moaned about my eating habits. Mainly the amount and the noise I made, as if you can help the noise you make. 'It's only mastication,' I used to say, while Fanny giggled. I knew it was a funny word, and it always got a laugh when you used it in class.

We did tend to argue at mealtimes, once my Mum started serving me first, and giving me as much as my Dad got. She maintained I was a growing boy and needed building up, especially if I was going to play for England. Then she'd laugh. It amused her, just the very thought. I'd put this down as my ambition in life when I went to grammar school.

'When I was a lad,' he'd say, 'I always got served last, often just scraps. Mind you, there was a war on.'

'We know,' I said, 'you've telt us.'

'During the war, we never had no sweets or oranges or bananas or meat or eggs.'

'Two negatives don't make an affirmative,' said Fanny, too bloody clever as usual. She'd just got all her O-levels, with A in everything, makes you sick.

'Yes, if you're going to college, Joseph,' said Mum, smiling at Dad, 'you'll have to mind your Ps and Qs.'

'Well I'm not going to college,' I said, 'not if you have to queue for a pee . . .'

Fanny groaned, but Colin laughed. It was his sort of joke, being nine years old.

'What does P and Q stand for anyway?' asked Fanny.

'I've never thought of that before,' said Mum. 'Perhaps your Dad will tell us, when he comes back from college. He'll be much cleverer then . . .'

'Will you just stop it woman, it's not a joke,' said Dad, getting up and leaving the table.

I've just made up that conversation, this minute, but then you do, when you're writing your autobiography. No one takes notes at the time. No one can possibly remember, word for word. But I took in feelings, without being aware of them, recorded scenes on my inward eye. Fanny and Colin probably can't remember them. They'll have different scenes, perhaps even different feelings. But I suspect that both me and Fanny drove Dad mad, in our different ways.

He was obviously very worried about going away. He had always been a great newspaper reader, a radio listener, a union and Labour Party man and all that, but in all his years as a working man, he had not written a word, apart from his time sheet. Not even family letters, or signed cheques or paid bills or notes to the milkman. Mum always did that. Now he was going to have to write essays, for the first time in his life. He'd left school at fifteen, with no qualifications, no bits of paper to prove he'd learned anything. It was probably slates in his day anyway, not writing paper. There was a war on, don't you know.

The week after he went off, I got picked for the North of England Under-15 team. I don't know how this happened, who had seen me, but Alf took all the credit, saying he'd gone above the County officials. My picture was on the front page of the *Cumberland News*, with a little story, all rubbish, and my Mum bought twenty copies to send to our relations in Scotland, in Canada and New Zealand, plus my Dad in Newcastle, in his hall of residence. She was dead chuffed.

I have to admit she was never against me wanting to be a footballer. If anything, my Dad was more worried. He saw me ending up with nothing, on the scrap heap at seventeen, after Workington Reds had chucked me out, with no qualification, no nothing. He knew the struggle he'd had to catch up, sitting special exams, having long interviews, before he'd got on to this course at Newcastle Polytechnic. He would have preferred me to have been like Fanny, so I could have gone to university and become a professional person. He could have accepted Fanny being like me, leaving school at sixteen, being a girl. She'll only get married, so he used to say, and waste all that learning.

I could have done well at school, no problem, they were all stupid, all idiots, and that was just the teachers. No, George Bott, Head of English, was a good bloke. He always told me I could do well, if I stopped messing around. I should stay on and try for university, even Oxford. Waste of time, so I thought, unless you happened to have no talent, apart from cleverness.

Some of the kids were pretty bright, such as Tom Graham, my best friend, who lived in our village, so we came in on the school bus together, with all the country kids, the hicks, the jerks, looked down upon by the Cockermouth townies. I can't believe it now, that we should have envied the kids who actually lived in Cockermouth, population 7,000, situation nowhere, amenities fuck all.

Tom did have straw sticking out of his arse. His dad was a farm labourer, from a long line of farm labourers, but he was dead clever, just as clever as our Fanny, but normal with it, I mean, one of the lads, messed around, chased girls, followed football, though he wasn't much good. I got him a game for Cockermouth Boys cos he was my mate. I told Alf I wouldn't play any more unless Tom was in.

I used to hang around the village with him on Saturday evenings, or when we had the money we'd get the bus into Cockermouth and hang around Main Street, eyeing up girls together, not that we got very far, not at fourteen, especially as we needed both eyes to avoid the hard lads, who were out looking for trouble. There were some real heavies, even then, especially on Friday evenings, when gangs came over from West Cumberland, hoping for aggro. We were just hoping for girls.

At school, all the so-called goers in our year, the fourth year, went out with sixth formers, and would tell us to piss off, kiddo, when we tried anything. Playing for Cockermouth Boys didn't mean a thing. I was still that little fat git with the big mouth. When I graduated to North of England Boys, I hoped that would impress them more, but it was a bit of a mouthful, and no one knew what it meant.

The alternative was to wait till we were old enough to buy motorbikes, that seemed to pull them, judging by the tarts who hung around the leather lads outside our village pub, revving up their engines, getting their cocks into gear. Or we could join the junior branch of the Young Farmers club, perhaps get our hands up a few classier skirts. That was our only ambition in life, to get it away, so Tom got the forms and we joined the Young Farmers. For about half an hour. We went to one meeting and found out they were all older than us and there was no sign of sex. Just public speaking competitions, car rallies, squash tournaments, ploughing matches and helping old people across the road. Forget it, I said.

So it was back to more solitary pursuits. Not together. Do you mind? In the privacy of our bedrooms, though on the bus in the mornings we did compare notes. How many times in an hour, how many inches was your erection, how much came out, was it as thick as school custard or like skimmed milk. Tom did toss himself off once in school, in an R.E. lesson, at the back of the class with his desk lid up. Miss Henn came round and banged it shut. He had the scars for weeks.

'Better than having a fucking bend in it,' he said. 'Like yours.'

I wished I'd never confessed that. I don't know whether it was natural, the way it was built, or it had grown that way with me always using my right hand. I did try to use the left hand, teaching myself to be ambidextrous, as I'd done with kicking a ball, but in the heat of the moment I always forgot.

One day we played the South of Scotland Boys. At football, dumdum. They all looked undernourished when they came on the pitch, with baggy shorts and their dark blue shirts hanging loose on their skinny, spotty bodies, whereas our North of England team had five lads who looked like Mr Universe with thighs like tree trunks. Two of them were already training at Man.United. We got hammered 4–1, and I was rubbish. I hardly got a touch. They were magic on the ball, and just tore our defence apart. I had to come back and defend most of the time, which is what our manager said. It was my first match, so I thought I'd better do what I was told. I gave away a penalty, lashing out at their winger, a real clever cunt, who had beaten the whole of our back three. Defending was never my strong point.

The match was in Dumfries, and I got dropped off in Carlisle and had to make my own way home by bus, which took forever, and I arrived home in a right temper, blaming them, blaming the ref, blaming our manager, knowing my mum would take my side and fuss around, making me something nice to eat, such as chips. She'd cut down on the chips when Dad was at home, to help his weight problem, but now he was away I could have them all the time.

She was standing at the front window when I got in, her hand to her head, looking very worried. Fanny was away on a school trip to France. Colin was sitting watching television.

'You having a vision,' I said, banging in, dropping my bag in the hall. 'Come on woman, chop chop, I'm starving.'

I could see she was upset about something. I presumed it was one of her headaches, but I chose to ignore it, not wanting to hear her problems. Dad usually came back at weekends, but this weekend he hadn't, because of an essay crisis, so he said. He was studying for a certificate to give him a proper qualification to look after the Naughty Boys, and they were piling on the work, which he was finding very hard.

She smiled and went into the kitchen to put the chip pan on and get some fish fingers from the fridge while I slumped in front of the telly.

'I'll have some, Mum,' yelled Colin, without looking up, hearing a noise from the kitchen.

'You don't know what she's making,' I said, giving Colin a kick. At nine years old, he was already twice as fat as me.

'Shurrup you,' said Colin, still without looking away from the television.

From the kitchen, I heard Mum give a little yell, so I sighed, got up and went through to see what had happened. She was staring out of the window.

'What's the matter, Mam?'

'There's been someone out there,' she said. 'All this evening, watching the house.'

'Just one of the lads, messing around, come on, hurry up. I'm going to meet Tom in half an hour.'

'Oh, I thought you were staying in tonight. You said you'd be too tired after football.'

'I am,' I said, hobbling, 'but I'll be okay in half an hour. Can I have some beans as well?'

'It's my Keep Fit class tonight,' she said, standing at the stove. 'Oh well, it doesn't matter I suppose. I hadn't got a lift anyway.'

I looked out of the back kitchen window, but could see nothing. One or two of the boys did prowl around the grounds in the evening, in their so called free play hour, which was why we always kept the doors and windows well bolted. There was no danger, but they might nick things if you left them lying around.

'I did see someone, I'm sure of it,' she said. 'A bearded man in a raincoat.'

'The village flasher,' I said.

I wasn't quite sure what a flasher did, but there had been a report in the *Times and Star* about a bloke exposing himself and stealing knickers from people's clotheslines. This struck me as funny, not dangerous. I presumed flashing just meant opening your flies, giving everyone a quick look, so what was wrong with that? Sounded harmless. They made jokes about it on comedy programmes on the telly, like Benny Hill.

She made me my tea, with apple crumble to follow, my favourite, but I had to eat it at the kitchen table, not in front of the telly, house rules. I was just finishing when there was a knock at the front door. She almost jumped in the air. Living in our sort of house, on what appeared to be a private estate, miles up a private drive, you didn't get chance visitors. Door-to-door salesmen didn't get that far, or Jehovah's witnesses.

'You go, Joe,' she said.

'Bloody hell, I'm eating, Mum.'

'And don't swear.'

I opened the door and there stood a podgy, smooth-faced looking bloke in a raincoat who took his cap off, presumably having expected my Mum to answer. He had nasty crinkly hair, all greasy and brushed to one side.

'Mum, it's your bloke in a raincoat,' I said, going back to the kitchen, leaving him standing at the front door. 'He says he's called Benny Hill.'

She wiped her hands and took off her apron, making faces at me for being so rude.

'Mrs Swift? Is your husband at home? This is my card.'

I went into the living room, carrying my pudding, and sat down beside Colin in front of the telly. I thought it was perhaps a club man, collecting some money, though it was a funny time to come, Saturday evening.

'Hello Joe,' said the man, coming into the room, all smiles, followed by my Mum. 'You done well this afternoon.'

'Oh aye,' I said, sounding just like my dad when he wants to give nothing away, but half wondering where I'd been this afternoon. It seemed a long time ago.

'I represent Carlisle United,' he said, sticking out his hand. 'My name's Ken.'

'Oh aye,' I said. My stomach gave a little jump and I could feel a bit of sick coming into my throat. I'd either eaten the crumble too quickly or it was excitement. I was trying to be cool and hard and not let on my insides were all over the place.

'Turn that stupid thing off,' said Mum, going over and turning off the television. Colin groaned, but she gave him a look.

'Won't you sit down, Ken, and have a cup of tea.' She was all beams and nods, her headache and her fears now all forgotten.

'That would be very nice, Mrs Swift, but only if you're making one.'

'You didn't call earlier, did you?' she asked. 'About an hour ago? I thought I saw someone in the back lane with a raincoat like yours.'

'Not me, Mrs Swift,' said Ken.

'Now I think about it, he had a little beard, which you haven't.'

'You're very observant tonight, Mum,' I said.

'Christ,' said Ken, then he apologised for blaspheming. 'That would be Newcastle United. Big bloke, big beard. He's called Reg. If he does call, just be careful, that's all. He's not officially a Newcastle scout. He's strictly freelance. But anyway, that's up to you, Mrs Swift.'

While Mum made some tea, Ken discussed the afternoon match, how I'd come back and defended well, better than I'd done in the previous game he'd watched me play. This was a surprise, that I'd been watched already.

'What about the penalty I gave away?'

'Over-enthusiasm, that's all,' said Ken, smiling. 'Anyway, you've obviously no idea how to tackle. We'll soon sort that out.'

'How do you mean, like?'

Ken then explained that he'd like me to go through to Carlisle once a week after school for training. Since that year they'd been in the First Division, they'd been building up a proper youth policy. I couldn't sign any forms officially, not till I was fifteen, when I could become an apprentice professional.

'Carlisle is probably the best team in the country to join as apprentice, at this moment in time,' said Ken. 'Oh thank you Mrs Swift, two sugars please.'

'Yes, they've done awfully well,' said Mum.

'With the big clubs, in the big cities,' continued Ken, 'young lads can get lost. They get very homesick.'

'Oh I'm sure,' said Mum.

'And with a big club, with so many players, your chances of getting in the first team are frankly, Mrs Swift, bloody bugger all, excuse my French.'

'Are you still in the First Division?'

'Oh Mum, give over,' I said. 'You're out of date.'

'We plan to be back in soon,' said Ken. 'Don't you worry. Our object is to consolidate our position, build up the background staff and the young talent. And that means you, Joe.'

'Oh, do you really think so, Ken?' said Mum.

Ken then explained that my expenses would be paid, coming through to Carlisle once a week, and something for a meal, so I wouldn't be out of pocket. They liked to do things properly, even though they were still a little club.

'And don't forget Brunton Park has the best pitch in England,' he said. 'Solway turf, you can't beat it. Same stuff they use at Wimbledon, did you know that, Mrs Swift? When they first laid it down at Wimbledon, there were little Solway shrimps, jumping out all over the place.'

'Oh, isn't that lovely,' said Mum.

I gave her a look, warning her not to be so soft. Ken was concentrating on charming her, praising the tea, admiring the furniture, the cocktail cabinet, Fanny's piano, saying what a nice house, a lot nicer than some of the houses he had been into in his time.

He arranged to come another time, when my Dad would be at home, as naturally he wanted to see him, and explain everything. As he left, he handed my Mum an envelope.

'Open it then,' I said, as soon as Ken had gone.

'No, I think I'll leave it for your Dad to open, when he comes tomorrow.'

'Don't be daft. Open the rotten thing, or I will.'

I tried to grab it from her, but she held on to it.

I'd read a story in the *Sunday Express* about the big clubs making underhand payments of up to £10,000, all illegal of course, to encourage young stars to join them. One dad had been given a free car, which turned up at his front door compliments of a famous club, the day his son signed apprentice forms.

I realised you'd have to be a star with the England boys before that sort of thing happened, being sought after by really big clubs, not Carlisle United. All the same, Carlisle had recently been in the First Division. They were bound to be offering something good.

'Come on Mum,' I said, 'it might be a thousand quid. You could buy your own car.'

Dad had taken his Mini with him to Newcastle, as he was driving back on the Sunday.

She slowly opened the envelope. Two tickets fell out. They were for Carlisle's next home match, against Rotherham.

'Bloody hell, the mean buggers.'

'Joe, don't talk like that. I think it's very nice of them.'

'Rotherham, they're rubbish,' I said, picking up the envelope and shaking it, just in case there was anything stuck inside.

'I think you're getting ideas above your station, my lad.'

'And why shouldn't I?' I said. 'They've come for me – because they know I'm good.'

'Oh Joe,' she said, shaking her head.

'I might join them, or I might not, see how I feel, so there.'

I banged out of the house and ran all the way into the village to tell Tom my news. My amazing news.

Until that day, I had seriously begun to think nobody was ever going to watch me.

Ken's Kuts, Wallsend

Dear Joe,

Thanks for letting me see it and I've followed your progress with great interest seeing how it was me what started you off as you well know like. That day I hadn't gone to see you but went to look at a goalkeeper called Green if I remember, from Kirkcudbright, but Queen of the South got at him first, and he was no good anyway. I'd recommended nobody to Carlisle for a long time, so I had to do something, or I'd lose my retainer. I was actually freelancing, part-time, getting my expenses only, but there's no need to change that, that's all right. I don't know why them lawyers worry about them tickets being illegal they don't know anything, all clubs gave free tickets, and the rest. You were not bad that day, not good but not bad, but I took a chance because of one thing you rarely see in lads of fourteen – confidence. You certainly still have it, from what I read like. I hope it helps where you are now, you'll need it. About the greasy hair, I don't like that, not at all, and I would be obliged if you would delete same. It was Brylcreem. I was a barber at the time, which I still am, here in my own place in Wallsend, so if you want a free haircut, or something for the weekend, then let me know, yours in sport,

KEN

5

I got the bus to Carlisle for my first training session. I could have got the train, but it stopped running three years earlier. Big City kids have it so easy.

Mr Bott organised it so I could leave school early that afternoon, as the buses were few, even though my form master was already moaning on about how much work there was to do, just another year to O-levels, Swift, the groundwork has to be done in the fourth year, everything depends on it, are you listening, Swift, all the usual schoolteacher shit.

I remember thinking that if you lived in a big city like London it must be a doddle, or Manchester, or Glasgow. Not just the transport, but the choice of so many professional clubs within a short distance. We lived about thirty miles from Carlisle, though it felt like three hundred. Apart from them there wasn't another professional club anywhere around, not since Workington and Barrow dropped out of the Football League. Going further West from Workington, you come to New York. Their new soccer league was getting started. I might try them, if Carlisle don't want me, I thought.

I was wearing a multi-coloured shirt with a long pointed collar which I'd just bought at the Co-op, at least my Mum had bought it for me, special offer in their winter sale. As I was leaving home Fanny said it was disgusting and out of fashion, in fact it looked sixties. That was all I needed. I worried all the way there. The Carlisle lads would obviously make fun of it. I had it buttoned up at first, like that bloke in Madness, can't remember his name, then on the bus I undid it as it was too tight.

I got out at the bus station and had to sit down to work out where I was. My Dad had done a map for me and said it was easy, straight down Warwick Road for a mile, then I'd come to the ground on the left, no problems. I've always had a poor sense of direction. When I stay in hotels, or strange bedrooms, and I've stayed in a few, then I have to leave chalk marks on the floor so I can find my way out in the morning. Or the night, if I'm making a quick exit. That problem doesn't arise at the moment. Not enough room here to swing a sheep, never mind shag it. Hold on. I'm jumping ahead. I vowed to myself I wouldn't do that. I hate books where they describe things that haven't happened yet.

Warwick Road was much longer than my Dad had said, and a lot busier and scruffier, then I found I'd been walking down Botchergate, so I had to come all the way back to the bus station and start again. I was carrying my boots, an old pair, getting a bit small for me, but very comfortable, and a clean pair of underpants. My Mum had insisted on that, saying I couldn't travel home in dirty ones, what if I have an accident. You mean shit myself, I said. Don't be vulgar. A road accident, knocked over by a bus and taken to hospital.

I was a bit worried about the underpants. They were Y-fronts, a bit baggy, as I hadn't really a lot of equipment to fill them with, not at that time, aged only, let me see, I was just about to be fifteen that week. In my first match for the North of England I'd noticed two of the really big lads putting on special jockstraps, sort of slips, with a thong at the back, like strippers wear, not that I'd seen a stripper, except in dirty mags. At the back, you could see their bare arses, but at the front there was a sort of pouch which kept their balls in place. I'd never seen this before, and didn't want to ask where you got them. I knew Cockermouth Co-op wouldn't sell them.

My Mum had also made me take a towel. Mum, they'll supply towels, it is a professional football club, not the Wolf Cubs. You never know, she said.

I felt I was about to go into the big time. I wondered if I would see Chris Balderstone, who was a brilliant cricketer as well as a classy footballer. A bit slow, but I liked the way he never looked rushed. Ray Train had been my favourite, in their First Division team, always

45

rushing around, and a great tackler, for a little feller. I knew I still had to work on my tackling, if I was going to stay in midfield. Perhaps they'd change my position. Put me up front again.

Brunton Park looked a bit old-fashioned and decaying, not as impressive or as modern as St James's Park, the only professional ground I'd been to before, when we lived in Durham, but then Newcastle has traditionally always been a top club, with a huge following. Carlisle, so my Dad said, trying to put me off, was one of nature's Third Division (North) teams, which is where they were in his boyhood. I said they don't have North and South Division any more. They will have, he said. You wait.

I found the main stand, as there was only one proper one, but I couldn't see the Players' Entrance, which was what I was looking for. Or any door that wasn't locked. There seemed to be no one around. I walked round the side and came to a cinder track and then a field, full of sheep. You never see sheep at St James's Park. Only on the pitch, har har.

I came back and eventually found a little door which was open. I wandered through, down dark concrete corridors, and found myself on the pitch. The surface was brilliant, really lush, so I took a few imaginary shots at goal, did a few quick dashes, till I heard someone shouting at me. It was a groundsman, ordering me to get off, saying I was trespassing. I said I'd come for training, Ken had sent me. He didn't know anything about that. There was no training tonight, never is, not on Monday. Training for boys was on Tuesdays and Thursdays, I should know that.

I slammed every door when I eventually got home, kicked several bits of furniture, then crashed into the kitchen, looking for some cheese to make toast and cheese. I'd missed tea, and was starving.

'It's all your fault, Mum,' I shouted in a really bad temper. 'You last saw Ken that evening I was out, when he came to see you and Dad. You stupid woman. You might have got the right date. And why is there never anything to eat in this stupid house . . .'

'Come here my lad,' she said, suddenly arriving in the kitchen and grabbing me by the ear. She was in a right paddy, something I'd not seen before.

'You were the last person to speak to Ken,' she said. 'He rang you last week, remember, wanting to talk to you personally, remember?

That was when he gave *you* the details about training. I could hear you saying, "Yes, yes, you've said," in your usual rude way. I knew at the time you weren't listening properly . . .'

'So it was your fault,' I said, wriggling free. 'If you thought I'd got it wrong you should have checked for me . . .'

'You horrible boy,' she said.

I ran upstairs to my bedroom with the toast and cheese. I knew it was all my fault. I was too furious even to get in a bit of quick self-abuse, the normal escape from the cares of the world.

I worried about what I was going to tell them at school the next day. I'd told everyone I was going, which was a mistake. They'd all want to hear how I'd got on. I couldn't say I'd buggered up the dates.

They cancelled, I said. Freak hurricane in Carlisle, the pitch flooded, giant shrimps jumping all the way up Warwick Road.

A few weeks later another scout arrived from Carlisle, in a bow tie and suede shoes. Trevor his name was, so smart my Mum thought he was the new doctor come to see my Dad. He was getting near the end of his college course now, and had some exams coming up, and was complaining about pains in his stomach, which we all thought was just nerves. Fanny was also about to take some important exams, to get into Oxford, but she was boasting she'd stopped revising. She'd already done everything she needed to do, what a creep.

Trevor not only gave me exact details of the next training session, but agreed to pick me up and take me there by car, which was great.

On the way there, he told me that every club had layers and layers of scouts. There were staff scouts, working full-time. Even Fourth Division clubs had at least one of them. Then you'd have scouts under contract in certain areas, covering the whole of Great Britain, working exclusively for a certain club. They would have their own jobs, teachers, or clerks or whatever, but be paid a retainer and expenses to work most evenings and weekends, plus a bonus, should a boy they find eventually sign forms as an apprentice professional.

Then there were freelance scouts, covering a smaller area, who would work for any club who rang them up and sent them to cover a particular match or check a particular boy. They got expenses only. In turn, all scouts had their own informal network, with teachers, parents, local league officials tipping them off on anyone likely coming through.

Often they would go and see kids as young as twelve, and bring them in for training.

I remember wondering why they had taken so long. With all that coverage, why had they missed me, when I'm so good? I didn't say it. No need to start off being marked as a bighead.

'We had a huge investigation when Kevin Keegan signed for Liverpool,' said Trevor. 'You've heard of him?'

'No, who's he?' I said, sarcastically.

'We have a good scout in the Scunthorpe area, so we should have done better. I looked up the records, and he had given him two good reports, but then another scout saw him and gave a poor report. I was about to go myself to see him, but I had to go to Scotland on a vital mission. When I got back, I'd missed Scunthorpe's last match of the season. During the summer, Liverpool gets in and signs him. Bingo.'

'Hard luck,' I said. I hadn't meant to be sarcastic. I wanted to know everything about everything to do with football.

'I'm sure a lot of clubs were like us. We usually have a good chance, signing on Fourth Division players. We had known about him, but we missed the boat. We do try, but we're not perfect.'

So that was a relief. Perhaps heads might roll for having missed me at twelve, or even at seven, when I played that brilliant game in the lotties.

I'd got it into my head it was going to be a proper training session, with the whole first team squad, perhaps me and Chris working on a few setpieces. It turned out to be a Trial, for schoolboys, mostly my age, but some younger. We split into groups of five first of all, with one in the middle, knocking the ball in and out, first-time passes. Then a bit of heading, keeping it up in the air, round in a circle, which not many could do, including me. Heading always gave me a headache in those days.

Then we had a match, which was a shambles. We didn't use the full pitch, just across the middle, and there were too many players, almost as bad as the lotties. I don't know how they could tell if anyone was any good from all that, but I was asked to come again, either Tuesday or Thursday, if I could manage it, being a country boy, living a long way away.

I went for the next few months, once a week, but it was always a struggle, dragging all the way there, all on my own, missing buses, being late, then coming back fed up, feeling I hadn't learned much anyway, that it was all pathetic, that they didn't really know who I was, with so many lads coming and going, getting trials, doing quite well, then never being seen again. In a season, even a little club like Carlisle was giving trials to about five hundred boys. I much preferred playing on Saturdays, with Cockermouth, or the North of England.

It all seemed pointless. It was like Mitchell's market in Cockermouth on sheep sales day, farmers poking and pointing, whispering and gossiping, then shaking their heads, clucking their teeth, moving on to the next batch.

The Carlisle coaches appeared just to be observing, not really training you, waiting and watching, mostly waiting till you got older and bigger, if you ever were going to get any bigger, in which case they might have to fatten you up, like yearling sheep. There were some kids so titchy you could hardly see them on the pitch, yet they were still given their chance. I was about average, not small, not big, except round the tum and the bum, which they were always going on about, telling me to cut out the sweets.

I was always surprised when kids I thought were really good, who were told they had a good chance of making it, just gave up, like that, overnight, never turning up again, preferring to lie in bed, or chase girls, or play snooker, appearing not to care any more about football, even though they were obviously good at it. There must be loads of people out there who are as good at football as those who have made a profession out of it. What makes the difference? Ah, we shall see, folks, stick around.

'I'm giving up training,' I told my Mum one day. 'It's boring.'

'Fine,' she said. 'Suit yourself.'

'But don't you think it's a waste of time, Mum?'

'How do I know? You're the one who goes. You're the one who wants to do it. You're the one who says he wants to be a professional footballer . . .'

My Dad said thank God, he always thought it was a daft idea. I had seen dads almost in tears at Carlisle, when the coaches made it clear there was no point in coming again. My Dad meant it. He thought it was a dodgy career, with enormous wastage, dependent so much on luck, on injuries, on fashion, on being in the right place at the right time, all true, oh wise one, and the money wasn't all that brilliant anyway, unless you were at the very top, and then only for a short time.

His main point was that unlike most football-mad kids of my age, I did have alternatives. I was not a complete thicko. If I was, then he'd say fine, give it a chance, what was there to lose, but I could do well at anything, if only I put my mind to it, go to university and have a proper career. Why not just save football for Saturday afternoons, and just enjoy it? I'd always get a game.

I'd thought only about football since I was seven. It was my only passion in life, what I dreamt about, read about, fantasised about. It even beat wanking. I knew no pleasure greater than coming off a pitch, absolutely knackered, purple in the face, sweat pouring out, hardly able to stand up straight, aches in every bone, yet feeling absolutely exhilarated, intoxicated, liberated, satiated. Yup, and over the moon. I'm talking about having won, having played well. Losing, playing badly, well we don't talk about that, do we. I can't bear it. That's when I lose my head, when things go wrong, especially if it's my own fault. I know, don't tell me, it's part of the process, the pain we have to bear to point up the pleasures.

Carlisle offered me apprenticeship forms when I got to fifteen, which was the age in those days – today it's sixteen. I could join them full-time, get £10 a week and get a proper training. My Dad said no, definitely not, he wouldn't sign or agree to anything, not till I was sixteen and had sat my O-levels. Even then, he thought I would be daft. I should go into the sixth form, do A-levels, then think about football.

I told them it was pointless. I hated school work, all the teachers, all the subjects, and would fail everything as I'd just skived for four years. I was going to be a footballer. Now. And I didn't care what he said.

He persuaded my Mum that doing my O-levels was the best course, and he also got on to Carlisle. They agreed it was wise to get some academic qualifications. They would wait till I was sixteen. No bother.

Then out of the blue, Newcastle United came for me. They asked me to come for three days' training at half-term. They would fix me up with digs. No problem.

I'd taken over the midfield in the North of England team, bossing everyone around, and had started scoring lots of goals, mainly from free kicks and penalties. I'd signed nothing for Carlisle, but I didn't tell them about Newcastle, just that I had a lot of school work to do in the holidays.

Arriving at Newcastle, I could sense right away it was a bigger, wealthier, better-organised club with more facilities. I felt so proud to be going there, to the club I'd always supported. At school, most lads supported Man United. I'd always followed Newcastle, thanks to my Durham days.

Yet I can't remember much about those three days. Apart from the fight. There was this lad called Mitch, small, red-haired, nasty bit of work, always moaning, always complaining, a right fouler. For the whole two days he had kicked me every time I played against him. He was also midfield, so-called creative midfield, trying to run the show.

We'd only just started training on the last day, doing press-ups, and hadn't even begun any ball work, when he tripped me up. So I head-butted him. A natural reaction, the sort of thing I did in the playground if anyone gave cheek. A coach tried to separate us, one of their reserve players, helping out with the schoolboys, and I head-butted him as well.

I was sent for an early bath, then got the train straight home. Goodbye Newcastle, so I thought.

I arrived home much earlier than expected, so my Mum and Dad were out, which was just as well. Dad was at home at the time, the last week or so before his exams, but they'd gone out to some friends who were having a twenty-first wedding anniversary do. Fanny was in Cockermouth, at some history lecture at school. It was just Colin in the house – and the babysitter. He was already in bed, fast asleep.

That made me even more bad-tempered, finding a stranger sitting in our house. It was stupid anyway, having a sitter for Colin, he was ten, but they always overprotected the little fat sod. It was a local farm lass, Maggie Satherthwaite, whom I vaguely knew, so she wasn't a total stranger. She was big and hefty and very cowlike, about eighteen. She didn't think she was cowlike, mind you, in fact she thought she was Gina Lollobrigida, always fussing with her long dark straggly hair.

She had hardly ever spoken to me, treating me like a kid. Until that evening.

'You can go now,' I said when I stormed in, throwing my bag down, then going to change the telly programme she was watching. She jumped up, pushed me so violently that I fell over a stool, and changed the programme back.

I got up, furious, and tried to get at the tv, but she barred my way. We struggled, pushing each other, till she put her arms round me, pinning me from behind, so I couldn't get at her *or* the tv.

Her huge breasts were pressed against my back, not really cowlike, now I felt them, in fact soft and giving and bouncy. I tried to lash out with my feet but missed. In the process my leg had gone between her legs. She laughed, mocking my lack of strength, compared with hers.

'You touch that telly again and I'll bray yer,' she said. She held me for a few more moments, then let me go.

I went into the kitchen and started banging around bad-temperedly, looking for something to eat, opening cupboard doors and slamming them.

'Who stole your scone then?' she shouted, still mocking me.

'Shurrup you, pigface.'

'Ooh, that's not very nice.'

'I said you could go,' I repeated, when I'd made myself a giant doorstep of a sandwich with Kraft cheese, mayonnaise and pickles. I was standing at the living-room door, watching the telly, just to see what she had put on.

'And who's going to pay me then? Will you pay me, Little Joe, for my services, now that you're a big famous footballer? So what's it like at Newcastle then, in the first team yet?'

'Get lost,' I said.

'Tell me all about it then.'

'Piss off.'

'Ohh, I can tell something's gone wrong with diddums. Come on, son, sit down on the sofa and I'll turn the telly off. It's rubbish anyway.'

'Piss off,' I said.

'Not till eleven o'clock,' she said. 'Then I'll piss all over you. Eeeeh . . .'

She made a gesture with her skirt, a sort of bolero thing, swishing it to the side, then she crouched on the sofa, as if about to have a piss, cackling like an old hen at her own wit.

'Ha ha, fucking funny,' I said.

'I'm telling your Mam you swore.'

I banged up the stairs to my bedroom. She shouted after me not to make so much noise. If I woke Colin she'd murder me.

I got undressed and was about to have a quick bash on the old organ before I got into bed, thinking there will be no need to hunt out an old *Radio Times* for the corset adverts, or flick though my Mum's *Woman's Journal* for the fashion photos, not tonight, not when the feeling of Maggie's breasts was still so fresh in my mind, and the touch of her legs, and the glimpse of her fat white thighs and the hint of her fanny when she had swished her skirt. Oh God, I can feel it coming now.

Was that just her stupid corny joke about 'services'? Why did she ask me to sit down beside her on the couch? Had my mind been too full of the head-butting scene to realise I was being offered IT, my big chance, on a plate, or at least my Mum's new sofa?

I got dressed, slowly, brushed my teeth, then I washed my balls and my cock, to get the erection down and make sure it was clean. I'd wet my grey flannels at the front, through washing my genitals with the trousers on, so it looked as if I'd pissed myself, or cheesed myself. I went to my Mum's bedroom to look for her hairdryer, but I couldn't see it. Instead, I shook some talcum down my flies, and then took my shoes of and did my feet. I was sweating already, and my socks were smelling, as they usually were, even when they were clean on.

I was shaking with expectation and excitement, but at the same time ready for disappointment, feeling I had imagined all the signs, perhaps even looking forward to it, knowing I could come back to my bedroom and have a real good wank.

'I thought you'd come back,' she said, smiling, reaching out to put down the sound on the telly and switch off the overhead light. I nearly turned back at that stage, as if I'd fallen into a trap. But I had such a hard on by then I had to sit down to hide it.

She unzipped me almost as soon as I'd sat down, and I came, all over her hand. She said not to worry. It didn't bother her. We could wait a bit. So we did, with her gently holding me, caressing me, at the same time slipped off her skirt, and then her knickers. I came again, even before I'd got on top of her. Not to worry, she said, just lie still for a bit.

We were getting going again when the phone rang. I started to get up, but she said ignore it. It stopped then started again. I thought it might be Newcastle, ringing to tell my parents what had happened, probably to say that was it, they didn't want me any more.

The phone rang again, and eventually she got up, moaning and groaning.

'Oh fucking hell,' she said. 'I'll have to answer it. It'll be your Mum, checking everything's okay.'

She got up putting her skirt straight, and picked up the phone.

'What? Oh dear, that sounds terrible. Oh, I'm very sorry, Mrs Swift. No, everything's all right here. Joe? Oh, I think I can just hear him, hold on, he's coming in the front door now. Yes, Colin, he's fine, sound asleep. Don't worry. I can stay the night if you like, if it helps. I just have to ring my Dad and tell him. Byee . . .'

What an evening. Three dramas, all at once. My Dad had his heart attack. It was just a few chest pains at first, at the party. Then he sort of collapsed, and my Mum had to get the emergency doctor.

That was the night I got my end away. If you can call it that. I certainly did, boasted like mad about screwing this older woman, she was all over me, couldn't get enough, I had her panting for more.

Then there were two phone calls. The first was from Newcastle, telling me not to come back again. The sods. The next was from London. Offering me a trial.

Upper Rigg Farm

Dear Mr Swift,

    I am returning your package. Margaret, or Pamela, as I gather she now calls herself, has not been in touch with us for many years, not since she left home at nineteen and went to London. You do know we adopted her. She has had nothing to do with us since then, or anyone else round here. She pretends she never lived in Rigg, or anywhere near. I'm afraid she has disowned us all, after all we did for her, but that's what happens, you see. You just do your best and leave it to the Good Lord. I've been telt she's married and is now Lady something, in Cornwall, I think, married to a big landowner, pots of money, though she's never sent us nowt, not that we'd ask. Hoping this leaves you as it leaves me.

                   M. SATHERTHWAITE *(Mrs)*

6

I arrived in London in a heatwave, you must remember it, so the effect was overpowering, everyone wilted, everyone was moaning, everyone was saying it's worse than the tropics. Even if I'd arrived on a freezing cold day, London would have seemed tropical to me. It was so totally foreign and exotic. The moment I got off the train at Euston, the foreignness hit me, making me feel small, insignificant, vulnerable. I was sure people were looking at me and thinking you don't belong here, you're not a Londoner, get back to the sticks, you hick, crawl into your cave, you crud.

There was no one to meet me at the station, which was daft, why should they, on a Sunday evening, not as if I was anyone special, not as if they had paid one and a half million for me. Remember when that was the record price paid by Man.Utd. for Bryan Robson from West Brom in 1981, ask me another. The whole football world was agog. How could anyone be possibly worth that? Chickenfeed today. You can't buy a decent Third Division player for a million now. Someone with their own knees will cost you two million.

The train journey down had been so slow, with Sunday work on the lines, and we halted for ages just after Penrith. By which time I'd eaten my emergency supplies of four Mars Bars, three packets of crisps, plus two Cokes, meant to last me all the way, so my Mum had said, perhaps even for a few days, just in case they didn't have such stuff in London.

I got on the Tube, with difficulty, clutching the address, changing to the Piccadilly line as directed, scared to ask anyone in case I couldn't understand their answer. The smells and sounds were so strange and confusing. I thought Newcastle was overwhelming when I'd gone there, but London was a whole new country, all of it mad, bad and hellish to know. Would I ever cope? Would I ever be jumping on and off a Tube like a native? What was I thinking? In a couple of years I'll have my own Jag. Bugger public transport. That's what I told myself, trying to cheer myself up, force a smile out of my tight nervous little arse of a mouth.

I had been down to London a month previously, with my Dad, for the trial. They'd paid for everything, including taxis. It all happened in a whirl. The sudden phone call that night, the command to come, the discovery that they had huge dossier on me, then the offer of apprenticeship forms, sign here, thank you, you won't regret it. How could I refuse a First Division club?

Now I would have to manage London on my own, a working man, what a laugh, like everyone else. I was sitting in a corner beside a large black man with a large black woman, wearing dead flash clothes, and an Indian woman in a sari with three little kids, also very well dressed. They were squashing me, but I didn't want to protest, or push them in any way, as I didn't know the rules, the codes, how to act and react, which was silly, as I was a Britisher and they must be, well, foreigners. I got such a surprise when I heard them speaking. They were all broad cockney. I was the foreigner.

I'd never seen black people before, not up close. We didn't have them in Cockermouth, nor had I seen any in Carlisle, or Newcastle for that matter. I'd never come across a Jew either. Catholics were about the most exotic and unusual people I'd come across. In Cockermouth, a foreigner was someone who came from Keswick.

I had to get off at some place called Turnpike Lane, which sounded olde worlde, and I was up and ready, three stops ahead, clutching my case, just in case these nasty Cockneys played a trick on me, whisking me on to the end of the line and I'd find myself in Cockfosters and never be heard of again.

I then had a long walk, through horrible streets, along Lordship Lane, till I came to 29, Newbiggen Street, N17. Mrs Jarret opened the front door the moment I knocked. She must have been looking for me through the net curtains. She was big and beefy, a widow woman in her fifties who looked as if she stood no nonsense and ate young lads for breakfast.

'You're bleedin' late,' she said.

'It was the train, I came on the train . . .'

'I didn't think you flippin' flew,' she said.

It was a two-storey redbrick terrace house, and the front door opened straight into her living room. I could see a tea table was set for two people, with plastic doilies, but she directed me straight up the stairs.

'Your bedroom's first on the left. Just dump your stuff, wash your hands, then come and eat your tea, I'm not waiting no more, is that clear?'

Wash your hands. What does she think I've been doing with them? I dragged my case towards the stairs. It was old and battered, last used by my Dad when he went away. Then I remembered I'd promised to ring home, the moment I arrived, tell them I was safe, find out how Dad was. It was his operation that day.

'Er, can I use your telephone please, er, Mrs Jarret?'

'You can not,' she said. 'Only for incoming calls, if you don't mind. I've had enough of that nonsense. You can use the one at the end of the street.'

I moved towards the front door, but she barred my way, grabbing my arm with her massive fleshy fingers. I still had no muscles on my arms in those days, and not much anywhere else. Ask Maggie.

'Not now,' she growled. 'Do you fink I've nothing better to do all evening than wait for you? Up those stairs, my son.'

So I went up slowly. I opened my bedroom door, swearing to myself under my breath, already wanting to go home.

What a fright I got. There was someone already there, lying on one of two single beds, reading *Reveille*. He jumped as well, then he grunted, a sort of hello, not in any accent I could recognize, then he went back to reading.

It was daft really, to have imagined I'd be on my own. I just hadn't thought. I said nothing, slowly opening my case. I took out a packet from the top, looked to see if he was watching, and shoved it under my bed. Then I got out my best shirt and new hipster flannels, bought by my Mum in Binns, Carlisle, specially for London, and looked around the room for somewhere to hang them up. There was a wardrobe, smelling of mothballs, which was full of his stuff, so I put my trousers on a wire hanger and hung them on the wall from a picture rail.

'She'll be having you by the balls for doing that,' he said, without looking up. I won't try to catch Danny's Irish accent. I'm useless at accents, either imitating them or writing them down.

'So where am I supposed to put my bloody stuff?' I said.

'Up your bloody arse,' he said.

'Thanks a lot.'

'I thought you was Scotch? She told me you was Scotch. Lying bastard.'

'No, I'm from Cockermouth.'

'Where the fuck's that?'

'Near Carlisle,' I said.

'You what?' he said, still reading.

I opened the wardrobe again, pushed his stuff to one side, watching with one eye to see his reaction, and hung up my shirt and trousers.

He glared at me, trying to look tough. He was my height, but thinner and weedier. If it came to a fight, I should win. And if it came to headbutting, he'd have no chance. He didn't have a forehead, just a bit of freckled, mottled skin, indented either side, as if the forceps had slipped. He looked more like a jockey than a footballer.

'Fucking watch the material,' he said, without looking at me. He then threw down *Reveille* and picked up the *Cork Examiner* from under his bed.

I didn't realise at that stage that Danny had only arrived in London five days before me, his first ever trip to the Big Smoke, so he was as fresh behind the balls as I was, but he was trying hard to lord it over me, pretending he was already a city slicker, a dude who knew his way around.

We went downstairs together and sat at the tea-table. Danny was still trying to look like Big Mick, while I felt like Wee Alec, nervous and anxious. I was starving, as I'd had nothing since Penrith, apart from some more biscuits and crisps and two cupcakes and a Coke from the buffet, spending the little money I had.

There was a funny smell. Not nasty or bad, just strange. The cups and plates seemed southern and odd, but then I'd always found it hard to eat in other folks' houses, even neighbours back in Rigg. Other mums always did things differently. Tea and toast in someone else's house never seemed the same as in our house. I once hit Tom Graham, when he told me my Mum's tea was horrible. I said his Mum's toast was shitty. Yet we all bought the same stuff from the same Co-op van.

'Here, get this down you,' said Mrs Jarret, slapping a plate in front of me. 'This will put lead in your pencil.'

It did look like lead, lumpy and solid, just lying there, newly-dead lead. I poked a fork into it, from a safe distance, and blood came out. Ugh. Liver. I hate liver.

Danny laughed. When Mrs Jarret had left the room, he pretended to be sick, which made me really feel sick, with lumps of sick coming into my throat, tasting of cupcake.

'Right, young feller, I want every bit of this eaten up,' said Mrs Jarret, arriving with Danny's meal, plonking a huge plate of chips and beans and sausages and a fried egg in front of him. That was just what I wanted. It wasn't fair.

'Pass the sauce,' I said to Danny, seeing some condiments on top of a mahogany dresser. While he leaned back, I grabbed some of his chips, just as Mrs Jarret returned and caught me, slapping my fingers with a large serving spoon. She'd brought me some green-looking shit in a dish.

'Actually, Mrs Jarret, I have had tea already. I'm not really all that hungry.'

'You'll eat that up, or else,' she said, folding her ams and glaring at me.

'What is this, er, anyway.'

'Spinach,' she said. 'Just what the doctor ordered. To go with the liver.'

'I don't think I've had spinach before,' I said, turning it over with a fork. It had been boiled into a mush and could have been anything, animal, vegetable or mineral shit. Amazing to think I now love spinach, and any sort of green vegetable as long as they are totally fresh, and always underdone. Not that I get much choice in here.

'Don't think I like making two different meals, I do not,' she said. 'No fun for me.'

'Then don't do it,' I said, looking at Danny, wolfing down his chips.

'Club orders,' she said. 'Just my luck to have two difficult bleeders at the same bleeding time.'

She explained she had to build up my strength, but not my weight, whereas with Danny, she had to build up his bulk, as well as his weight, to give him strength.

'So he can have lots of carbodies,' she said. 'While you are on a preteen diet.'

'You what?'

She couldn't pronounce the words any more than I could, but she knew what she had to do, and knew it worked, having had apprentice professionals in her care for the last decade, seen them swim into her pool and flounder around as little shrimps, then move on as mighty sharks.

'But he's the same height as me,' I said. 'We should be having the same stuff.'

'They'll have checked your old fellers,' she said. Me and Danny caught each other's eyes and smirked, thinking this was some rude Cockney expression.

'Don't you worry, old son,' she said. 'They know that Danny's dad is a little skittery thing, is that not right Dan? While your dad is probably big and fat and hefty, am I not right.'

Danny was nodding his head, while still stuffing his ugly twat face.

'I'll have to ring him,' I said, standing up, grateful for the excuse to leave the table. With one ham shank of an arm, she forced me down again.

'They don't leave things to chance these days,' she said, 'not like them old days when apprentices were allowed to eat any old rubbish. They now study your genes.'

'That's lucky, cos I've brought a pair, which I'd better go and unpack,' I said, trying to rise again.

'Ha bleedin' ha, we've got a joker here, have we,' she said, eyeing me up. 'Just be careful with your jokes. I know all the tricks, don't you worry. I've seen it all before.'

I don't know why she was issuing this warning to me. I'd done nothing, said nothing out of place, still feeling nervous and apprehensive. Did I have a bolshie look I was not even aware of? Teachers at school often used to tell me off before I'd opened my mouth.

I did manage to swallow most of the liver, with great difficulty, and forced down enough of the spinach to keep her happy, washing it down with several cups of tea, which was also horrible, but not as bad as the food.

She screamed when she saw me putting two sugars into my first cup of tea, pulling the cup from my lips as I was about to drink it, and poured it down the sink. I explained that I had had two sugars in my tea all my life, since I was a baby. I couldn't drink tea otherwise. What else could I drink? I hated water. I'd just fade away, and the club would blame her.

She hit me over the head with her tea towel and told me not to be such a pain. In the end, we compromised on one sugar per cup, for the first month, then I'd cut it down gradually to nothing.

'Bloody hell,' I said, muttering to myself as she cleared the table. 'It's a bloody prison.'

'What was that?' she said.

'Nothing,' I said. But I could see she was half smiling as she went into the kitchen.

Danny offered to take me for a walk round the block before bed, get some fresh air, show me the local park.

She said that was a good idea, but we hadn't to be late. Tomorrow was a big day and we'd need all our strength. We would soon know about it tomorrow. We wouldn't be able to walk anywhere, not after tomorrow.

I gave Danny a punch in his ribs as soon as we left the house, calling him a fucking creep. He'd said nothing all the meal, letting me walk into it, and I bloody didn't want to have a stupid walk, to some stupid park. I hate walking. Always have done. Still do.

'Don't be a fucking eejit,' he said, quickening his stride as we walked down the street. He turned round a corner, and walked straight into a pub.

'You get them,' he said, sliding into a corner, walking sideways, as if he was a spy. 'Mine's a Guinness.'

Cheeky sod. I ordered two, both halves, though I'd never had Guinness before. Shandy was all I'd tried, but I still preferred Coke.

When I came back, I couldn't find him at first, then I saw him in a side room at a pool table, setting up the balls. I'd never played pool before. Our local pubs didn't have such things, not in those days. He hammered me, first few games, till I got the hang of it.

The Guinness was horrible. I couldn't believe it had ever caught on. Surely everyone's first taste must be like mine – revolting. But I'd paid for it, so I slowly forced it down. That's what London seemed to consist of so far, forcing things down. Perhaps that's what Life was going to be like? Hey up. No philosophy.

All around, people were laughing and shouting and enjoying themselves, much more than in the North. They had spilled out on the pavement, sitting on benches with umbrellas up, women and blokes eating French bread and sausages with young girls drinking fancy drinks with cherries in and making fancy talk, all of them sounding so clever, so confident and cocky. They were probably just clerks, earning bugger-all, but they seemed so sophisticated and their girl friends so fashionable and desirable, but of course out of reach to a hick like me. I hadn't even learned the language.

I can still smell and hear that pub now. My first London experience. It was another country, another time. Yet it vanished so quickly, that feeling of newness, of being a stranger.

'Your turn,' I said to Danny.

'No, you get it, I'll give you the money.'

'Get stuffed,' I said. I'd had to repeat my order three times in the first place, as the barman said he hadn't understood a word I'd said, snot-faced bugger.

Danny eventually went to the bar, as he was dying for another Guinness more than I was. I could hear the barman talking to him, something about a birth certificate, had he brought it yet, then he came back and said we're going, this place is fucking useless.

'Serves you right,' I said. 'You little runt. I wouldn't serve a twat like you anyway.'

'Fuck off,' he said.

We went into another pub, not as smart or well-decorated, much more crowded and very smoky, full of blokes with dogs, all arguing loudly and violently about the football season ahead, saying Arsenal were going to stuff Spurs. I kept well out of the way, not knowing if the violent language was real, or only cockney posturing. I slid into a corner while Dan went for the drinks. He managed it without anyone questioning his age.

'Oh Christ,' I said as he sat down. 'I fucking forgot.'

I got up, went over to the bar, wandered round, not wanting to ask, as they wouldn't know what I was saying. I finally found a phone and dialled home.

'Hi, Mum, it's Joe.'

'Who else would it be?'

'I've arrived okay.'

'You're at Mrs Jarret's, are you?'

'Yes.'

'What's she like then? Sounds very noisy. Is she having a party?'

'What? Oh yeah. To welcome me. No, it's just that she has a few people here.'

'Is it a boarding house?'

'What?'

I was holding my left hand over my ear, trying hard to listen above the pub noise. The last thing she'd said, when she'd put me on the train at Carlisle, was not to hang around pubs, or get in with the wrong crowd.

'It's all fine,' I said. 'I'll ring you tomorrow, after the first day. Nowt to say now. Oh, how's Dad . . . ?'

I could only faintly make out the answer. Something about a pacemaker. They'd put one inside him. Sounded weird. I thought pacemakers were people in races, who set off dead fast.

'Bye then.'

'Take care, Joe. Hold on, Colin wants to speak to you.'

But I'd hung up. I didn't want to speak to him anyway.

That night in bed, Danny produced an old fashioned Dansette record player from beneath his bed and put on an Abba record, keeping it low. She didn't know about it, he said, no music or radio was allowed in our bedroom, not after ten.

'She's not a bad wee soul,' he said. 'Better than any fucking nuns.'

I reached under my bed and got out my package.

'Is it a dirty book then,' said Danny. 'Give us a look.'

'Get stuffed.'

It was a six-pack, of Penguins, special offer, which I was saving for emergencies. I slowly ate each one, spinning them out, all to myself. Bugger Danny. He'd had a proper tea.

Danny switched his music off, and then the lights. After about five minutes, I could hear a fumbling and thumping noise from under his blankets.

'You dirty bugger,' I said, knowing he was doing what I was doing.

'Goodnight, cunt face,' I said.

'Goodnight, shite hawk,' he said.

Manuel's English Bar

Dear Joe,

I have no objections to the references to me in the
chapter you have sent me so far but I do not like the
language and that's a fact but I suppose that's up to you.
A course I know all about carbohyrobes, even if I can't
spell it, that was my little joke, you must know that, you're
not the only clever one. But if you do not tell the REAL
TRUTH about what happened at Newbiggen Street then
I will, so help me, I've had it up to here, people thinking
it was my fault, the *News of the World* will be very pleased
if I rang them, I shouldn't wonder, you'll see.

ELSIE GONZALEZ (*Jarret as was*)

7

On the morning of our first day Danny was made to eat a raw egg mixed with milk for breakfast, so that fettled him, that larned him, neither of which expressions he seemed to know. It was one of Mrs Jarret's own specialities, always worked in the past, she said, for building up the weak. I was given some shit called muesli which I'd never seen before. It tasted horrible, and she wouldn't let me put sugar on it, but I was allowed some toast, wholemeal brown, more shit, with margarine and not butter.

Then we set off. Into the future? Okay Tom, just testing, but it was the first step, which could well have been the last step. Out of the ten apprentice professionals – six of them brand new – heading for Spurs that day, by the law of averages, only one would ever make it into the first team as a regular. Another two or three would get into the reserves, then be given a free or modest transfer and manage a career of some sort, in the lower divisions or non league. The rest would just disappear, and never play professionally again. Tough shit. So it goes, another future gone.

But on that morning, who was to know who would survive? Certainly no one at Spurs. The greatest coaches in the world can't tell at sixteen which kid will make it. They know who should, who at sixteen gives out all the right signs, but signs can be confusing, can disguise what is inside and has still to come out, sorry, Tom, we'll quit the homilies, and now back to me.

I wanted to get to the top. Or nothing. I couldn't bear the thought of second best. Perhaps I had in my mind that I could always do something else. I didn't know what, but Mr Bott and my Dad had always said I could make a success of many things, should I put my mind to it. I was confident – but worried that my worth would not be recognized, that I might fall amongst idiots and halfwits.

Danny was unconfident – but totally unworried, as far as I could see. His ambition in life was very simple – never to go back to Ireland. He thought he had now achieved that. By starting at a big club, whatever happened in the future, he had been here, received the best training. He was therefore quite prepared and even expected to fall through the divisions, ending up in Hartlepool at twenty-seven, then he'd run a pub or a newsagent, no preferably a newsagent. He could put in his day reading all the dodgy mags on the top shelf, then spend his evening in the pub. At sixteen, he only had two interests in life, sex and booze. Football was a poor third.

We walked up Tottenham High Road together in the blazing summer sun, a scruffy, boring, tatty road which goes on forever and is all the same, cheap and featureless, with nasty furniture showrooms full of nasty stuff. Danny stopped from time to time to look in the windows, and sometimes shop doors, if there was a likely-looking girl at the counter, opening up the shop for the day. I kept my head high, no not pride, not walking tall to disguise the tum, but to catch that first glimpse of the floodlights, towering in the sky. They looked like the masts of a giant battleship which had sailed up the High Road and then got stuck. The moment I saw them, I felt nervous, my stomach began to turn and I thought where am I, what am I doing, but I didn't say a word. I couldn't explain this to Danny. He had his nose against a window, watching a girl up a pair of steps.

No one spoke to us, no one probably even looked at us, and why should they, just another couple of lads going to work, though we did both look pretty smart, in our new flannels, our best shirts. It was mid July, and the rest of the world was still thinking about the Wimbledon champion or who might win the Open Golf. No one had yet got round to gentle thoughts of football.

We got to the White Hart pub, which I'd never noticed on my first and only visit, and turned right into a short lane, a rather poky entrance for the vast edifice which lurks behind. I looked up at the enormous sign, TOTTENHAM HOTSPUR FOOTBALL CLUB. It had never been my club. Queens Park Rangers had been the only London

club I'd vaguely followed, just because of Stan Bowles, and I'd vaguely
followed him cos when I trained at Carlisle I wore a training top they
said he had worn.

We had to report to the boot room. The other eight apprentices
were already there, trying to look busy, part of the fabric, pulling out
a large wickerwork skip, then getting down boxes marked white tops,
black sox, counting out the contents and putting them in the skip. The
room had no light and was small and crowded and smelled of polish
and embrocation. No sweat, no signs of sweat. No one was sweating,
not yet, so early in the morning, so early in our life, tra la.

We stood at the door and watched, Danny because he was a skiver
and me because I could see there was more than enough people
loading the skip already, trying to look busy, trying to disguise their
nerves and awkwardness, pushing each other to drag out the skip into
the car park. We should have joined them. By standing idle, we were
given the job of fetching a heavy weighing machine and humping it
into the boot of the coach. I was sure I had pulled a muscle, even
before we'd begun.

On the coach to Cheshunt, which was then the Spurs training
ground, we sat at the back, all us apprentices, not saying much,
staring out of the window, reading *Melody Maker* or *N.M.E.* At the
front were a couple of reserves, poor reserves, must have been, else
they would have had their own cars. There were no first-team players
with us. The Gods were making their own way to Cheshunt.

'Swifty, is it true you shag sheep where you come from?'

I looked round. It was Tel, a very pale-faced Cockney lad I'd met
during the trial. He had a wiry body with the most enormous thighs,
a sure sign of his superior status, of his advanced experience. He
was seventeen, and had been an apprentice for six months already,
confidently expecting to be offered professional forms very soon.

In the last two years, playing for Cockermouth or North of
England, nobody had picked on me, not since Cally and the
Under-Thirteens. It was an old taunt as well, one I'd heard many
a time before. As the only country lad amongst the apprentices, I
might have expected it. Even Danny was from a city, the city of
Cork, as he kept on telling everyone. Of the others, five were
from the London area, one from the Midlands, one from Fife in
Scotland and one from Bristol. I should have been able to think

of an immediate reply, but I was caught off balance, my mind elsewhere.

'We'll have to have a look at his chopper in the showers today,' said Tel. 'See if it's got any wool on it.'

Everyone laughed, especially the brand-new apprentices, pleased to see someone else being picked on.

Cheshunt was amazing, nine acres of lush lawns right in the heart of suburban Hertfordshire, with three full-sized pitches, extensive dressing rooms, a proper dining room and a rose garden. I gazed around, taking it all in, and was told off for not helping to unload the balls – forty of them, one for every player, from first-team star down to apprentices. At Carlisle there were never enough balls to go round in training, and they were all worn.

The first-team stars were slowly arriving, in their new Jaguars, Rovers, Volvos and MGs, standing around talking to each other in their Mediterranean tans, immaculate casuals and expensive hair. I could hear Glen Hoddle being asked by another player about some TV programme he'd done, and asking how much he'd got. 'Enough,' he replied. I'm going to start one-word replies from now on, I thought, much smarter.

We were all trying to listen and gape as we unloaded the last of the stuff from the skip. Tel said he'd heard Archibald was now on £250 a week, straight up, no messing, and we all oohed and ahhed, sucked our breath and muttered fucking hell.

The reserves arrived in second-hand Cortinas and Capris and looked equally stocky and adult, but somehow not quite as tanned, not quite at ease, their hair not as fashionably coiffured. There were a couple of dozen spectators, men with dogs, schoolboys on holiday, plus a handful of teenage girls who nervously and respectfully tried to get the stars to sign autographs as they arrived.

The first team changed in their own dressing room, but once out on the pitches we were all equal, senior and junior all mixed up, working together. Me and the five other brand-new apprentices were given our club number. Everyone has one at most big clubs, from one to forty, which goes on all your kit and stays with you till you leave. I was given number eight, and made to feel pretty privileged, because a coach told me that was the club number which Danny Blanchflower had. A good sign, I thought. Not so good was the fact that the previous incumbent had been given a free transfer to Torquay.

We started with simple physical exercises, to limber up, then each person was given a ball and told to go through various routines, heading, keeping it up, bringing it down. Then we worked in pairs, one-touch passing, and I found myself with Garth Crooks, oh ecstasy, and I mucked up the first pass I gave him, trying a flash slice off the side of my left foot, and sent it straight at a dog. The dog went away limping and I saw Garth laughing, either at me or the dog, or both.

Then we moved on to groups of fives, doing further passing movements. There were whistles going all the time, coaches shouting instructions, telling us to change partners, or move on to the next routine. Nothing lasted too long, which was good, but a lot of people were getting a right rollicking for making mistakes or not trying hard enough.

After an hour we moved on to another pitch and an ex-Olympic weightlifter took us for weight training. This was hellish, even though the six of us, the new apprentices, were taken on our own and not given such arduous stuff to do, being seven-stone weaklings, or in my case, an eleven-stone weakling. Okay, eleven and a half. For five foot nine, I didn't think that was bad, but I was told that when I got up to eleven and a half stone of muscle, that would be permissible. As long as I was eleven and half stone of fat, I would be referred to as you fat git or alternatively you fat cunt. I got abused and ridiculed and shouted at non-stop from that day onwards about my weight. Still happens.

'They're trying to fucking kill us,' I said to Danny. He couldn't reply. His mouth was down to his knees and his eyes had disappeared.

Then came a match, which was what I'd been waiting for, a chance to show off in a proper game, register my presence with the Gods, who of course had no idea who any of the new apprentices were. We were put into four teams of ten each and I thought great, it'll be a knock-out competition.

I hate training when there's no element of competition. I know many players, and most coaches, say that the object of all training is to compete against yourself, as that is the ultimate and purest way to improve. Bugger that. I don't even like learning skills on my own, or doing something in a vacuum, not since I was a kid practising against the wall. I did all that in the cradle. What I like best is doing something better than someone else, whether it's tiddlywinks or taking World Cup penalties. It's beating the other fucker that gets my adrenalin going.

We did play as four different teams – but all on the same pitch, at the same time. Bloody stupid, if you ask me. It was chaos and I was useless. I couldn't get used to seeing two goalies standing in the same goal. The regulars knew all about it, and enjoyed it, as it was easy to skive, but I ran around like a blue-arsed lunatic, getting nowhere and running into people. Even the dog.

I was knackered when it finished. Before I could drag myself back to the dressing room we boys had to collect up and count all the balls, just in case one of the spectators had nicked one. I moaned and groaned and was told I was on a soft option by one of the coaches. It was true we apprentices did have very few extra duties, none of them arduous. In the old days, such as the fifties and sixties, so one of the older coaches told me, the apprentices did all the rotten jobs, cleaning the boots for the first team, sweeping out the dressing rooms and even painting the grandstand. That still happened in some clubs, the less affluent ones, even in the First Division, but not at Spurs any more.

'So we're the aristocrats,' I said.

'Aristocunts, in your case,' he said. Personally, he thought we were all spoiled rotten, we had it too easy, didn't know we were living, yawn yawn, the usual stuff I'd heard all my life.

'Do you fancy this then, Swifty?'

It was Tel, prancing bollock naked out of the showers with his cock pulled back between his thighs, speaking in a high pitched voice.

I was sitting on a bench, trying to get my boots off, but I hardly had the strength.

'Or what about this?'

He was now bending over me, shoving his big hairy arse into my face.

'I bet this is what you really fancy, eh Swifty. Seen one of these before, eh?'

'Yeh, thought I recognized it,' I said. 'It's a fucking sheep.'

Everyone laughed. Tel stood up, not at all amused, and moved down the dressing room to his own peg. He picked up a towel and halfheartedly started flicking the end at Danny, who sat smiling gormlessly but not retaliating.

We had lunch in the dining room – chicken soup, roast beef, with tinned fruit and custard for afters, no cream, cos I asked. I expected we would all be sent home as I'd been told that training, even for full-time professionals, was mornings only at Spurs, as at Carlisle and Newcastle and all British clubs. I'd seen all the dirty kit being taken away to be washed, so I'd thought that's it, thank God, I can now go home and sleep. I hadn't realised that in the four weeks of pre-training, they often had an afternoon session as well, to build us up for the season ahead.

However, as this was the first day, it was being kept easy, so the coaches said. All we were going to have in the afternoon was a fun run, just to limber us down. Bloody hell. Not my idea of easy, or fun. I'd always hated cross-countries at school, but you soon knew how to hide or where to take short cuts.

For this run, there was no escape. Fresh kit, newly washed, arrived as we finished lunch. Danny couldn't get over this. Being from the bogs, he only ever got clean clothes once a year, on his birthday. Two coaches on bikes stayed at the rear of the run, swearing and shouting at the stragglers, which included me.

I can't run. I mean the act of running, pointless running, from here to there, is beyond me. I don't even like walking and avoid it if possible. God wouldn't have invented cars if he'd meant us to use our own feet all the time. I have been known to get the car out to go twenty metres to buy a newspaper. I always piss in the hotel-room sinks to save crossing the carpet to the bathroom. I will take a lift to save one floor, even if it means waiting till they've built the lift. I'm saving myself, see, my legs and my lungs, for when I need them. On the pitch. I can run forever, without even thinking about it. That's my job. When I'm not working, I'm not working, am I, so why use my legs. Most footballers are the same. In fact many can't walk. They stagger, bandy-legged, or roll from side to side. I've walked beside Maradona, off the pitch after a match, and he sways as if he's in agony, no, not because of any of that, just because he tuned his body to run with the ball, not to do anything pointless like walking.

We came across several workmen digging a hole and they started shouting Arsenal Arsenal, then we went past a girls' school and heard some of them whistling at us and shouting sexy legs, give us a flash. I had no breath or strength to reply. I was tired when I began, after the morning's exertions, but I was totally knackered by the end of the run. I don't know how I got home to the digs afterwards. I think Danny had to help me.

Yeh, that stupid, gormless git turned out to be a brilliant runner, and was in the leading pack all the way round. After tea, he tried to get me to go to the pub again, but I refused.

I lay on my pit, resting, thinking what have I done, how am I going to cope, I'll never manage those stupid weights, or all that running, this wasn't what I came into football for.

There were so many better-trained, much fitter players than me, all ahead of me. Some of them must be just as talented, just as motivated. How can I get ahead of them, never mind catch up? People know them already. They don't know me, or how good I am. I'm just that fat little git who can't lift puny weights or run a cross-country, the one who hit the dog when he tried a flash kick.

I must have dozed off. Mrs Jarret was shouting for me, yelling in my ear that I was wanted on the phone. I didn't know I was allowed on the phone, then I remembered she'd said she didn't mind incoming calls, if they were urgent, and not from girls or fans. I thought, fat chance of me ever having girls, or fans.

'Hello Joe, what do you know.'

It was Mum, with her usual corny opening.

'Ugh,' I grunted.

'How did it go?'

'Rotten. I'm knackered.'

'Oh that's good.'

'Huh.'

'Your results have come.'

'You what?'

'You passed all seven and got two As – in English Lit, and R.E.'

I'd almost forgotten about my O-levels. It seemed years ago that I'd taken them. Home and school were another world.

'How did Tom do?'

See, having said I'd forgotten, I was now being competitive.

'He sat eight – and got eight As.'

'Jammy thing.'

I should have taken eight, not seven, but they wouldn't let me take French, as I'd failed the mock, so that's why Tom took one more than me.

'You haven't asked about Fanny.'

'How's Fanny?'

'She's got into Oxford.'

'Oh that's good,' I said, thinking I'll have to keep that quiet. It's one thing being a clever dick myself, getting seven O-levels, which will probably make me a genius in the dressing room, I'd better not boast about our Fanny getting into Oxford. They'll probably think it means Oxford United.

I went back to bed and fell straight asleep, dreaming of playing at Wembley in a mortar-board and gown with Tel polishing my medals.

G.L.R.

Dear Joe,

Joe who? No, only kidding. But I have to say I don't remember you coming to Spurs, not as an apprentice anyway, but then there were so many. I think I had moved on to Charlton before you had made your big mark. I was of course mega in those days, and you were only mega round the backside, don't mind me, just my coarse humour. I've no recollection of that training session with you, and I don't think I would have been so unkind as to laugh at your mistake. What happened to the dog, by the way?

Anyway, best of luck with the book. (And with your present predicament.) That chapter did bring back many memories for me of the good times I had at Spurs.

Incidentally, I arrived with five O-levels, so don't get carried away that you're some sort of genius. I hope you'll make it clear that all footballers aren't thick, despite what some journalists and authors have written about us.

Yours in sport,
GARTH CROOKS

8

'How's it going, young Joe,' asked Mick, sitting down beside me on the coach back from Ipswich. We'd played a morning game against their youth team, before a monster crowd of twenty-three and two dogs, and managed a one–nil win. It had been a boring match, but I'd scored the winner in the last five minutes, coming up to the edge of the penalty area , holding the ball as if about to pass, then darting through and beating the goalie.

I was feeling well pleased and didn't want Mick McNutter droning on in my ear all the way home. He was one of the senior players who helped out with the youth team, a small but enormously stocky Scouser. For years he had been a reserve defender, forever on the fringes of the first team, but it was now said that his playing days were over, thanks to a nasty knee injury. He was only twenty-five but had got it into his head he was my father figure, ready to sort out any personal problems.

It was two weeks into the season, six weeks since I'd started, and I personally thought I had no problems. Other people might have problems, not me, especially those with stupid ideas and stupid systems.

'Not bad,' I said, picking up Danny's copy of *Penthouse*, trying to ignore Mick. Dan usually sat with me, but he'd gone to the back row to play cards with Tel.

'Not bad? You're with one of the greatest clubs in England, in all Europe. It's gorra be more than "not bad".'

'That's what I said, not bad. Could be better.'

'Perhaps that's your fault, Joe. *You* could do better, wajathink?'

Oh no, I'm not going to get a load of Mick's cheap shit psychology. The last thing I need.

'Look, you're squashing me,' I said. 'Watch the material, eh.'

'Nice suit, that,' said Mick, running his hand along the crease in my trousers. I could feel his podgy fingers through the shiny blue manmade fibre.

'You're not a fairy, are you,' I said. 'Cos you can go and touch up Tel. He loves all that.'

That was probably a bit rude to a senior player only doing his best, but after six weeks I'd lost any awe of the full professionals.

'New, is it,' asked Mick, looking up at the rack where I'd thrown my jacket. Everyone else had their jackets in plastic containers.

I knew he was getting at my suit. On Saturdays when we were on show to the public, even when it was only twenty-three spectators and two dogs, we were meant to wear dark grey suits, not anything flash.

This afternoon a few more people might see us, as the first team was at home and we were going back to White Hart Lane to watch them, from a respectful distance of course.

We were also meant to have our hair cut short. Not a skinhead crop, as we might then be mistaken for Park Lane end yobs, but neat and tidy, in a military fashion. Our youth team photograph had had to be retaken because one criminal, namely me, had his hair too long. I was now trying to grow it long again. No reason really, just that everyone else had it short. Same with the flash blue suit. I hate doing or wearing what I'm told to do or wear.

'What did you think of my goal?' I asked Mick.

I know I shouldn't have brought the topic up. It's a weakness, to look for praise, as my mother was always telling me, suggesting you are insecure or uncertain, but that's bollocks. It shows confidence, because you are also inviting criticism, and you have to be confident to take criticism. I can, because I consider most of my critics are idiots.

I was really just making conversation, getting it round to something interesting, namely me. I can discuss me and what I've done for hours.

'Your goal was a bit lucky,' he said.

'Cheeky sod,' I said, laughing, but suddenly feeling angry.

'It went through the goalie's legs.'

'That's where I aimed for.'

'It was also lucky that our forwards were running off the ball, as they've been told to do. That was why you got clean through.'

'Thanks.'

'Though one of them was offside, so you were lucky the ref gave it.'

'Anything else?'

'Yes, you shouldn't have been there in the first place. You know where you were told to play.'

'But I scored! Bloody hell. I scored the winner. No other fucker looked like scoring.'

'That's not the point. You're in the youth team, still learning the game, not playing for England in a World Cup final.'

'Not yet,' I said.

Mick had the intelligence to smile, not indulgently, more quizzically, leaning back in the aisle and looking at me, as if changing the focus and distance on his mental viewfinder.

'If you're ever going to learn to tackle, you've got to stick at it, not give up because you get bored. It's for your own good.'

'Oh my good Gawd,' I said, 'not that again.'

Was I already picking up a cockney accent, in only six weeks? Possibly. Despite what Mick and the other coaches imagined, I had been learning a few things.

For our three matches so far I had been put into a defensive midfield position and told to stay there for the time being, stop any bugger getting through, then get rid of the ball quickly, and let Danny do the creative bit. In training, I was doing tackling practice all the time, and heading, my other main weakness, so all the clever buggers were always telling me.

I had tried to stay back in the first two matches, both draws, telling myself it might be useful to be able to do it, for any emergencies or team injuries during a game, and it would also help make me an all-round player. But I hated it.

Mick actually thought I had a future as a defensive midfielder. With my bulk, and my bum, he saw me as another Dave Mackay. Never heard of him, I said, just to annoy.

I had no intention of staying as a defensive midfielder. I'd started as a striker, moved myself to a midfield attacker, and now this lot were trying to push me even further back. I'd end up as goalie at this rate.

I also hated push and run, which we had to do in training matches all the time. This was the style of the old Arthur Rowe Spurs team, and they still talked about it. You give the ball at once, one touch if possible, then run like hell into space, just to give the ball another one-touch. Forget it. That's for automatons.

British coaches are often criticised for producing conveyor-belt robots, with massive thighs and small brains, who will fight till they drop, all true now I think about it, have you seen Wimbledon recently, but it's not their passion for physical strength which worries me – it's their obsession with speed. Coaches want the ball got rid of quickly, and hate people who try to keep it. I love the ball. I want to hold on to it, make it my friend, caress and care for it, not kick it away like a hot turd.

Coaches want the ball kept moving, that's the sort of stuff they can teach you, and which most halfwits can learn. And they get results – that's if people do what they're told, don't muck around or disobey orders, as I used to do. In all my career, I've never seen or been given dribbling exercises. You know, people being taught to take on other men, to waltz round them, nutmeg them, do tricks with the ball, beat people with a bit of wizardry. British coaches can't cope with that, so they stick to passing and running, kicking and tackling, heading and shooting, all the lumpen qualities that footballers do need. Oh well. I suppose it's no different from most human activities.

You can teach skill. You can't teach talent.

I just thought of that now, in trying to remember times past, sitting here quietly, on my own, with bugger all else to do, trying to form in my mind what was bugging me all those years ago, what I was revolting against, but without at the time being able to put it into words, or even coherent thoughts. Some good is coming out of this bad confinement. Hey up, we'd better get back on that youth team bus. We'll now let Mick have his say about the theory of football.

'We're looking for four things in young footballers,' said Mick. 'Are you listening, Joe?'

I pretended to stifle a yawn. If he's rehearsing for his F.A. badge, I'm not going to help him.

'Do you know what they are, Joe?'

Even worse. He thinks he's a schoolteacher, asking those bloody stupid rhetorical questions which all classroom wallies love.

'Firstly, we are looking for footballing ability – able to control the ball, pass it, shoot, head, trap it, people who look comfortable on the ball. So you've got that, Joe.'

'Thanks, o wise one.'

'Secondly, we're looking for a football brain. It doesn't always go with footballing ability. It means the capacity to read the game, to alter the game, to avoid the obvious pass, to be creative and act one move ahead of everyone else. That's what's most lacking in schoolboy football. You see them running all over the pitch like fucking cows with their tits chopped off.'

'You what?' I said.

'You've got a footballing brain as well,' he said. 'We spotted that right away. Two out of two so far. It's in all the scouting reports on you.'

'Do I get the coconut now or later?'

'Thirdly, physical.'

'Oh I see,' I said. 'You're now going to make personal remarks about my big arse.'

'I mean physical ability, the third attribute. That's not a matter of weight and height, though they matter, but what you do with your height and strength. You've got some way to go there Joe, though the tackling is coming along, and the heading, and we'll soon have you lasting a whole ninety minutes. Today you looked knackered in the second half . . .'

'I was saving myself to score the winning goal.'

'Fourthly, now what do you think the fourth quality is that we're looking for in a footballer?'

'Sex appeal? Size of chopper? Nice hair? No, I've got it, arse licking. You must have the ability to be a right creep and say yes sir no sir to every bloody coach, manager, director and official you're ever likely to meet.'

'Have you done?' said Mick, sighing.

'No no, hold on,' I said. 'How could I forget – luck. That's what we all need, isn't it Mick. Lady Luck.'

He paused, thinking. Luck was obviously not in his list of priorities, though in his case, it was in the end the only one he had really needed.

'I'm thinking of Character, Joe. That's the fourth and the most vital element – and the hardest to tell, when someone's still young. It's no use having all the football ability in the world, unless you've got the character to use it, the determination to make the most of what you've got, to train and practise and improve, to rise above misfortunes, to rise above temptations, never to be satisfied and think you know it all or have it all, but always wanting to do better . . .'

Oh God. It wasn't his F.A. badge he was in for. He was turning football into a religion. As it happens, I agree with that. It's my religion, what I worship, what I believe in. I just happen to prefer a different sermon, with a different message. Joy and light, that's what I'm after, not hard graft and discipline.

'And it's your character, Joe, that's what we're all worrying about.'

'Well don't,' I said.

'We can give you guidelines, try to teach you things, keep an eye on you, but you must care as well. In the end, it's in your hands . . .'

'You mean like wanking, Mick.'

Mick stared at me wearily, shaking his head, moving as if to get up and go back to his own seat, then suddenly he flung himself down again, pushing me hard against the side of the bus so I could hardly breathe.

'And just for a change, try not to be such a smart cunt.'

Mick went off to his own seat and I looked out of the window, trying hard to appear Not Bothered. In the reflection, I could see him taking out a little notebook and scribbling away. J. Swift is a knowall. J. Swift has a big mouth. J. Swift has talent but is too clever for his own good. I'd read all that before. In five years of school reports. So what's new.

But that little lecture did affect me, despite myself. I sat there worrying about the impression I was giving to the world out there. You always assume they'll know when you're just trying to be funny, amuse the lads, saying something for the sake of saying something.

You hope they'll even know when things blurt out of your mouth that you didn't mean to blurt out. So it's a worry when you sense a reaction you didn't intend, that something has been taken the wrong way.

Thicko Micko thinks I don't *care*. That's the one word that got me in his stupid monologue. Fuck him. See if I care, about him thinking I don't care. Next time, he can practise his psychology shit elsewhere.

Or was he seriously trying to tell me something? Had he been told to warn me about something? Such as at the end of the season, I could be on my bike, just another apprentice who never made the grade?

Perhaps I didn't fit in, I thought. What if my talent, such as it is, is suitable only for schoolboy football, where I can boss the others around, where the others have such little confidence. What if they really think I haven't got what it takes to be a full professional? It's their bloody job, after all. They've had years of experience, with all sorts. It's silly to think I'm just being picked on. They want me to succeed. That's the point of the exercise. It made me feel depressed all the way to Tottenham.

Then just as we got into White Hart Lane, I thought okay, so what if they are seriously telling me what they seriously think, so what if they are worried about me making it, what if I have to admit they are only trying their best? Then tough shit. They are all bloody *wrong*.

I smiled for a moment at myself trying to cheer myself up, then I thought oh no, that could be worse. Imagine being chucked out unfairly, because of their stupidity, because they can't see how good I am.

People can overcome such a blow. You often hear about rejected players who then try twice as hard, just to prove their first club wrong. Look at David Platt, given a free by Man United, then later sold to Bari for six million quidlets. Yes, but you don't hear about the ninety-nine per cent you don't hear about.

I don't want to go through all that, either way. I want to do it first time. I want to succeed now.

It was still bugging me all afternoon, as things did in those days, going round and round in my stupid head.

I tried to avoid standing around with the other apprentices, saying nothing, unable to communicate. We all looked such pathetic dummies in our new suits, always too big, our clean faces as if our mums have just washed us, our shy but polite smiles, eager but self-effacing grins. Was I really like that, part of that lot? Yup. There was no way to avoid it.

You have your pass, your right of entry, but you have to flit in and out, be there but not seen, taking care not to disturb the air which the Gods are about to breathe. You can't of course go into *their* dressing room. That's a hanging offence. So you wander around the parts where your presence does not offend, such as into the general office where one junior secretary may know your face but have forgotten your name, unlike the stars, whose first names are branded about by every jerk in the club. There may even be a letter for you in the pigeonhole marked Apprentices, oh rapture, from your mum of course, not a fan or a tv contract, asking why you haven't written or phoned since you left home and your Dad's sick with worry.

You pick up your seat in the Main Stand, not a good one of course, they're not going to waste good tickets on mere apprentices, somewhere low at the front at the side, where you sit with the other apprentices, all looking scrubbed and bandbox fresh and as self-conscious as hell because there are season-ticket holders all around, not of course the ones with the best seats, who make loud comments, such as I thought the police were getting younger every day but bloody hell, the bloody club is signing on bloody infants now.

I had no tie on, my only sign of rebellion, for which Mick would doubtless take me aside at Cheshunt on Monday, but I did stay with them, dutifully in the row, rather than bunk around for an empty seat elsewhere, trying to distance myself from the rest of them. That was me then. That was my status. But all the time I was impatient to be off, and up. Life seemed to drag along so slowly, with nothing appearing to happen.

I hate watching football anyway. That may surprise, but I think most players would say the same. You want to be out there, doing it, not watching other fuckers getting it wrong.

I hate any sort of sitting still, and that is not typical of most footballers. They love sitting still, doing bugger all, going bugger nowhere, looking at bugger nothing. It's their favourite hobby, along with cards and crumpet. Once training is over, they flop, their mind and body fold under them and they become one-dimensional, discarded toys on the carpet of suburban life, waiting to be wound up for the next game, for the whistle to command them back to real life.

It's not stupidity or lack of intelligence. It's how we've been programmed, how we've been trained. They don't want us to have any distractions. Thank you Mick. You bastard.

Somewhere Bloody Hot

Dear Joe

Great to hear from you, you old wanker. As you know, I'm now the national coach of the Western Gulf States F.C. On £100,000 a year – and that's just the expenses – my own chauffeur and stretch limo, ten coaches under me who don't understand my scouse accent, but then they are Yugoslavs! Remember them? Seriously, it's great out here. Best job I've ever had. Don't let's talk about the worst one. You was there.

You should try it. They'd love you. Some of them have even heard of you! I tell them I taught you all you know, so I was pleased to read your stuff, as it bloody proves it. They won't read it of course, not out here. They'll probably ban it like that Salmon Rusholme because of the Oh God stuff. I've just applied to be reserve coach at Workington Town and mentioned your name, so do us a favour, Joe, pull any strings you can. And I won't sue!

Yours

MICK

9

'I'm going to bingo,' said Mrs Jarret after she had given us our lunch. It was about a week later. I'd lost house points for not wearing a tie. Been given a black mark for long hair. Threatened with detention for giving cheek to sir.

'Ugh,' I said. It wasn't her usual bingo day, not that I was concentrating, or even interested. I was slumped with Dan in front of the television, watching *Magic Roundabout*, wondering what to do, trying to make major decisions about the rest of my life, such as should I slump here for another couple of hours and then watch *Blue Peter*. It's very catching, doing nothing, when nobody is offering you the chance to do something.

'I want that thing off now,' she said, standing at the front door with her best poplin raincoat on, bright sludge colour, clutching her handbag, plastic snakeskin. She'd put lipstick on, yuck, and her high heels, which always seemed daft just for bingo. All she met there was a load of other old bags like herself.

Dan had decided he could fuck her, stupid sod, no really, he said, if he had to, if there was no one else left in the world, he'd give her one, no problem. It made a change from fucking the Queen. That was his usual topic, last thing at night in our bedroom, before we went to sleep. If you had to, who would it be – the Queen, Princess Margaret or the Queen Mother? I'd say you Irish bastard, leave our sex symbols alone.

I like to think I've always had taste, though let's not analyse that too much at the moment, and don't send me any photographs, please.

But Old Ma Jarret, bloody hell, that was going it. How could he even think about it? She was at least forty-five with stringy bleached hair and was so fat she fell out of her clothes, even with her best raincoat tied as tight as possible.

'You've both got a lot to do,' she said, glaring at us.

'We're knackered,' I said.

'Yeah, give us a break,' said Dan.

'I have to report your progress to the club,' she said. 'You know that. I'm not going to say you've been doing your studies if you ain't.'

'We're going,' said Dan. 'Just as soon as this is finished. Honest.'

'You'd better.'

She left us alone, still watching the television, looking at it and through it without actually taking any of it in.

Dan had enrolled at Tottenham Tech to do his City and Guilds in bricklaying. Enrolled, but never been back since. I was supposedly studying for A-level English at North London Polytechnic, or is it the Polytechnic of North London. I hadn't been able to find it in the phone book. Wasn't my fault. I had tried.

The club, like all modern clubs, likes to think that their sixteen- and seventeen-year-olds are still pursuing their education, following some other form of training, acquiring a useful qualification or skill to fit them for the big wide world outside the hothouse called football. They don't like being accused of ruining young lives, even though they know that most of the seventeen-year-olds will end up on the street, out on their arses, their hopes of a life in football gone for ever.

But you don't think like that, not at seventeen. How can you get up the motivation for another life when since the age of ten, football is all you've ever wanted to do? And now you are doing it. So you think.

'Right, let's go,' said Dan, jumping up. He'd been silent for five minutes, waiting for Mrs Jarret to disappear down the street.

'Where?' I said.

Dan ran upstairs to our bedroom and returned clutching his pay packet.

'The pub,' he said.

'It'll be closing.'

'Then we'll have to hurry. Get your finger out.'

'I can't be bothered.'

'Oh come on, man,' he said, trying to drag me up by the arm. He was stronger now than two months ago, and I was lighter, but he still couldn't budge me.

'It's bloody boring, that pub,' I said.

'Better than sitting here on your own,' he said.

'I'll manage,' I said.

'You're not scared are you? That somebody will see us at the pub and you'll get reported?'

'Fuck off,' I said.

'You're in the shite already, mate. Your card has been well and truly marked.'

'Piss off,' I said.

When he'd gone, I watched a Pakistani-language programme for a while, which was surprisingly interesting, so interesting I gave it about ten minutes, then I switched to an Open University course on Great Art, which was quite stimulating, so stimulating I gave it all of five minutes, then I thought bugger this, I don't want to be interested or stimulated, I'm a footballer, not a professor.

I wandered round the kitchen, looking for hidden biscuits, secreted sweets. Mrs Jarret had a sweet tooth, but she now put her goodies well out of my way. I could go to the corner shop, and get fresh supplies, and the latest copy of *2000 AD*, my favourite reading, but that meant a three-minute walk.

I stood at the window, looking nowhere. Out there, beyond Lordship bloody Lane, out in the heart of mighty London, life was full of excitements. There might even be someone out there, looking for me, yooo-eee, I'm here darling. Why did I say darling? Perhaps I'm into fellers. I wouldn't be surprised. Danny's fixation with cunts and tits puts me right off. No, just testing, just teasing.

Most of the other apprentices came from the London area, so they had their old haunts, networks and friends to knock around with in the long, draggy hours when training finished for the day. The professionals of course had wives or regular girlfriends or business affairs to attend to. And money. Not a bloody lot you can do as an apprentice on twenty quid a week.

I knew no one in the whole of London, eight million strangers, or is it ten million. One day, they'd all know me. Ah ha. What as? Not a footballer, the way things were going. Mass-murderer, that was probably my best bet. No, too dramatic. A streaker at Wembley. Could be the nearest I'd get.

I could go to Oxford. Fanny had said I must come and see her, please do, but I wasn't sure which direction that was, and I didn't want to go anyway. I was a footballer, not a student. Supposed to be. So it said on the front page of the *Cumberland News* when I signed for Spurs. What do they know? Oh God, I was just so *bored*.

Wham, bam. The front door opened and in burst Danny, so quick, so unexpected, it seemed like a film beginning, jamming you to your seat so you can't move.

He was followed by two girls, tottering on ridiculous high heels, both of them giggling. Danny had a six-pack of beers, while both girls were carrying a bottle each. One of them, small and blonde and tarty, started swigging from a large bottle of British sherry. The other, thin and dark-haired, had a half bottle of vodka. They were probably about fourteen, going on twenty-five.

'Where's the party then, Danny boy?' asked the blonde.

'Yeh, you promised us a bloody party,' squealed the other.

'Keep your hair on girls,' said Danny. 'And your knickers. For the moment, anyways.'

'Oh, hark at him, cheeky sod.'

They hadn't seen me at first, standing at the window.

'Heh Joey boy,' shouted Danny, putting his arm round the blonde. 'You're in luck. I've fixed you up. Don't think much of yours, mind you . . .'

'Fuck you,' said the dark-haired one.

'Get some glasses then, you wanker,' said Danny. 'Don't just stand there, like a spare prick at a wedding.'

'Talking about yourself, Dan,' said the blonde, trying to grab him by the balls, to see if he had a spare one. He yelled out, in mock agony, then jumped upon her and they fell on to Mrs Jarret's best mock leather sofa, pretending to wrestle.

Hold on. I'm imagining this. Let's slow it down. I went into the kitchen to get some glasses. How had he picked them up? Must have taken all his week's wages. And their language. Girls in Cockermouth didn't say that sort of thing, or do that sort of thing, not when you'd just met them.

I found four glasses, washed them out, and came back into the living room to see them all going upstairs. I stood at the bottom, wondering what to do, was it Dan's private party, or could others join in?

'Come on Joe,' shouted Dan. 'Linda's got the hots for you.'

I could hear Linda swearing, hitting him, then it was all shouts and laughter, plus a few bangs and crashes.

I went slowly upstairs. Dan was already on his bed, lying on top of his girl, Mandy, stuck together in a French kiss, then she pushed him off so violently he fell on the floor.

'I'm dying for a fucking fag,' she said.

Linda, who was sitting on my bed, smoking, handed her a cigarette. Mrs Jarret did not allow smoking anywhere in the house, not till boys were eighteen, club rules, so she said.

Dan got up and pulled out his record player and put on an Abba record. He then got the glasses and poured everyone out a drink, mixing things together. It tasted horrible, but the girls didn't seem to care, knocking it back almost in one gulp, then demanding another.

I sat with Linda on my bed, my arm half round her, wondering what to do next. She smelt of Woolworth's talcum and her hair was stiff with lacquer. She'd kicked off her shoes and was nodding her head and swaying her body in time to the music, or it could have been the drink. They'd probably had a few in the pub before Dan had met them.

After a few records, Linda announced it was time to get dancing, and she grabbed my hand and tried to get me to dance with her. I can't dance. I don't know what you do and I always feel stupid, trying to do it. I said not now, thanks, I need a few more drinks, before I can dance with anyone.

The girls danced together, laughing and giggling, whispering to each other, still smoking, still drinking while they danced.

Mandy managed to get Danny on his feet. He was as hopeless as me, but more willing to try. He clung on to her, being stupid, pretending to be drunk. I noticed that Mandy had put her hand down his trousers, and was slowly unzipping him. His trousers fell to the floor so he was standing in his underpants. She then flung him on the bed and got on top of him.

I didn't see what happened next as Linda started on me, going for my flies, rolling me over, kissing and cuddling. She pulled me on top of her and I could see and feel her bare thighs. She had no knickers on. I hadn't noticed them coming off. The sight of her pubic hair was enough for me, and I arrived before she had begun.

'Fucking hell,' she said. 'Is that the best you can do?'

Over on the other bed, Mandy was standing up, lighting another cigarette.

'We thought you two was in training. Our dog could do better.'

'And mine,' said Linda. 'And he's got a bigger willy!'

They both roared at their own wit. Mandy pushed Danny right off his bed, which made them laugh even louder.

Linda tried to push me off my bed, but she wasn't strong enough, so she got up and joined Mandy on Dan's bed. I lay back on my bed thinking how did all this happen, how are we going to get rid of them, who are they anyway?

I could hear the music being turned up at top volume and I leaned over to tell Dan to turn it down. He was on the carpet, between the two beds, his eyes closed, groaning and moaning to himself.

On his bed, Linda and Mandy were both stripping off. Oh no, I couldn't manage it again. Once was bad enough. When they were totally naked they lay side by side, their hands round each other. Dan opened one eye. Even he looked horrified.

'Well if you lot can't manage it, we girls will have to stick to-gether.'

As they screamed and roared, the bedroom door opened and there stood Mrs Jarret.

'What the hell's going on here? I've never seen anything so disgust-ing in all my bloody life . . .'

She sniffed the cigarette smoke, turning up her nose as if the smell itself was suspicious, glared at the empty bottles, looked hor-rified at the naked girls. She decided to attack the loud music first, so she marched to the record player and tore the record off the turntable. The screech of Abba, caught short in the middle of *Mamma Mia*, was equalled by the screech of the girls, followed by the screech of Dan saying she had buggered up his record player.

'Come on Carol,' said Mandy. 'Let's get out of this dump.'

'Yeh, it stinks.'

The girls jumped off the bed, grabbing their clothes, pulling them on as they staggered for the door.

'Yes, get yourselves out,' shouted Mrs Jarret, trying to hit and kick them as they fled past her. Then she turned to us.

'Out! And that means both of you.'

She started pulling my clothes out of the wardrobe, and then Danny's, throwing them at us across the room. Dan was still struggling with his record player as his clothes landed over his head. Then she got our cases out from under the bed.

'I never want to see either of you again.'

I shoved my stuff in my case and went downstairs, followed by Dan.

'Where we gonna go now,' he wailed, as we stood in the street together.

'It's all your fucking fault.'

'What we gonna do?' said Dan.

'I don't know,' I said, 'but I'm not doing it with you.'

I headed off down the street, on my own, determined to leave London for ever and never return.

Siempre a su servicio en:

Marqués de Salamanca, nº 5

(Junto a Correos)

TORREMOLINOS

Dear Joe,

Thanks for the second chapter now received. The post to Torremolinos is very slow as at present, out here, I blame it on all the Brits leaving and this country is falling to pieces. I am relieved to see you have told the TRUTH. When I sold my story to the *News of the World* when you became famous and when I had to leave as people were saying things about me, it was not my fault they took a few diabolical liberties in their story, about the drugs and the rubber and whips and that. You have said enough anyway in your story so I am relieved so don't blame me any more as I am only a poor widow. I hope this finds you as it leaves me. The girls if you can call them girls did not tell you their real names and you have called one of them Linda then Carol. I think they were runaways from the North if you ask me, probably Watford.

Yours,
ELSIE GONZALEZ

10

I got to Euston and caught the last train to Carlisle. Without a ticket. In my rush to leave I'd not brought my money with me, such as it was. Twenty quid was all I'd saved, hidden at the back of the wardrobe in case Dan nicked it.

All the way I stayed in the lavs to avoid any ticket inspector. I was shit scared I was going to be found out, but each time they moved on after banging on the door.

At Carlisle I got off the train, letting everyone leave the platform while I decided what to do. I went to the Gents and waited, then I remembered there was a mail-van entrance which led out on to the Viaduct. I worked my way round to it and was just about to leave the station when I felt a hand on my shoulder.

'Where are you going, son?' It was a railway policeman, taking my arm and holding me against the wall.

'For a train.'

'Where to?'

'Workington.'

'There isn't one. The last went hours ago.'

'I mean Glasgow.'

'You got off that train. I've been watching you.'

He had started off dead nasty, but now that he was looking me over carefully, studying my neat clothes, short hair, he was deciding I was not a hooligan, liable to escape or knife him.

'You in the army?' he asked, loosening his grip.

'No,' I said. I didn't want to mention Spurs. I didn't want them dragged into it, though as I was never going back why did it matter? If I ended up in court, it would make the *Cumberland News*. They'd done that story when I joined Spurs. I didn't want them to do one, now I'd left. Oh God, the humiliation.

'Where's your ticket?'

'I've lost it.'

'Come with me,' I said.

He led me to a little office, through a door in a sandstone wall, sat me down at a table covered in teastains and took down details of my name and age and home address.

'You can ring my Dad,' I said. 'He'll pay my fare, I mean for another ticket, for the one I lost . . .'

He picked up the phone and dialled home. It rang and rang, but there was no answer. Oh bugger. That's all I needed. Where the hell could they be? I'd have to spend the night in a cell.

'He might be on night duty,' I said, giving him the number for the Boys' Home. He got through right away and asked for Mr Swift.

I could hear my Dad sounding confused. He never was quick on the uptake, not like Mum, always smart at sussing things out.

'He's what? Our Joe? Where? But what's he doing there? Oh, God. Okay, I'll come . . .'

He arrived about an hour later, looking not just furious with me, but absolutely shattered, as if he hadn't slept for days. He paid the money, signed various papers, apologised for me, then bundled me in the car.

We didn't speak till we got well out of Carlisle, on the Thursby road.

'So what have you done?'

'Nothing,' I said, all sulky.

'Don't bugger around with me,' he snarled.

'I've left Spurs.'

'Christ, what a time to choose.'

'Not my fault.'

'Don't be bloody childish.'

'It wasn't my fault,' I said. 'They're all stupid. I should never have joined.'

'You've only been there a couple of months.'

'I made a mistake.'

'Have they chucked you out?'

'No, course not. I just can't stand it any more. I hate London, everything . . .'

I'd given him a chance to sympathise, feel sorry for me, but he didn't seem to be listening. His knuckles were tight on the steering wheel and I could hear his teeth grinding. Since his heart attack, he was supposed to keep calm at all times, and do little exercises when he felt stress coming on.

'Millions of kids want the chance you've had, and you've chucked it away.'

'You never wanted me to go.'

'Don't be so stupid. Of course I did.'

'Well you never said.'

'Have you been giving them lip, being a bloody knowall, as usual?'

'No,' I said.

I wished my mother had picked me up. She would have listened properly, taken my side, not attacked or criticised me, until she had heard the whole story, or as much as I was prepared to tell.

We got into the house. It was in darkness. I presumed Colin and Mum were in bed. I dumped my case in the hall and went into the kitchen. I'd have to sleep in the little bedroom, Colin's old one. He'd taken over mine when I'd left. I hated that little room. Why had I come back home anyway? No one wanted me here. Or anywhere. I opened the fridge door.

'Oh bloody hell,' I moaned, staring into it, with the door wide open. 'There's nothing here. I'm starving.'

I felt a blow on the side of my head which made me stagger across the kitchen floor. My father had hit me, the first time in my life that he had ever touched me.

'That bloody hurt.'

'Good,' he said, standing over me, as if about to strike me again. 'You deserve it. You cheat on the railways, you throw up your job, then you come home and start complaining to me that the fucking fridge is empty . . .'

I'd never heard him use that word before.

'I'm telling Mum,' I said. 'Where is she anyway?'

'It's taken you bloody long enough to ask,' he said, staring at me. I opened the back kitchen door and ran off into the darkness, stumbling through the grounds, falling over piles of wood which had been cut since I'd been away. I got to the front gate of the estate and stood, wondering what to do, where to go. The last time I'd run away from home I'd had a spotted handkerchief with some belongings. Now I had nothing, not even any money. I could hitchhike somewhere. Get to Glasgow then a boat to America and write home in ten years' time, when I was a millionaire, sending them food parcels for their stupid fridge. It wasn't meant to be a criticism. Mum would have known that. It was fury, with myself.

I walked into the village, past the pub and the village school, all locked up for eternity. I came to Tom's cottage, which appeared to be in darkness. His dad's vegetables were lined up for inspection, each row at the alert, even in the dark, when no potato or onion could possibly expect to be wakened up and inspected.

I went round to the back and saw that his bedroom light was on. I could see the shape of Tom's head at the window, leaning over a table, doing an essay, what a creep. I threw up some stones till a curtain was drawn and a window opened. I could see Tom's face peering out, trying to identify the noise.

'Playing away tonight, are we Joe?' he said at last.

The window closed, then his back door opened and he led me in.

'Cup of tea,' he asked.

'Yeh, gan on,' I said.

He motioned me to be quiet as we went into the kitchen, saying his old folks were asleep, then we went up to his room with a mug of tea each.

'Free mug?' I said, sitting on his bed, examining the face of the Queen on the Silver Wedding mug he'd given me.

'Yeh, we all got one at school.'

'I knew I should have stayed on.'

'Come back,' he smiled. 'All is forgiven.'

'What's the essay on?' I said, getting up and looking at his school books, not remotely interested.

'Paper,' he said. 'I find that's always best. They won't accept them carved on wood or chiselled on stone, so what you doing here then?'

'Oh nothing,' I said, sitting down. 'I've left Spurs.'

'You daft bugger.'

'Not you as well. I've just had all that from me Dad. He's chucked me out.'

'What happened?'

'He beat me up when I said the fridge was empty . . .'

'I mean at Spurs, you tosser.'

I explained how I hated the training, how I was being played out of position, made to do stupid things, by stupid people, how I hated London, hated my digs.

'So you decided to leave.'

'Yeh.'

'Why now, this evening?'

'I don't want to talk about it,' I said.

'Something must have happened.'

'It was this cunt Danny I share with, an Irish git, it was all his fault.'

I went through the whole saga, blow by blow, but for some reason I didn't describe the two scrubbers naked on the bed, and what they were doing to each other. That would really have been too humiliating, telling a mate.

Then I described Mrs Jarret coming in, and chucking us all. Tom laughed at Mrs Jarret throwing things at Danny, and the girls running out, half naked.

'What were they like then, these two tarts? Did you get it away with both of them, or just one at a time.'

'Shurrup, eh, it's not fucking funny.'

Tom always wanted to know about my sex life, as he didn't have any, and he certainly hasn't any at the moment. I used to tell him about mine just to get him excited, poor bastard.

'So what you gonna do now?' he asked.

'Dunno.'

'Join Carlisle United?'

'Get lost.'

'What then?'

'Dunno. But I'm not going back to Mrs Jarret's. Or Spurs.'

'Were you homesick? I bet that was it.'

'Give over.'

'I would have been homesick. It's only natural. First time away from home, big club like Spurs, big place like London. Is it true in London that nobody knows their neighbours? Hmm, that can't be true. You did manage to get to know a couple of the locals . . .'

'Ha bloody ha.'

'Perhaps you should have gone to Newcastle, or some other Northern club. At least you wouldn't have had language difficulties . . .'

'If you're just going to take the piss,' I said, starting to get up.

'No come on,' he said. 'Don't be daft. It does take time to get adjusted, when you come from a little place, where you've been used to being the big fish in a small pool. You're not used to being a nobody, are you Joe.'

'I'm going.'

'Didn't Georgy Best run away when he first went to Man. U? And Graeme Souness at Spurs? Well, then. It happens all the time. Just have a rest for a few days, calm down, settle yourself.'

'Oh God,' I said, sitting down again.

'And you're bound to have missed your Mum and Dad.'

'I didn't miss me Dad. My ear is still bloody sore. Look, where he hit me, the rotten sod.'

'Well he's having a hard time, poor lad.'

'How?'

'Didn't he tell you?'

'What?'

'Your Mam's in the Cumberland Infirmary. Taken in three days ago. Brain haemorrhage or something. Sounded serious, but she's supposed to be stable. Your Colin's with your gran in Newcastle.'

'Oh Christ,' I said. 'That's all I need.'

'And don't say that to him either,' said Tom.

'Oh fucking hell,' I said.

'You do tend to think of yourself, and no one else.'

'Fuck off,' I said.

We sat silently. Tom picked up his essay, and began to read the first page.

'So what do you think I should do, Tom?' I asked, after a long pause.

'Go home. Tell your Dad you didn't mean to complain about the fridge. Go into Carlisle tomorrow and see your Mam.'

'Yeh, of course.'

'She's the one who always wanted you to become a footballer. And she backed you when you chose Spurs. Remember . . .'

'Oh God, don't remind me . . .'

'Tell Spurs you came home cos of your Mam, you were worried about her, upset and all that, not your normal state.'

'I didn't know about her.'

'Yeh, but they don't know that,' said Tom. 'Stay a few days, help your Dad, then go back. You've got to give it another go.'

'I can't go back to Mrs Jarret's.'

'I bet it's happened before. If she's been taking in apprentices for all these years. Some of them must have brought girls into their bedroom. Tell you what. Send her some flowers first thing tomorrow. Say you're sorry, before she can report you to Spurs . . .'

'Flowers? Bloody hell. Whajathink I am?'

'It's the best thing to do. Then you can find different digs. They must have others.'

'Thanks,' I said, getting up. 'But I'm not sending any bloody flowers. That's really soft. Anyway, I haven't got any money . . .'

I stayed at home one week. And went to my mother's funeral. I don't want to go into all that. It happened. Life was never the same again. There's nothing else to say. It happened.

Here, today

Dear Joe,

Two points I'd like to include here, before you go any further.

1) I paid for those flowers to Mrs Jarret remember, and you never paid me back.

2) Your Dad did send you a letter about your mother going into hospital, because I posted it. You obviously never got it before you left, though he presumed you did, which is why he waited for you to ask about her.

She was a great woman, your mother. You owe a lot to her, you stupid bastard.

TOM

11

I never felt like a Reserve. Even from the beginning, I told myself I was simply passing through, another staging post, another notch on the crotch, whereas I seemed to be an Apprentice for ever. I suppose I elongated that stage, looking upon myself as an apprentice from about the age of ten, long before I became a real one, with a capital A.

I ceased to be an Apprentice when I was seventeen and a half and was upgraded, oh joy, into a Full Professional. Where are they now, Danny and Tel and all the other apprentices I once shared showers and hopes with? Who bloody cares? They had their chance.

By the time I reached eighteen, I'd had ten games in the Reserves, and after each I expected the call to come, the first team needs you, your true worth has been recognized at last, arise Sir Joe. I used to lie awake at night, not scoring goals, for that was taken for granted, or being brilliant, ditto, but listening to the crowd chanting, 'Joe-oh Swift, Joe-oh Swift, Born is the King-ing of Whi-ite Hart Lane.'

Then for a brief moment I did get depressed. We were in the dressing room at Highbury one day, after beating their Reserves 2–1, in front of a fairly decent crowd of two thousand, a bloodbath as usual, with everyone kicking everyone else, sometimes each other, matches against Arsenal tend to be like that, when I heard Willie running through all the Reserve games to come before the end of the season, listing the so called soft ones.

'That's it over then, lads,' he said, doing his hair in front of the mirror, which always took him for ever, as his hair was down to his waist. 'Fucking easy from now on.'

103

I caught his eye in the mirror for a moment, but he looked through me, intent on his hair, talking to himself. He was being serious, not taking the mick or messing around. I was appalled. Firstly, he was only looking forward to the easy matches. I looked forward most to the hard ones, as a chance to get stuck in, to show them, to shine. Secondly, and that was what depressed me, he was assuming he would be in the Reserves for the rest of the season. He accepted that was his place in life. Stupid bugger.

Or was I being unrealistic? After all I'd only had ten games. Someone like Garry had had three years in the Reserves, but tried as hard as he'd ever done, which paid off, as he'd just been promoted to the First Team Pool.

That season, if I remember, the First Team Pool consisted of eighteen. That meant the twelve or thirteen first-team regulars, who in a season expected to see their names on the team sheet every week, depending on injuries, tactics or loss of form. Then there were two or three who were regular first-team subs, one of whom travelled with the team, as cover for certain vital players, or vital positions, but who usually ended up on the bench. Finally there were a couple of younger players who showed promise, but were still unknown to most supporters, who might make it to the subs bench four times in a season, probably managing one game towards the end of the season. It was worth being in the Pool. You got paid more money and shared any extra loot that was going, should the team progress in the Cup.

The Pool was always announced at the beginning of the season, and wouldn't change, unless people left the club, so if you were not in at the beginning, you hadn't much chance of making it for another year. I'd just become a Full Pro as the season began and did not expect it, but now, after ten games, I was fancying my chances, working out that if certain players left, and better players didn't come, I might have a chance, even though I wasn't in the Pool.

Willie Woodbine was in the First Team Pool. At eighteen he had been Wonder Willie, hailed as the new George Best when he had come down from Scotland to Chelsea, a Wembley Wizard in the making, his face in all the papers, usually coming out of all the clubs. He'd left them after some row, then gone to Watford, where he had practically disappeared, mainly because he couldn't find it on the map from London, so he said in some interview, obviously a joke, but one which didn't please the Watford management.

Spurs had brought him back to London, but after one good season he was injured, went into the Reserves, and now looked like languishing there. He was still only twenty-two, but he looked ten years older, with bags under his eyes and lines down his face. Footballers do age quickly, and no wonder, having your body beaten to death in training every day, but it was night-time wear which had worn out Willie, plus the bookies.

I'd just found myself a flat, thanks to Willie and one of his contacts, off Green Lanes, a bit further from the ground, but at a very reasonable rent, only £20 a week, well a rented room really, supposedly a studio, but at least I didn't have to worry about landladies any more. I was now saving up for a car which I planned to buy once I'd passed my test.

'It's your big day, son,' said Willie one day after training at Cheshunt. 'I'll give you a lift in my new motor.'

He swaggered outside, dressed in a purple shirt open to the waist and white trousers with black buttons on the outside, signed a few autographs for some dopy-looking girls, then led me to his car, an E-Type Jaguar. I was most impressed, even though it was about ten years old and painted a lurid purple colour to match his shirt. I was pleased to be offered a lift. Willie usually went off in the afternoons with one or two of his first-team cronies.

I got in and he started up the engine which was very noisy, spluttering and choking. Willie revved it up even more. Several first-teamers walked round it, putting their hands to their ears, then tried to push it over while we were still inside, just for a laugh, the sort of the thing Willie would have done.

'Going back to the Lane?' asked Garry, rushing over. He was in a dark suit, white collar and tie, official uniform for players in public, but not necessary for training days.

'You must be joking,' said Willie.

Garry said his car, an old Vauxhall, was being serviced, but he'd promised to go back and help with some youth trials, what a good lad. He still lived with his parents in their council house in Barnet, aged twenty-one, much to Willie's derision, whereas he approved of me, determined to find my own place at only eighteen, which was why he had helped me to get it, and at a fair rent.

He was a good lad, Garry. Willie had ignored me at first, when I got into the Reserves, but Garry had helped me a lot, on and off the pitch, and had even invited me to his home for a few meals. Everyone liked Garry, though they mocked him all the time, especially Willie.

'Come on then,' said Willie. 'Get in, I'll drop you off.'

Garry got in the back seat, where he had to crouch, worrying about his suit. He was my height, but looked bigger as he was so stocky. Willie was incredibly thin, with no waist or chest, and in his clothes it was hard to believe he was an athlete of any sort. Stripped down, he did have strong muscular legs, the better to take all the battering he'd had in his career. Willie was the sort of flash winger whom all full backs wanted to flatten in the first minute. And usually did.

'Did you get any more money then?' asked Willie. Garry had been in to demand a pay rise, not having had any for a year.

'No, they can't afford it.'

'You don't believe that crap, do you?'

'Well they have spent a lot this season.'

'So you're leaving,' said Willie, smiling at me, winding Garry up.

'No, why should I?'

'Cos you're a failure, son.'

'That's your opinion, Willie.'

'If you were good enough, you'd be a first-team regular. You're not, so you're a failure, isn't that right, Joe?'

I didn't say a word. I'd just started to knock around with Willie, and still didn't feel quite accepted. They were both technically first-team players. Willie certainly was, supposedly only playing in the Reserves while recovering from injury. I was pleased to be in their company, especially Willie's. He was always entertaining, as long as he didn't happen to be picking on you.

'The thing is, I understand their problems,' said Garry, thoughtfully. 'I know why I'm not in. I probably wouldn't pick me again either, not when I played like shit against Everton.'

That had been his only first-team outing so far this season. He'd been put in the middle of the back four, and had not played well, booting the ball up the field every time he got it, playing for safe. He'd been told to do that if he got into problems, and not try to be clever, but they hadn't meant him to belt it into the Mersey every time he got it.

'You've given up,' said Willie. 'Otherwise you'd go in there and give them an ultimatum. Play me, or else.'

'What about you?' said Garry.

'I've been injured, remember?' said Willie, winking at me in the mirror. 'And I'm on first-team wages, so no sweat. It'd cost them a fucking fortune to get rid of me. My agent's seen to all that, don't you worry.'

'I'm not worried,' said Garry, looking very worried.

'Joe's the one who should worry,' said Willie. 'How the fuck's he gonna replace Glenn? The whole fucking world thinks the sun shines out of his arsehole.'

Willie was jealous of Hoddle, of the way the media had fallen in love with him, just as they had once raved over Willie. I wasn't jealous of Hoddle. I just thought he was brilliant, and felt privileged to be in the same dressing room, nor did I consider he was standing in my way. I felt I could play his role, as the creative midfielder, but in a different way, offering different skills, such as work rate and strength. I saw myself getting into the first team, playing with him, in a complementary role, but there were three people already ahead of me, plus Garry, who normally also played midfield.

Yes, I said strength and work rate. Those bastards had been right. It was what I had been lacking. Now I had it. All their stupid training and weights and endless exercises had paid off. I was now twelve stone, and carrying hardly any fat, well not much, though it was a struggle. I considered myself the best midfield tackler in the Reserves, and the best distributor of the ball, two skills which rarely go together, and by far the best at dead balls. Willie, who also played midfield when he was forced to, was faster, and could beat more men, when he put his mind to it, which wasn't often.

The car swerved violently as Willie suddenly braked. We climbed the pavement, passing several startled pedestrians, and drove through the open glass doors of a secondhand car showroom.

'Is it in yet?' he shouted towards someone at a far desk.

'Willie, lovely to see you Willie, my son,' said a smiling fair-haired bloke I recognized as Dez, one of Willie's many hangers-on.

'Don't give me the spiel. Where's the stuff?'

'No problem,' said Dez, walking over.

'That means it isn't in,' said Willie, reversing out of the showroom, just as violently as he'd come in, and zoomed off again.

I didn't ask what he was expecting. Not necessarily a new car, though Willie changed his every month. Possibly some electrical gear, a telly perhaps, fresh off the back of some lorry. He had promised to get a new telly for my flat, latest model, very reasonable, as long as I rubbed the serial number off the back the minute I got it.

He stopped again, outside a furniture store this time, and went in to look at a new suite, saying his missus was moaning on that she needed one. He was greeted once again like an old friend.

'Twenty per cent off for cash, as it's me,' I could hear him saying to the manager, slapping him on the back. He put his hand in his back pocket and pulled out a load of paper.

'You do take luncheon vouchers, do you?'

There was a lot of laughs and backslapping. Some packages were being exchanged.

'Don't wrap it all up, I can't take it now. What else you got for me then, you old wanker?'

Garry and I sat in the car as he negotiated some deal. Garry was getting impatient. He had agreed to take a youth trial in fifteen minutes.

'You should be careful of him, you know,' said Garry.

'How's that?' I said, innocently.

'Well he does have dodgy friends.'

'Such as you and me,' I said.

Garry sighed, not wishing really to badmouth someone, simply wanting to warn me, as the younger, more impressionable player. What impressed me about Willie was his attitude, which I knew was all wrong, and the coaches told him so on the hour. He reminded me of lads I'd played with at school, who had skill, but didn't give a bugger. Willie had somehow slipped through the scouting net, his Wrong Attitude intact. I liked to hear him rubbish some of the values I'd grown to accept in the last two years, defying the need to train hard, keep healthy, out of trouble, uphold the good name of the club and all that stuff. There was part of me in him, in that I was still willing to defy authority and received wisdom, but I'd become more calculating, taking what I considered was good and useful, while still rubbishing a lot of things. The big difference between us was that Willie had lost something vital, if of course he'd ever had it. Burning ambition. He lived for today. I lived for the next match, the next stage.

We dropped off Garry, only a few minutes late, then Willie insisted on taking me to another car showroom where he said I would get a very good deal, cos they owed him a few favours. He tried to get me to buy a car, there and then, sign here, I'll fix the deposit, no problem, even though I had no money and hadn't passed my test. I managed to resist the temptation.

From there we went to his bookies, to pick up some winnings, so he said, and get a few tips, and then to a golf club somewhere in the North London suburbs, not to play, but to use its private bar which stayed opened all afternoon. Willie had three Bacardi and cokes. I had half a Guinness, spinning it out, as I had a driving lesson later that afternoon.

'Right, she'll be getting her knickers off now,' said Willie looking at his watch. 'I better take you to your pad, unless you want to come and watch me on the job.'

'I'll wait for the film,' I said.

'Nice one, Joe,' said Willie. 'As it happens, I wouldn't put it past her.'

'You wouldn't put what past her?'

'Another nice one. Going for the hat-trick now, are we?'

In the car, he explained he was going to see this older woman, very glamorous, very wealthy, who was sex-mad and loved inviting star players to her home in the afternoon, to use her swimming pool, watch dodgy movies, then jump into bed with her. Her bedroom had a one-way mirror in the ceiling. She liked super fit blokes who could fuck her till she screamed, such as Willie. And she didn't mind being watched.

He was getting me quite excited, just by his description, even though I didn't believe half of it.

'You can join me if you like,' he said, as we arrived outside my flat. 'Come on as sub at half-time, when I get knackered.'

'I've got a driving lesson,' I said.

'Another time,' he said. 'Cheers.'

I was pleased to be asked. I might not yet be in the First-Team Pool, but it looked as if some of the first-team perks might be coming my way.

2, Soho Square, London, W1

Dear Mr Swift,

My client, Mr Dai Davies, JP, managing director of DD Motors, has instructed me to tell you that if he is identified in your book, either by name, by the distinctive bald hairstyle he once affected as a footballer, by his Welshness or in any other way, he will take steps to stop the book's publication and sue for considerable damages. Since his enforced retirement from Tottenham Hotspur FC, Mr Davies has become a most respected figure in the motorcar distribution world, and is this year president of the East Ham branch of his trade association. Anything which holds him up to ridicule or disrespect will be viewed with the utmost seriousness.

As for your lawyer's suggestion of changing his name to Willie, giving him another surname and making him Scottish, then we reserve our position with regard to this one.

Yours sincerely,

WOODBINE AND WOODBINE (*Solicitors*)

12

I was picked up for my driving lesson, a double one as my test was getting near, so I didn't get home for over two hours. I thought at first I'd had a burglary. My fridge door was open, and everything was melting. I had little in it, as I never cooked and always had takeaways. I checked the ice cream in the freezing part. That was still okay. Phew. I decided I must have left the fridge door open myself, rushing off to training in the morning.

The phone rang and it was Garry. He was over the moon. Someone had been injured and he'd been told he would definitely be in the first team for Saturday. He hadn't expected to be sub, or be in the first team squad.

'It's all the helping with the youth team,' I said, just as a joke. 'I'll have to try it.'

'Piss off,' he said.

'No, really, the boss knows he can rely on you to do the business.'

'He wants to see me in the morning,' said Garry. 'I wonder what for.'

'It'll be the money,' I said. 'You'll be getting a rise as well, you lucky sod.'

On Saturday morning I had a long lie-in. The Reserves had played midweek, so we didn't have a game. We were expected to turn up and watch the first team, though we didn't have to, not like being in the youth team. I decided I would, just to give Garry moral support.

I had ice cream for breakfast, as I wasn't playing, and couldn't be bothered going out to buy bread and cereal, then I re-read last night's

Evening Standard. It had a bit about Garry being in the team, with a quote from him saying this was it, he was going to establish himself in the first team this time, Spurs was the club he had supported as a boy, the only one he ever wanted to play for, so his future was definitely at White Hart Lane, no question.

About eleven o'clock, I went out to buy a morning paper, to see if they had any Liverpool team changes, but they had nothing in. I was thinking of going back to bed, or perhaps cleaning the flat, doing some shopping, or ringing my dad, which I did every Saturday, when I remembered, or watching the kids' programmes on TV. Or perhaps have some more ice cream.

Now what was the weather like, how many flies on the wall, what sort of ice cream exactly was I eating, Marine Ices or Walls, did I get out of bed on the right or the left that morning, hold on, I must be able to remember *everything* about that day. Yeh, you've probably guessed by now just why I'm lumbering you with all these boring details. How could I ever forget them?

The phone rang at three minutes past midday. It was the club, one of the girls in the general office, rather offhand, I thought. Telling me to come in, at once. I was to be sub for the first team against Liverpool.

Should I go on the tube? No, first-teamers didn't slum like that. But I had no money for a taxi, the extra driving lessons had taken all my cash. I rang Garry, to tell him my good news, see if he could give me a lift, but there was no answer from his home. He must have gone already, along with his parents.

I rang my Dad to tell him to listen to the radio, as the Spurs game was to be the commentary match – and I might be coming on. He wasn't in. He was at work. I got Colin, who had the telly on loud in the background, obviously watching it while he spoke to me. He said what, you what, listen to what, on the radio, oh no, our radio's bust, then he hung up.

I went on the bus, thinking this might be the last time I'd ever go on public transport. After today I'd be a star, with a chauffeur-driven car provided by a grateful club, correction, I'd be with some wealthy woman in her Rolls, complete with a one-way mirror at the back.

In the car park Old Les, who did bits for the Spurs programme, came over to say well done, Joe, but nobody else said anything to me.

Some of the national reporters were hanging around, trying to speak to Hoddle and the other real stars. I was ignored. They wouldn't know till they got their duplicate team sheets half an hour before the game that I was sub. It would still be meaningless anyway, as my name was not known to them.

I hung around the general office, trying to look casual and relaxed. I had no tickets to pick up, to put in envelopes and leave for my friends or relations. My inclusion as sub had been so late, nobody had thought of giving me the usual first-team share of free tickets. And anyway, who were my friends, my personal hangers-on? I didn't have any. As for my relations, my Dad was three hundred miles away, and working.

I was looking out for Garry, to go into the dressing room with him, but couldn't see him, so I was forced to go in alone.

I could hear Willie's voice, so I presumed he must be the other sub, holding forth, telling some long story about being chucked out of a club, then the police picking him up and him telling them he was Jimmy Greaves.

I changed in a corner, listening to the chat, but saying nothing. I asked Johnny Wallis, the first-team trainer, where Garry was. Hadn't I heard, he said. Just two hours ago, he'd been struck down with a stomach complaint.

What? I could hardly believe it. Garry was a diet freak, only ate the healthiest stuff, a nonsmoker, nondrinker. How ironic. Poor Garry. But that was obviously the reason I'd become sub. Willie was playing in place of Garry. The other two likely reserve midfielders were injured, so I'd jumped the queue and been given my chance. A chance to sit on the bench and get acclimatised to a first-team atmosphere, so the Boss explained. That was clearly the most I should expect.

I went out in my tracksuit for the kickaround, and heard the crowd politely clapping and shouting out a few individual names. Nobody kicked the ball to me. I did a few speed exercises, running ten yards like hell, then doubling back, just to look keen, draw attention to myself.

When the ref came out, I was given all the tracksuit tops to carry off the pitch. It was at least a job, something to do, but I hated them all, every player out there, about to perform, while I had nothing to do.

It was weird sitting on the bench, watching the match. I'd never done it before. The first thing I noticed was how curved the pitch was, sloping from the middle to the side, for drainage purposes. You don't see that from the stands.

The biggest surprise was how little you can see from the bench. No wonder managers like Beckenbauer and Dalglish stand up for the whole match. You can't follow what's happening on the far half, or see the other touchline, estimate distances, see who's running, see where the spaces are. The whistle goes for things you never saw happen.

However, when play's on the near side, on your side, it's like watching giants. Players seem bigger, stronger, fiercer. You see every bead of sweat on their body, hear every oath, every command, and feel every crack of every bone when they collide.

I don't want to go on, I thought. I'm scared. They're all zombies. Their eyes are glazed. They are so wound up they don't know what they're doing. Someone is going to get killed out there. Our coaches were equally wound up, screaming and shouting, urging our lads to get them, get stuck in, go in for the kill. That seemed to be the main instruction. Not that the players could hear a tenth of what was being screamed.

Of course I wanted to go on. What was I saying? That's why I was here. That's what I'd waited for all these years. That's why I was listening for every thwack, waiting for someone to be injured, a terrible thing to think, but that would give me my chance.

At half-time, there was no score. In the dressing room they all sat steaming like racehorses, heads down, while new orders, new formations, were given out, muscles massaged, wounds attended to. I made myself busy, passing round tea, getting fresh tie-ups and pads, making no comments. They were the fierce warriors. I was simply a handmaiden.

Ten minutes before the end, when it was still nil-nil, Hoddle was brought off. The crowd booed, not realising he had been injured. I could still hear the boos when I ran on, hoping they were not aimed at me.

I'd expected to be told to stay back and defend, hold out for a draw, but I came on with instructions for the midfield to be rearranged. My job was to play wide, head for the wing, take on their fullback, and get in quick crosses, while Willie was taken off the wing and told to play up front in the middle, as a second striker. I hadn't played wide for years, but I went on and did as I was told, waiting to get the ball. I don't think anyone noticed me coming on, as the crowd were still upset about Hoddle.

Once I was on, and the match restarted, I didn't feel at all nervous, nor could I hear the crowd, which was strange. I ran up and down like an idiot, gave a couple of one-twos, but never got the ball back. It was as if the team hadn't realised I was on either.

It was seven minutes before I got the ball in any space, and it came from a bad clearance, not a pass. I made towards the corner flag, stopped and put my foot on the ball, while their fullback stood off, waiting for me to commit myself. I knew I should put in a quick cross, as instructed, but that was what their defence expected. Out of the corner of my eye I could see them all lined up, waiting. I pretended to cross, but instead I curled my foot round the ball and dashed past the fullback, with the ball rolling towards the byeline, about to go harmlessly for a goal kick. I got it, just on the line, and with my left foot I sent it high into the goalmouth. I ended on my arse, sliding against the advertising boards. It was a hopeful ball, not meant for anyone in particular, but it landed just under the bar. Their defence had hesitated, convinced it was going out, then they panicked. Someone sliced at it, it rebounded, hit a defender on his back then went in for an own goal.

It was their mistake, not my skill. I hadn't meant to try to score, just to get it across, as instructed. The crowd went mad, cheering and jeering, delighted with the Liverpool mistake. Most of our players didn't realise the cross had come from me, or soon forgot, as we were urged back to defend for the last three minutes, which we did, holding out to the end.

Afterwards, Willie took the major credit. He realised the ball was still in play, so he said, and had watched it coming down, then he'd got a touch to it, which was what caused the panic. In fact, he might have got the last touch, but he didn't want to claim the goal. It probably was his goal, but an own goal was good enough for him, so he modestly told the reporters in the car park afterwards. He'd scored enough in his life, and would be scoring a few more this evening, har har.

Several reports said the ball went out of play when it was crossed, but the wind caught it, though they didn't mention who had crossed the ball, the bastards. Others said Willie had scored after a deflection. Another bastard. My part in it had been forgotten. Either way, it was deemed a fluke goal. Why should they mention me anyway, an unknown, who'd just come on, only touched the ball once, and done nothing else of note.

Willie roared off afterwards, forgetting to give me a lift, the sod. Everyone else was deciding which club they were going to, or where they were taking their missus.

I left on my own, feeling pleased to have been part of a first-team game, pleased I had contributed, but feeling deflated, let down somehow, back to being on the periphery.

I thought about going to the pub on the Cambridge Road where most unmarried reserves went to on a Saturday night. They'd all want to hear what happened in the dressing room, what was said, how I'd got on. I decided that first of all I would go to Garry's, check out the invalid, commiserate with his misfortune, if I could do it without gloating.

His mother let me in, making lots of faces, and I went into the kitchen where Garry was eating a salad.

'You've recovered quickly,' I said.

'What?' He looked startled, not having heard me arrive.

'Your stomach upset. What happened?'

'Nothing,' he said. 'I don't want to talk about it.'

He finished eating, cleaning his plate slowly and carefully, then he made some tea, for both of us. We discussed the other results, worked out Spurs' chances of jumping three places in the league on goal difference.

'So the doc treated you,' I said.

'What for?'

'Your stomach upset.'

'I didn't have one,' he said. 'I was getting my own back.'

'You what?'

'You know the boss saw me yesterday.'

'Yeh.'

'It wasn't about money. It was to say he was putting me in the team.'

'We know that.'

'But he also said it was just for one match. I hadn't to think I was now going to be a regular.'

'They always say that, so you don't get expectations . . .'

117

'No they don't. They don't say it's one match only. He made it clear Tony will be back in next week, whatever happens.'

'So what's wrong with that?'

'Don't you see? He was saying that even if I played brilliant, I would not be in. I had no hope, not a bloody chance in hell. So what was the point? I might as well play badly, because it won't make any difference . . .'

'I'm glad you didn't do that, you daft sod.'

'I thought about it all last night. I couldn't sleep. Then I decided this morning to get my own back. I'd tell him at the last moment I was ill. That would serve him right.'

It didn't make sense, but there was little point in arguing with him. He'd talked himself into a corner, with his own twisted logic. It was typical of so many reserves, waiting in the wings, over-analysing every decision, every word, every gesture from the Boss, tying themselves in knots of their own making.

He wouldn't come out for a drink, even for his usual tomato juice and a game of snooker. He was staying in. He couldn't be seen out, if he was ill, could he, even if he wasn't ill, know what I mean.

I went for a few drinks with the reserve lads, then got back to my flat just before twelve, intending to ring my Dad, tell him what had happened.

I could see the flat had been disturbed as soon as I got in. I opened my bedroom door and there on the bed was Willie, with a girl beside him. He'd let himself in with his own key, given to him by his mate who had fixed the flat for me. He was smoking a fag. She jumped up when I entered and started putting on her clothes.

'Out,' I said. 'I want you both out.'

'No sweat,' said Willie, slowly getting up.

'And keep your bloody hands out of my fridge.'

Through my mind went that scene with Mrs Jarret, and what a fury she had been in. I couldn't work up the energy to be really furious. I was calm and controlled. Sad if anything, but not angry.

'That was a good goal you got,' said Willie at the front door.

'What?'

'Your goal,' said Willie.

'I thought you got a touch?'

'Nah,' said Willie. 'I never touched it. Nor did anyone else. See you.'

So that was my first-team debut. A day me and Garry will always remember.

GRAND HOTEL
HARTLEPOOL

Centrally situated and a short walk from the station.
Fine ballroom and banqueting room.

Telephone: Hartlepool 66345. (STD 0429)

Dear Joe,
Nice to hear from you again. Since I joined Jehovah's
Witnesses, I don't seem to have heard from many of the
lads, but then I am on the road most of the time, working
for the Lord. I don't remember ever using the word
'bloody', but that is up to you, Joe, and your conscience.

Yours,
GARRY

13

I left Willie in bed in our room at the Gosforth Park Hotel, and went downstairs to reception. I'd been rooming with him for the last six months, since I got in the first team, and he was beginning to get on my nerves. He never stopped yabbering on, wouldn't go anywhere or do anything, had no interest in any place we ever visited, played stupid tricks all the time, his feet smelled and his jaw clicked when he ate.

We weren't supposed to eat before our pre-match lunch, but that didn't stop Willie. I left him in bed naked, scratching his balls, eating crisps, talking to some bird on the phone who had promised to come to our bedroom last night but hadn't, while watching children's telly.

It was a cup match, against Newcastle United, and we had come up the night before. With London clubs, and even most Midlands clubs, we travelled in our coach on the morning of the match. This was a vital match, and a long distance, so we were all here well in time, getting prepared, in the right mood, and all that shit. A right mood, my friends, is in your head.

We were supposed to have a long lie-in, resting till twelve, but I decided I'd have a walk around. Some clubs make you get up early, force you to have an early lunch about eleven, then you have to go back to your bedroom and rest till it's time to go to the ground. They even check the bedrooms, to see you're under the sheets. Bloody cheek. Spurs liked to think they treated you like adults, expecting you to rest sensibly before a match.

I threw my keys along the counter, seeing how far I could slide them. In just six months, I had grown used to hotel life, which was strange, because until then I'd never stayed in a hotel. I was already beginning to moan if room service was slow, there was no free biscuits and coffee maker in the room, or no colour telly. All bookings were done by the club, signing in, bill paying. We just had to turn up on time. Not that Willie took much notice of that.

'Hi there.' It was a woman aged about thirty in a dark executive-style suit, giving me a smile. She was standing waiting at the reception desk. I didn't recognize her at first, then I remembered that Willie had tried to chat her up last night, after we'd just arrived, but had got nowhere.

'Oh hi,' I said. 'Do you work here, then?'

'No,' she said. 'I'm here on a conference, just for the weekend. How long are you here for?'

'Just today,' I said. 'We'll be leaving about one.'

'Are you on a conference?'

'No, I'm working,' I said.

Her voice was quite posh, at least it wasn't regional, a sort of B.B.C. accentless accent.

'I hope it goes well,' she said, taking her room key, number 203, from the receptionist and going towards the lift. 'Have a nice day.'

I walked round the hotel grounds, smiling to myself. She obviously didn't know I was a footballer. She might not have known my name anyway, even if I had told her, but if I'd let slip I played for Spurs, that would have made a difference. It usually did. Willie told girls as soon as he met them, it was his way of pulling them, but then he had no taste, and would shaft any dopy scrubber that came along. On the pre-season tour he had gone mad, but then most players do, married or not. I liked to think women fancied me as me.

When I got back to the hotel the reception area was crowded with blokes in leather jackets smelling of Aramis and Havana cigars. The hangers-on, the hustlers and bustlers had arrived. One or two nodded to me, as I now knew most of them by sight, from the car park at Spurs, or in our away hotel, but they were mostly waiting for their particular player, to sweep him into a corner, smarming and smoothing, laughing and joking, picking up any team gossip, any titbit about their personal affairs.

'How's the flat hunting going?' said Dez. He was Willie's particular mate and I didn't recognize him at first in sunglasses.

'It isn't,' I said.

'I could have something for you,' said Dez. 'Something tasty. Keep in touch.'

'Got any tickets, Joe?' said a bloke I hadn't seen before, aged about forty, wearing a maxi sheepskin coat which almost drowned him.

'We haven't been given them yet.'

'I know that, sunshine, but when you do, can I have them?'

'Sorry, they've been promised.'

'Not to worry,' he said, putting his arm round my shoulder and steering me into a corner. 'How would you like a new motor?'

'I wondered what you had in those pockets.'

'Nice little MGB sports? How's that grab you, eh?'

'Sounds good.'

'Come here,' he said, pulling my ear down so that he was practically strangling me. 'This will sound even better. It's free.'

'Free?'

'To you, Joe my boy, it's free. I'm hearing good things about you, Joe. I can see a great future for you, Joe boy. I think we can do a lot of future business together.'

'What's the catch?'

'No catches.'

'So how do you open the doors?'

I pulled myself away and got my key and went up in the lift. It was almost twelve o'clock, time for lunch in a private dining room, specially reserved for us. We had to wear suits, when walking round the hotel, or going to the match, but for lunch we all took our jackets off, hanging them neatly behind our chairs.

I had steamed fish, the least horrible thing we were allowed. Most of the others had scrambled eggs. We all drank tea, great teapots of it, which arrived on the table first. The manager and coaches sat at one end of the table, talking together, trying to be hearty and friendly, pretending they were relaxed, just to relax us, but I could see they were as stiff as schoolteachers, worried as ever about the match to come, while pretending to be amused by Willie.

He started off swapping people's jackets around, moved on to throwing bread rolls, then he produced a bottle of beer, which he'd sneaked in, and was swigging from, waiting to be caught and told off. Alcohol was not allowed, pre match. Willie knew already that he was the travelling reserve, not likely even to get on the bench, so they were indulging his bottle of beer.

The directors and the club doctor ate at their own table, in another room, which was just as well. We all swore and discussed women and boozing, clubs and pubs, music and clothes and dodgy gear, as per usual. The presence of any directors was always a bit inhibiting.

After lunch, we got given our free tickets, only two each for an away match, then we all piled next door into a television room to watch the lunchtime football programme, jeering and booing at every statement from the so-called experts, shouting out obscenities during every interview, cheering if there were any clips from our games.

The door opened and the woman in the suit I had seen earlier popped her head in and looked round.

'Yes, this is the right room darling,' shouted Willie.

'Over here, I'm waiting for you,' shouted someone else.

'Get 'em off.'

'Bags me first.'

'Shurrup you lot,' said someone. 'She's the new ref.'

Everyone laughed and the woman looked embarrassed. 'I'm awfully sorry,' she said. 'I thought this was our conference room.'

'You can come and confer with me, darling.'

When she'd gone, there was another knock at the door.

'She can't keep away from me,' said Willie. 'Don't let her in.'

A young uniformed waiter entered, saying there was an urgent phone call for Mr Swift.

'If it's the *News of the World*, Joe, deny everything.'

'You're wanted in the maternity ward, Joe.'

'Her dad wants to talk to you.'

'I told you to wipe that number off the stereo, Joe.'

'And the doc told you always to wipe everything, Joe . . .'

I left them laughing at their own wit, and went to a phone in the room where we had had lunch. The trainers were still sitting, looking at lists and drawings.

'We can't manage it, Joe,' said my father.

'Where are you?' I asked.

'At home,' he said.

'Oh God, and I've got the tickets for you.'

'Colin's not well, not well enough to travel.'

'What's wrong with him?' I asked, as if I cared.

'He's had one of his attacks. He's wheezing really bad.'

'Oh well then, that's it, I suppose,' I said. 'You're never going to see me play.'

'Will you be coming then?' asked my Dad, plaintively.

'How do I know?' I said.

Everybody else's dad followed them everywhere, home and away, but my Dad had only seen me playing ten minutes for the first team so far. He'd come down for my full debut, at the end of the previous season, but I'd had to come off with an ankle injury after ten minutes. Nothing serious, and I played the next game, but he couldn't make that, as he was working. Before Christmas, he'd come to London, but the match had been cancelled because of snow. Another time he was coming, but the match was rearranged because of a cup replay, and he couldn't make it. This time he had agreed to drive across to Newcastle, his native city, just a couple of hours from Cockermouth, and would bring Colin.

'Come on your own then,' I said. 'You've still got time.'

'No, I'll just bring you bad luck anyway,' he said.

'Oh don't be stupid, Dad,' I said. Then I hung up.

I went down to reception, but there was no one there. I found Dez and the other hangers-on in the bar. I gave my motor car friend the two tickets, saying they were a present, no need for any money.

We went by coach into Newcastle. It rained all the way, which upset some people. I don't mind playing in the rain, unless it turns to mud. Rain makes the ball skid and less skilled players have difficulty controlling it. Never worries me.

There was a huge roar as we approached St James's Park. Our fans were being marched from the station in a long, wet crocodile, surrounded by police. They had just recognized our coach, hence the big roar. We all gave them a wave back. When the Newcastle fans spotted us, they naturally booed and waved their fists and gave us the v-sign. We sat in our seats, muttering fuck off cunts, but staring into space, giving no sign of having heard. No need for a brick through the window before the match had even begun.

We dashed from the coach, trying to keep our good suits dry, avoiding the local press and photographers. It was strange to be back at St James's Park. It seemed decades since I'd trained there as a schoolboy, well all of five years, but it looked so different, with different trainers. The crowd didn't know I had had a Newcastle connection, as no newspaper had yet done a proper interview with me, just bits and pieces, a few loudmouth post-match opinions. Otherwise they would have jeered 'United Reject, ah ha' the moment I came on the pitch.

I played brilliantly, and have reports to prove it, which is why I'm remembering the day so clearly. Everything I tried came off. Every pass found a man. Every movement worked. I scored the first goal dashing through from the edge of the box, my speciality, when they all expected a pass, holding off two men to slide the ball past the goalkeeper. The next I got from a free kick, curling it in with my left foot from about thirty yards away. Then I was brought down in the second half, trying to dash through again, and I scored from the penalty. We won three–nil. A hat-trick to moi. Good, huh?

Now was it being upset with my Dad which did it? Probably not. If he'd been there, you could have argued the opposite, saying it was his presence which spurred me on. Or being fed up that day with Willie, who was driving me mad with his stupid jokes and tricks? Being back in Newcastle, wanting to prove something? The wet conditions? The absence of Hoddle? Yup, now we're getting near. He was injured, and was out for several weeks. Instead of serving him, I served myself.

That was the day I started to dominate the midfield, playing the leading creative role, as well as breaking up their attacks. I took all the free kicks, dictated the tactics, made them all give the ball to me. It was all coming off, so they were more than happy to do so. Some days, some players do seem to be able to do anything, and everyone else realises it, just as some days you can do nothing right. I always knew I could dominate the midfield, but until then I had been forced to play a secondary role to other players, to subordinate my natural instincts. The only blemish was a booking, when I stupidly handed the ball when it was going miles over my head into touch. I'd begun to feel it was my ball, my game, so I could do anything I liked.

They all had a great time on the coach on the way home, knocking back the lagers. Some people even sang, which pleased the Boss. In his day players always sang, whether they'd had a good game or a bad one. That was what you did in the olden days. Thinks like Tipperary and Keep Right on to the End of the Road. Then it was fish and chip suppers all round. In the olden days.

Once in London, most of our lot went straight up West, to a new club where Dez had got them all free membership, and didn't get home till Sunday morning. So I was told later. Me, I was tucked up nicely in bed by ten o'clock.

I had arranged with the Boss earlier in the week that I would not be coming back to London on the team coach. I explained that my Dad was coming to the match, with my young brother, then I was going back to Cockermouth with them in my Dad's car to spend the weekend with them, coming back to London by train on Sunday. I'd asked if I could stay till Monday, as my Dad was a widower and all that, and I hadn't been home for some time. I was told the weekend was okay, but I must be back on Monday morning, sharp, for training as usual.

I had a few drinks in the players' lounge, saw our coach depart, then I took a taxi to the Gosforth Park Hotel, which was on the way home to Cockermouth, just in case I should be going home. I paid him off and went up to room 203.

I didn't know her name. I didn't know if she would be in. For all I knew she might already be in bed, on the job with her managing director, or downstairs in the dining room, eating with her husband.

'This is a surprise,' she said, opening the door. She was in a dressing gown and looked a lot younger than she had done in her executive suit.

'Come in. I'm just changing for dinner. Would you like a drink?'

She got me a beer from her mini-bar, then went into the bathroom to dress.

'I gather you did jolly well this afternoon,' she said from the bathroom. 'I heard the score on the radio.'

'Yeh, the lads done well,' I said. She laughed at my words. I was speaking the way footballers are supposed to speak, but not quite acting like one.

Willie would have been in the bathroom by now, jumping on her already. I was taking my time, waiting for her to lead, if she wanted to lead. I was quite happy just to talk to her, have a few drinks, leave it at that, then order another taxi and carry on home to Cockermouth. She seemed too classy for any clumsy or rough approaches. Too refined for anything crude. I was wrong of course. And I was right.

We spent the night together. The conference was almost over, so she said, and the dinner was purely a formality. Then all day Sunday, still in her bed, with short breaks for fresh air, fresh supplies from room service. And Sunday night. She said she had a few days' leave due anyway, before going to Belgium on a new posting. I thought, bugger training on Monday. Who scored all the goals and got us in the next round of the cup? I rang and said I was with my Dad, wasn't I, on compassionate grounds. Sorry about that, Boss.

What a lot I learned that weekend. About football, about life. I never knew there were so many positions I had not tried before. I learned how to be creative, how to dominate, to get rid of the ball at the right time, then to hold it till the last moment, striking at the vital second, bringing everything to a climax. That's football, that's life.

Yes, I played brilliantly that weekend, and have her letters to prove it. I never saw her again, alas. That's life. That's football.

BRITISH EMBASSY YAOUNDÉ
Avenue Winston Churchill
BP 547 Yaoundé
Cameroon

Telephone: 22.05.45
Telex: 8200 KN

Dear J,

How sweet of you to send me your report. It has been sent on to me from King Charles Street. I left Brussels some time ago. It was a jolly good conference and I remember it well. I realise you are getting in touch with me now as a matter of 'Copies to All Departments' and there is no need for me to comment further. I agree with all the points you have made. Well done. No need to add anything, such as my name. I would prefer to remain anonymous, as we are obliged to, under Foreign and Commonwealth Office regulations. My contributions were of course voluntary.

Oh, one little point. I can't remember sending you any letters after our meeting. I thought it was only a postcard, thanking you for all your help during our meeting? I would be obliged if you could return it/and/or them, care of Dept X, here at the Embassy. Good luck with all your future conferences.

Yours,
PP
(*Signed in her absence*)

14

So it's a home match this time, about a year later, 1985 or give or take a few centuries. And I'm in the present tense, as we're getting more up to date.

There are some players who can remember every game, every goal, the ref's name and occupation and name of mother, if any, and whether there was tea or Bovril at half-time. It's funny how you can remember early days, early doors, the ones which the fans usually forget. Then matches begin to fade and fuzz together. Except for one or two. Here's one. Catch.

I'm living in my new apartment in the choicest part of downtown Enfield, the first property I ever owned, two bedrooms, luxury kitchen, full CH, entryphone, plus waist disposal unit, which was how they spelled it, Mr Bott, not me, you know how good I am at English, on the estate agent's handout, the one Dez gave me the moment before it officially came on the market.

I'd been in it over a month but it was still a stranger to me. The five-seater luxury sofa retained its plastic cover, the exceedingly cunning breakfast bar had not yet been let down and the state-of- the-art cooker had not been switched on. That would mean reading instructions. I'd given up reading instructions. Famous people don't need to. When I get round to hiring my personal staff, I'd have people who would read instructions, plus carry money, open the post, do the shopping and make phone-calls for me. Going to the lav for me, that would be optional.

I had tried out the bed a few times, but I can't remember who with.

I seemed to spend most nights elsewhere, sleeping where I ended up, eating when people provided it for me, dining in restaurants which were more than keen for my custom. 'I'm buying a cookery book soon,' so I told the *Evening Standard* the week before. 'I need to find out how you make toast.'

Not a joke, really. When all you've done since the age of fourteen is play football, most other skills have passed you by. One part of your being gets highly developed, the ability to kick a ball roughly in the direction of the goals, plus the minor skills and attributes which go with it, such as big thighs, big thirst, big cock, but most other manual skills get left behind. I prided myself that I was not as totally cut off intellectually as most players. I felt in touch with current affairs, films, television, and I always made a point of sussing out every new town and country we visited, taking in the local sights, not just the local talent. During the last close season I read three books. Only one of which was on cookery. Can't remember the other two.

Football clubs like you to concentrate on what they are paying you to concentrate on, but there comes a time when they get a bit worried. If you're still unmarried or unattached at twenty, and not living at home with your mum, they start asking questions. Not are you a poofter, because of course all football coaches, the world over, believe there are no such things, not in football, go wash your bloody mouth out at once, you fairy. They want to know if you're eating properly, sleeping properly, looking after yourself. It's not you they are thinking about, of course, or your daily well-being, but themselves and *their* well-being, on Saturday afternoons.

I remember the first talk I had from the Spurs doctor, as a young apprentice, warning us about certain sorts of women, and if you got a certain sort of sore on the old John Thomas, come and see him, and he'd sort it out. I suppose today the apprentices all get talks on Aids when they sign forms. Poor sods. Must frighten them for life.

In every big club around the world there is of course someone whose job it is to sort out any paternity claims, keep at bay the women who allege they are up the spout cos of what you have done, you bastard. There's also usually someone with a hotline to the local nick when some idiot crashes his car, wrecks a hotel bedroom, thumps someone at a nightclub, gets too drunk and too disorderly.

They are used to dealing with such things. You get a right

bollocking, of course, but they can take it in their stride, as it's always happening. What they are not used to is players living alone over the age of twenty-one. They like the idea of you settling down, not necessarily married, not in this day and age, but shacked up with some suitable girl, which usually means someone totally dumb and devoted. They know that for the first season after marriage you will lose a certain sharpness and put on a bit too much weight. This is a known fact. All clubs have statistics to prove it. They then have to work harder on you in training, getting you trim and hungry again. Naturally being married, or living with a partner, doesn't make a blind bit of difference when you are in hotels or on tour and there are women hanging around hoping for favours. The clubs accept that. Boys will be boys will be bastards. But at least when you are at home they know roughly where you are. More or less.

Over the last year I'd had a few of those so-called fatherly chats, gentle enquiries about my domestic arrangements, even though I wasn't yet twenty-one. Eyebrows had raised about my close friendship with Dez, and my reply had been the same to all of them: fuck off, you nosy bugger.

I went downstairs to the front door of my choice apartment block, swept up my post from behind the double-glazed security front doors, and got into my new MGB GT, badly parked at an angle across our private car park where I'd left it last night, unlocked of course. Too boring to park and lock properly, when you've been out late, where ever it was I'd been out late. Can't remember now.

My free car of course, the second one so far. The only drag was having to have this larger-than-normal-sized sticker in the back window, telling the world which North London garage had supplied it. I had been appointed their sales consultant. Not exactly an arduous job, as all it meant was turning up once a month to their showroom, having a few drinks with important customers or chatting to their staff. Personally I thought they were getting my services cheap. I was also allowing them, at no extra charge, to announce a weekly 'Joe Swift's Choice of the Week' in the secondhand car adverts in the North London press. Next time I was going to demand a Mercedes.

I started opening some of my letters as I drove towards Tottenham, winding my way through the Saturday morning shoppers, then chucking the envelopes on the floor of my car. It was already covered with unanswered letters. I don't know how so many people had got my new address, in only two months. Most of them had just put Joe Swift, Enfield. Some cleverclogs in the post office had done the rest.

A woman with a crippled son wanted me to sign a birthday card for him. She'd at least enclosed a stamped addressed envelope. Ones who don't are straight on the floor. Yet another agent wanted to handle me. Straight out the window. A woman's magazine wanted to interview me on my sex appeal, for a fee of £100. Bloody hell. Cheeky sods. A school in Leighton Buzzard wanted me to open their fete, no chance, while a church in County Durham wanted an item of secondhand clothing for a celebrity auction, which I might consider. I usually throw old things out. Saves me washing.

'*Arsenal*!' shouted a lorry driver, shoving his fat face out of his cab window as I waited at a traffic light.

'Go fuck yourself,' I shouted back, throwing some old envelopes at him, then winding up my window quickly.

I got to the ground only five minutes late. We were supposed to turn up at one-thirty sharp, or we could be fined or punished. Oh yeah. So they're gonna drop me. Good one. I jumped out of my car in the car park, without putting the handbrake on, and threw the keys to a commissionaire, leaving him to park it.

I was immediately surrounded by a gaggle of leather coats, jostling for attention, plus a few radio and agency press. Too early for the nationals. They are still getting tanked up at that time on a Saturday. I strolled across the car park to the office in my new dark double-breasted blazer, very classy, so Sonia said when she gave it to me. Direct from her husband's factory. Or is she called Sandi? Something like that. Only met her twice. I also had on a white silk poloneck shirt, bought in Paris, so Sandi said when she gave it to me last night. Or Sonia. As you know we were supposed to wear dark suits, white shirts and ties, when on duty. For once, I was almost conforming. What a creep.

I went into the general office where the rest of the first team were standing around in their best gear, being formally casual and stiffly relaxed. If there were any apprentices or Reserves around, I didn't notice them. One never does.

The first-team players were signing get-well cards from local hospitals, team photos for schools, footballs for charity auctions, idly, as if their writing hand had nothing to do with them, while chatting and laughing amongst themselves. There's usually one player who has brought some special thing in to be signed, having been conned by a local do-gooding group or his relations, so you sign that a bit better, so it can be read, knowing that next week you'll want the lads to sign something for you. That day it was a stupid six-foot-high cardboard Spurs cockerel, to be raffled for Ethiopian relief. Or similar.

I went to my pigeonhole, bulging with the usual rubbish, just to see if there were any presents, any free things. It's one of the nice things about being wealthy. Poor people give you things. Stupid, isn't it. Just when you can afford to buy anything you want, after years of being hard up, you get things for nothing, from people who can't afford it. Most of it of course is from well-off people and rich firms, trying to con you, getting you to accept something, so that you will feel beholden. In just a year, since the fan letters and offers started flooding in for me, I had developed a very simple strategy. Accept everything: reply to nothing.

Other players thought this was pure greed, or utter rudeness. Most of them replied to everything, except abuse. I used to mock them, struggling to form their letters in their spastic handwriting, or getting girls in the office to duplicate replies. If they were real stars, they would have an outside agency to run their fan club and send out photos. Tax allowable, but what a drag, what a waste of time.

I've always enjoyed abusive letters. I bet there's been a lot recently, as you might expect, since I've been here. None has got through, of course. They'll be piling up somewhere. In the old days, I used to read them aloud on the coach, to amuse the lads, if time was hanging heavy. You can tell abuse immediately from the green handwriting, words underlined in red or in capitals, and endless PSs. Personally, I would have liked to have replied to many of them, sending equal abuse back, if I could have got up the energy. Even though it would have broken a lifetime's habit.

Shocked? You feel I have a duty to reply to everyone, as the Blessed Lineker does? My attitude to fans is that I didn't ask them to write. I don't feel I owe them anything. My job is playing football, not being nice to fans. If they like my football, then fine, if not, then piss off. If enough people don't like my football, I'll soon be told to piss off, then no one will write to me again. That's the way it is. I accept it. As for firms, they write because they want to take, not to give.

'Any telegrams or urgent messages?' I asked one of the senior secretaries, a middle-aged woman in a suit.

'Look in your pigeonhole, Joe. You know the system, Joe.'

'It's full of shit. Pigeon shit,' I said. 'Tweet tweet.'

I pretended to fly round the room, crapping over everyone, then landed on top of her, which wasn't very funny, but was very Joe Swift, aged twenty and a bit.

'There was one telegram, addressed to the manager,' said the secretary, pushing me away. 'You were seen in a nightclub at two o'clock this morning.'

'That was my brother. Anything else?'

'Just the usual press and tv requests for interviews.'

'Boring, boring.'

I went into another office to collect my free tickets. I put them all in an envelope, addressed to Sonia-Sandi, then I strolled back across the car park to the West Stand. There were now a lot more press around, local and national, trying to find out the latest on injuries, team changes, who might be sub. One of the local papers asked me about some problems with the new West Stand and what I thought of the latest facilities.

'Very good,' I said. 'I approve of the jacuzzis for every player and hot and cold running maids in every corridor.'

'Thanks, Mr Swift,' he said, solemnly writing it down.

'What time did you leave Tramps last night, Joe?'

'Who are you from?' I asked. It was another reporter, one I hadn't seen before.

'I'm doing a story for the *Mirror*,' he said, all smiles and charm. 'Was it two-thirty or three o'clock you left?'

'Piss off,' I said flatly, walking towards the players' entrance. It was the usual sort of wind-up question.

'We've had a story from a freelance photographer,' he said, running after me.

'Must have been my brother.'

'I didn't know you had a brother, Joe.'

'I mean the freelance photographer. All photographers are my brothers, unlike reporters, who are all shits, now piss off.'

'The photographer alleges you punched him and that he's considering legal action.'

'Medical action, more like.' I said. I was now getting angry, so I pushed him aside and went through the players' door.

I was last into the dressing room, as usual. I hate waiting, of all sorts. I threw my blazer across the room, but it missed my peg and landed on the floor. They could all see it was brand new, yet I was mistreating it. Many of them had their suits hanging neatly in plastic bags.

I picked up a programme from the treatment table and sat down on a bench to read it.

'Welcome to White Hart Lane,' I said, mimicking the Radio One tones of Willie Morgan, the club's DJ. 'The world-famous home of the North London Wankers.' Then I changed to the Boss's accent. 'Happen we got well stuffed at Leeds last week. If Joe Swift had produced the form we know he is reet well capable of, then someat might have gone reet for us. If he got his hair cut, he might see where t'goals are, and if he stopped screwing birds all night long, he might have more energy during day, ee ba gum, stick it up your bum . . .'

They all laughed. I did the same most weeks, and mostly they laughed, except for those I knew I was annoying. Hard cheddar. Some players like total peace and quiet in the dressing room before a match, but not me. It's always been part of my getting-ready process. Anyway, it's not a church. We're not getting ready for a bloody funeral, at least we hope not.

Some players were already undressed, naked except for their socks and boots, their studs echoing on the floor as they walked around. Some were in their jockstraps and shirts, but with bare feet. All players have their own rituals, their own sequence for getting ready.

'Just off to the library,' said someone, taking his programme with him to the bogs.

Several were being massaged by the trainers, lying on the treatment table, having last-minute attention to muscles or liniments and oils rubbed in.

'The big decision this afternoon,' I said, at last going to my seat, picking up my blazer from the floor and hanging it up.

'Is what are we going to do tonight, lads? I was gonna have yous all back to my pad . . .'

'Oh yes, likely bloody story.'

'But there's this new club opening. Cock of the North, it's called. It's only for big cocks. No, straight up. They have this brilliant security system. You have your cock photographed on your membership card, so you have to flash it to get in . . .'

Most people were not listening by now, deep into their final preparations. At last I started to undress, throwing off my clothes, trying not to look at the bruises and cuts, lumps and bumps from the last match. It's how you feel, not how you look. I felt pretty good, say eighty-five per cent fit. I don't think I'd felt a hundred per cent wholly fit and perfect since I was fourteen. You never do. You're always getting over something, worrying about some weakness, wondering what's going to play up next.

At ten to three there was almost silence in the dressing room. Footsteps could be heard above our heads and outside in the corridor. Music and meaningless roars drifted from the terraces. The Boss was going round, taking people aside individually, repeating personal instructions, then he stood in the middle, awkward and embarrassed, telling us who would take corners, free kicks, penalties, which defenders would mark which opponents, always to watch for Bryan Robson breaking through from deep. We knew all that. He'd told us in the team talk. He was just hiding his own nervousness, giving himself something to do.

Seven minutes before three, the ref came in, told us he wanted a good clean game, and inspected all our studs. 'Good luck, ref,' I said with a smile. I always said this. It was cheek, but he couldn't get you for it. I knew that he knew he wanted good luck, just as we all did.

At five to three, the Boss moved to the doorway, waiting for us, a sign that it was time. We all then shook hands with each other, round the dressing room. I used to smile at this, when I first got in the first team, at the solemn faces, the serious expressions, shaking hands with lads you'd been sitting chatting with for almost two hours. But now I took it seriously. It was a symbolic shaking, like touching wood, stroking totem poles, a sign language to the gods, wishing ourselves good luck – and even more important, no injuries in the ninety minutes ahead. At the doorway, the Boss shook us each by the hand himself.

There was a trickling, rumbling, gathering roar, as we clipclopped down the corridor, then the strains of 'Macnamara's Band' welcoming us on to the pitch, followed by a giant roar as we entered the field to the exaggerated delight of our supporters. From the Park Lane end, the opposition end, the roar was almost as noisy. When you play Manchester United, they bring enough supporters to outshout many home crowds.

I saw one or two Cadbury's Flakes being thrown in my direction from the Park Lane end. A few weeks previously, I told the *Daily Mail* I only had two hobbies, sex and Cadbury's Flakes, though best of all, I preferred sex with Cadbury's Flakes. They'd missed out this second bit, but everyone had remembered the Flakes. I picked one up, and pretended to eat it, giving an enormous chew, which our supporters loved.

The match started at full pelt, and got faster. It was one of those games where the ball buzzes like a pinball and the tackles come in before possession has taken place, innocent, overeager tackles, simply meant to send you straight into Tottenham High Road, not necessarily to Casualty. I got clattered early on, but I was coming to expect that. The ref was trying to keep the game flowing, and not blow up all the time, screaming warnings at us all as he rushed back and forward. He was one of those who like to make friends with you, like Joe Worrall, calling everyone by their christian name, as if you can ever be friends with a ref.

The midfield was a battleground, while the wings were quiet and empty enough for sunbathing. The first name in the book was mine, when I retaliated once too often, bringing down Bryan Robson, which of course had the Man U crowd booing me from then on, every time I touched the ball. I never mind that. It amuses me, to be picked on for special abuse. It doesn't upset my confidence, as it does with some players, who then start getting rid of the ball too early, just to stop the booing. I know the crowd is doing it partly for their own amusement, enjoying themselves, and will soon grow bored, when something else happens. In a sense it's a compliment, that you're worth booing, but it can take the edge off your concentration if you start waiting for the boos to begin.

Man U were gradually getting the upper hand, pushing us back, and I was being forced to defend more. I got caught on the edge of our box, looking for a way out without actually belting the ball upfield into space, which I would never do, as I consider that a blasphemy, an insult to the sacred art of football, though all coaches will tell you to do this in an emergency. As I farted around, in smaller and smaller circles, being pushed back, with everyone on both sides expecting I'd have to belt it, or knock it into touch, and me waiting to be fouled, so I'd get a free kick, I swivelled round and sent it about forty yards, high in the air, towards our goalie. Only he wasn't there, stupid sod. Luckily my aim was not as perfect as it usually is. It hit our bar, then rebounded safely into his arms as he dashed back.

Gawd, the Man U crowd gave me some jeers after that, but our crowd loved it. I pretended it had been deliberate, breathing on my knuckles and polishing them on my shirt, then I gave a little bow to the Man. U. end. Flash bastard, well I was only twenty. It was a mistake, though. Their boos were deadly serious from then on, really hating me.

I began to tire towards the end, too much defending, running back to cover, too many late nights, and they should have scored several times, but ten minutes before the end Robson went off injured. In the last minute I made a slow dash from the edge of their area, which looked like I was running into trouble, but I got past two defenders before the third pulled me down. I made the most of it, but we did get a penalty. I took it. And scored.

I ran forward to pick the ball out of their net, as they protested, which made the crowd behind their goal go mad, screaming and shouting, spitting and throwing things at me, suspecting I was going to time-waste, which was probably true, but at the time, I just did it, without thinking. Just like I did the next thing. I dropped my shorts, flashed them a quick bare bum, then hared back upfield with the ball, and put it on the centre spot.

The ref had been running back as well, and hadn't noticed what I'd done. He blew for time the second the ball was kicked off. Pandemonium all around. Absolute fury from the Man U crowd. Total ecstasy from the Shelf.

In the dressing room, it was brilliant. There is a natural though morally reprehensible delight in winning when you don't deserve it. It's not a matter of luck, and all matches contain moments of luck, just as all lives contain moments of luck, but a matter of justice. On the day, they had been the better team. We had worked hard enough, but they had worked better, and should have won. No question.

The best pleasure of all in football is a total win, when you do it with grace and style, fabulous moves, endless creations, countless openings, constant near-misses then a stream of effortless, unstoppable goals, every player giving of his best, till the whole team soars celestially above the sum of its parts and you can see, you can just see it in their eyes, that the other side is so demoralised they are almost in awe of you, desperate for the whistle. This does happen, once in a millennium. Usually, alas, just as you feel you are getting into such a stride, at least for a few brief moments, they start kicking the hell out of you, or they decide to regroup and all ten go back into their penalty area, and stay there for the rest of the match.

If winning in style is best, there is also a pleasure to be had from winning with no style, as we did that day. In fact there's the double satisfaction of an unexpected and undeserved victory, combined with knowing how they must feel, sitting across the corridor in the other dressing room, sick as bloody parrots.

'Can you just see Robbo's face now,' said someone. That broke us all up, once again. Is it being nasty, malicious, enjoying someone else's pain? Probably. But very human. We know next week, or the week after, it will happen to us. C'est le football.

As I came into the corridor, making my way to the players' lounge, looking forward to a drink with the Man. U. lads, unless they'd chickened out and got straight on their coach, I was grabbed by two Sunday paper reporters. They had sneaked in illegally, saying they were desperate for a quote, their first edition was already going. One of them shoved a photo at me, taken from the side, my arms round some blonde in a nightclub. I'd forgotten all this nonsense, about what I had done or not done last night. Playing a dramatic match is like tearing up your past. It wipes out what went before.

'You what?' I said.

'That is you, Joe, isn't it.'

So that was it. They were still in some doubt if it was me in the picture.

'We know you were there, till two-thirty in the morning.'

'Like fuck I was. I was in bed, but I'm not telling you who with. Now fuck off.'

I still wasn't clear what they were trying to pin on me. It's not illegal to be in a club till two-thirty, though I'd get a bollocking from the club for being out so late on the night before a match.

As I entered the players' lounge, one of the assistant secretaries gave me a note, saying the chairman wanted to see me on Monday. I grabbed him as he moved away, demanding more information. He muttered something about a possible fine. The board would doubtless want to get in first, before the Football League got in on the act.

'What the fucking hell for?'

'Bringing the game into disrepute. Remember what happened to Sammy Nelson.'

He was the Arsenal player who got fined £750 and suspended for dropping his shorts. I was about to deny I'd done such a thing, when he said that the television boys had the whole thing on film.

'It was just a laugh, bloody hell, they can't be serious.'

In the players lounge, we commiserated with the Man. U. lads, without sniggering too much. They only had a quick drink, but at least they turned up. Our lads had quite a few, getting ready for the bigger few we'd have that evening.

In the car park, as I was getting into my car, one of the trainers came up and said the Boss wanted me in tomorrow.

'What the hell for?'

'Extra training. He thinks you're not fit enough.'

Bloody hell. On a Sunday. He must be joking. Who got that goal? What is happening round here?

My good mood was evaporating fast. Those reporter shits had really annoyed me. Then the stupid board making a fuss about a stupid bare arse. Now the Boss taking it out on me. I should have been the hero, not treated like a child, or a villain.

As I drove through the gates, a commissionaire dashed out.

'There's an urgent message for you. In the office.'

'Oh bloody hell,' I said, but I got out, leaving the car running. 'That's all I fucking need.'

The soreness suddenly hit me. I could hardly walk. The euphoria of winning had been disguising the pains, but now I limped and lumbered across to the office.

One of the secretaries handed me a bit of paper. It was a message from someone phoning from Ipswich – Bobby Robson. I was to join the England squad on Monday.

Telegraphic Address: 'STADIUM' Manchester
Telephone: 061-872 1661/2 (Office)
061-872 7771 (Ticket and Match Enquiries)

MANCHESTER UNITED Football Club Ltd
OLD TRAFFORD, MANCHESTER,
M16 0RA

Dear Joe,

I don't quite remember that match, not the way you describe it, but then you try not to remember such matches, especially ones where I got injured. I do remember the bum incident. I have it in my personal video collection, specially redone in slow motion, and I often show it to to my friends at Christmas. It scares the life out of them. Better than any horror movie.

Yours in sport,
BRYAN ROBSON

15

1986 and I'm getting ready to go out, making big decisions, what evening suit to put on, my old one or my new one. The old one is vintage, at least a year old, bought at Burton's in a hurry when I had to go to the Supporters' Player of the Year award. My new one is dead flash, state of the fart, well fashionable, but I did buy it at least half an hour ago, so it already feels as dated as the old one. I know. I'll put the old one on, double breasted, no ribbons, no tat. Saturday night, so it's going to be all right.

It's what you live for, as a footballer. Saturday night, win or lose, you can forget. What am I saying, the whole world lives for Saturday night. If I try hard, I can remember the excitement of Saturday nights in Cockermouth, going with Tom into town with such anticipation, walking the length of Main Street, convinced everyone was watching us, looking for action, testing out at least two pubs, walking back down Main Street, then straight on, back to our village, actionless. Well, that didn't take long. Some memories are not worth remembering.

A quiet night tonight, just a little dinner engagement, nothing strenuous, nothing too late, nothing too tiring. I wonder who I'll end up with. Nobody too tiring, nobody too noisy I hope. Tomorrow afternoon I'm joining the England party, for our big match on Monday.

No, not that match. It's six months later and I've now played three times for England. Three games, but not consecutive games, not in a flow, not a natural progression. That's the nature of international football. Even if you don't miss a game, it still feels like a new beginning. You need about fifty caps to feel established, that you belong. I felt no nearer belonging than I did on that first match – a goalless draw against Turkey, don't talk about it, please.

Where's my bloody school tie. People steal things in this house. Colin, have you seen it? If that Fanny has taken it. It's not my fault. Oh God. Mum, help me.

For a moment, hunting around for my bow tie, I did think I was back home. She never saw me play for Spurs, poor soul, poor me. There's not a day goes by when I don't think of her in some way. It's subconscious, no words, the communication is private. Is that why I can't bear to have any woman moving in with me, keeping them all at bay? Don't answer that, Doc Freud. I don't want to know.

I found my bow tie down the back of the new sofa, six-seater, still covered with plastic, like most things in my new place. Enfield? That was ages ago. How could I have lived in that grotty little modern block? Suburban North London. One shudders at the thought. The answer is I didn't live there. I just passed through, now and again, then sold it, at a large profit. Now I'm in Regent's Park, don't you know, right next to the Park, your actual Regency Terrace, an exceedingly elegant first floor apartment which me and the Queen are rather proud of. It's her pad, really, but she's living elsewhere at the moment, somewhere in Victoria, rather downmarket if you ask me, near that station, surrounded by gaping tourists, poor lass. I've leased it from her, through her chaps at the Crown Estates. Cost a fucking fortune, even before I moved in. I like to be central, near the evening action.

Footballers are so corny. They will act like footballers. They marry hairstylists, buy a semi in the suburbs, then a mock-Georgian detached out in the pretend countryside. I remember once going to a party at Mike England's, when I was only an apprentice at Spurs, so that was good of him, and his house knocked me out. It wasn't a footballer's house. For a start, it was architect designed, really original and amazing, and I thought I'll do something like that, if I make it. No I didn't. I thought *when* I make it. Now I have.

A young woman, equally classy, comes in to do for me, no jokes please. I rarely see her. She has a degree in Mods or Mod Cons or something, and is the niece of my lawyer, Arnold, the one who arranged the lease for me and who has offered to take over all my legal and accountancy affairs. She comes in mornings, tidies up, fills my fridge with convenience junk, opens the post, answers anything vital, pays the bills, all the boring stuff that people marry wives for.

I got my electricity cut off in Enfield, another reason for leaving, and never paid stupid things like ground rent and maintenance. The club had to sort that out, just as they have sorted out a few other nasties over the last year. That nightclub photo was nothing. By chance, I'd shafted some society bird called Paula or Pansi who was also sleeping with a Cabinet Minister and the Editor of a posh Sunday paper. Good laugh, that story, though not such a good laugh as the bare bums. That's still running. On the Shelf, you see lads with bare bum masks, or inflatable bare bums, which they wave in the air. Makes a change from inflatable bananas. Remember them? For a whole season, you saw them at every ground.

Only two bedrooms this time, both quite small, but one enormous main room with double windows. I'm not expecting to put many people up. My Dad says he's not coming to London ever again. It took him eight hours on the train when he came at the end of last season for Spurs-Arsenal. He still hasn't seen me play for England. I've given up inviting him. Right, that's the picture.

The intercom went. Out of my very elegant front windows I could see the inelegant sight of Dez, lumbering out of his Lotus Elan. I smiled at his unhealthy, fleshy frame, and shielded my eyes from the dazzle of his two-tone blonde hair, his gleaming rings and his new evening-suit jacket. It had purple brocade lapels and white velvet buttons and he was wearing it with a frilly pink shirt. There were countless proper agents and managers, or legal chaps with letters after their name, such as Arnold, begging to handle me, but somehow Dez Dainty had taken me over. It amused me to have him around. I felt at ease, treating him as one might treat an old school-friend. Like shit in other words.

'You look like a fucking ponce,' I said, as he swaggered in. 'Come here, make yourself useful, you wanker. Tie this.'

'I don't suppose you had ties in Cockermouth, did you,' said Dez, his fat fingers getting to grips with my collar. 'Cover yourself in woad, did you mate, when you went out of an evening, sheep shagging . . .'

'Not that again,' I said, grabbing his balls with my hand behind my back.

'Oh, gerroff, that hurt, you cunt,' said Dez, pretending to be mortally injured. 'I'll need them tonight.'

How strange, you might think, two grown men, in evening suits, in an elegant flat, one of them quite well known, both on high incomes, behaving like, well two grown men in evening suits. I'd recently got £1,000, half in oncers in my back pocket, for turning up at some sales conference at a posh hotel, an invitation which Arnold had opened, and negotiated the fee, and after the brandies and cigars, that's how they all behaved. Like drunken yobs. I've had an invite to the Oxford Union, well there aren't many footballers around who are thought capable of speaking in sentences, but I'm not going, am I, though Arnold is all for it. I know without knowing it that after a few drinks, they'll be ball grabbing and debagging, only with classier accents.

I went into my bedroom and put on my jacket, admiring myself in the mirror. Dez was on my phone, without even asking me, arranging some transport.

'Gorgeous,' said Dez, coming up behind me. 'I could fancy you myself. And so will everyone else when they see your sexy picture.'

'What sexy picture?'

'I'll tell you in the car.'

Dez was driving, another way in which he made himself useful. I wasn't banned at the time, but I'd just been done for speeding, not my fault, I was late for something, can't remember what, coming out of the Sportsman Club. I was only doing seventy, in Tottenham Court Road, well it is one-way. Luckily the two coppers recognized me and were very grateful for West Stand tickets, four of the best, so I didn't get breathalysed.

'When I put the picture idea up, they all loved it,' said Dez. 'Every fucking Sunday paper, all wetting themselves . . .'

'Well, they would, if it was one of your ideas, Dez. They're as half-witted as you are.'

'I think we'll do it for the *News of the World*, whatja fink, Joe boy? Could be ten grand in it, exclusive, just for one naked picture. Not bad, er.'

'I'm not showing my prick in the *News of the World*.'

'Your bum, you nutter. The same one you flashed at the Park Lane End. Ten grand is ten times what you was fined, so that can't be bad.

I should have thought of it months ago. You can't see nuffink on that telly shot.'

'What about the club? I'll be done for bringing the club into disrepute again, and all that shit.'

'No chance. We'll say it was snatched. You'll be in a shower, right, getting out, right, when this paparazzi cunt who's got in the Spurs dressing room, right, so it's their fault, okay, he snatches you from behind, showing your behind, gerrit. All done in a studio of course. It'll probably make a centrefold.'

'Brilliant,' I said, laughing. Dez's ideas were not quite as dignified as Arnold's, but much more fun.

'"Joe Swift: the Bare Facts",' said Dez. 'I can just see the headline now. Or "Bum's the Word". Gerrit? Instead of Mum's the word.'

'Just keep my Mum out of it,' I said.

'Only one problem,' said Dez, as he drove through the Park, turning up Leo Sayer on his radio.

'What's that, Dez?'

'Have you got a hairy arsehole?'

'I haven't looked recently.'

'Cos you know what happens with hairy arseholes.'

'Amaze me.'

'Little bits of shit get caught in the short hairs, know what I mean, Joe?'

'You would know, Dez.'

'Too true squire, it's with having a lovely big fat arse.'

'You said it,' I said.

'It can be agony when you're driving,' said Dez, fidgeting in his seat. 'So what I do, right, when I'm at traffic lights, right, I lift up one side of my arse, like this Joe, and I try and winkle out the little hard bits of shit . . .'

The car swerved across Baker Street, almost ramming a double-decker and two taxis, while Dez pretended to be taking down his trousers.

'Give over, you stupid sod,' I shouted at him, grabbing the wheel. He burst out laughing, having caught me. I really did think he was going to pick bits out of his arse.

'Actually, now I think about it,' he said, roaring across Oxford Street into Mayfair. 'If you have got a hairy arse, it could be dodgy.

Seriously. No one wants to look at a bloke's hairy arse over their Sunday breakfast.'

'I dunno,' I said. 'Nancy boys might. Or Arsenal supporters.'

'Good one, son,' said Dez. 'Hold on, panic's over. Just had a thought. They could do the same as they do with the tarts in those old-fashioned dirty mags.'

'What's that, Dez.'

'You know how their fannies come out looking dead smooth, with no hairs at all? What they do is touch them up with an airbrush. You don't mind being touched up with an airbrush, do you Joe?'

Dez was still laughing as we arrived at the hotel in Park Lane. He left his car, for a flunky to park, and we went in.

For a moment I felt slightly nervous, like that first day at Cockermouth School, how would I cope with all the superior grammar cads, would they be horrible to me, should I leave now? Then it passed.

We entered this glittering room, with chandeliers and thigh-deep carpets, liveried waiters darting round with trays of champagne and a pompous toastmaster with his nose in the air asking for names like a schoolteacher then beaming down like a real arselicker when he heard the name, as if every guest was world-famous, announcing it publicly in a deep poofter voice. He got mine right, and gave me an extra dollop of brown nose, but he beamed just as hard and phonily when Dez gave him his name, as if recognizing him at once as the well known international twat, then he announced it loudly – Reg Dainty! Did I larf. That put me in a good mood right away.

Once we moved around, sorry circulated, I could see that behind all the flash frocks and the stiff shirts they were basically barrowboys and cockney crap turned millionaire nobodies, with a smattering of smalltime somebodies from television and show business. I soon began to feel superior. No grammar cads here, just cockney cunts. How will they cope with me, will I be horrible to them, should I leave now?

It was my first Black Tie Ball. That was what the ticket said, adding 'Carriages for 2 a.m.', so I had expected something a bit posho. Most of the types seemed familiar, from other West End charity and sporting gatherings which Dez had dragged me to in the last year. Each ticket was marked £50, bloody hell. Dez must be lashing out. Showed how well he'd done out of me.

The women had their hair piled high and were dripping with

jewellery. The men were in even fancier dinner suits than Dez's. They looked like old dwarfs, tanned and lined, mummified human beings, dug out of the grave for the night. There were a few younger people, some of whose faces I vaguely recognized.

'Joe, lovely to see you again,' said a creep with an Irish accent I'd never met before, but then I recognized him as the slob presenter on a cruddy TV show.

He was setting up a new show, so he said confidentially at the top of his voice, a breakthrough in panel games, with big, but big names, and he'd just love me to be on it some time, as he knew the younger audience would really go for me.

'It *is* a family show,' he smirked. 'So sorry Joe, no mooning!'

'You'll have to ask Reg, my agent,' I said, nodding towards Dez. 'He handles everything for me.'

'Yes, but I always wash my hands afterwards,' said Dez.

I steered Dez away quickly. I recognized a younger popstar I'd seen on *Top of the Pops* last week, and edged my way towards her, but Dez got in first.

'Hello, darling.' said Dez, getting one arm round her. 'What are you doing later?'

'Flying to LA,' she said, moving away so quickly Dez was left with his arm in the air.

I refused the champagne, which I hate, nasty fizzy sickly stuff, give me a good glass of Burgundy any time, and went to find our table, number six, so the seating plan said. At the top was seated Sid Flatman, owner of a string of strip clubs, which shows you how smart the do was. He had probably been sitting there since the last Charity Dinner, being too fat to get out of his seat. He said hi, nice of me to come, it was his table, he'd bought all eight tickets, but if I had any tickets for the England game, say no more.

At the other end was an old bloke I thought at first was dead, slumped in his seat, eyes glazed, skin like a walnut, mouth dribbling. Beside him was Sonia, obviously waiting for me to sit in the vacant seat beside her. Oh fuck. Wait till I see that sod Dez.

I liked her well enough, she could be quick and funny, which is what I look for most in a woman, oh yes, that comes first. Sexy comes second, and she could be far sexier than some women I've known half her age who just lie there, waiting for you to light them up. Sonia was into quick combustion. She looked pretty stunning, for a woman of, I dunno, she said she was thirty-two, which could be true, more or less. I hadn't seen her for a while and had no real intention of beginning all that again. She wanted arrangements, would I turn up on Wednesday afternoon at four-fifteen when her husband would be away. I never know where I'll be in half an hour, never mind next Wednesday.

Sonia had bought five tickets from Mr Flatman, so she explained, and had given two to Dez, so hoping I would come. I gave her a kiss as I sat down, which is what you do in London, oh, I know it all, but remote, in the region of her shoulderblade. I turned to my right, hoping the person there would be worth talking to, but Sonia had my arm and was turning me back to introduce me to the old bloke, pushing him to wake up, pay attention, dear, this is the famous Joe. He had this heavy foreign accent and I couldn't understand a word he was saying. This was her husband.

I eventually said hello to my right-hand side, a young girl, hardly more than sixteen, by the look of her, with long blonde hair, no make-up and a simple black dress. I asked if she was a model, which was stupid, as models don't like to be taken as models, and she said she was a student, home for the holiday from Switzerland.

'I'm at a finishing school,' she said, in a soft but very posh accent.

'What are you finishing?' I said. 'You look finished to me.'

'Hmm,' she said nervously, 'not really. You see I want to . . .'

'Hi Joe, long time no see,' said a loud man in a cumberbund sitting opposite, pushing across the table to shake my hand. He insisted on introducing me to Tracy, a tarty-looking girl beside him. If you're filling in the table plan that just leaves Dez, next to Tracy, and I wasn't speaking to him, the bastard.

The cumberbund said his name was Hugo something, and I disliked him straight away. He boasted about his very successful marketing company, his big plans for expansion, how he had seen my first England match, and knew I was a winner, just like he was. What a shit.

Before the meal began there were several speeches about the charity the money was going to, and how honoured they were that so many famous sportsmen were present. I had only seen me so far, but there could be others scattered amongst the three hundred people at the various tables.

To my surprise, the chairman then called on Bobby Moore to stand up. He was at a far table, miles across the dining-room, but I recognized him at once as he stood up shyly, nodding modestly. All the guests cheered wildly, banging their tables, then Bobby Moore sat down again, not having said a word. Very strange. Other famous players were asked to stand up, acknowledge their presence, such as Geoff Hurst, Alan Ball, Rodney Marsh and Kevin Keegan, and accept the pointless applause, just for being here. Weird. Imagine being cheered just for being alive. Old Royals, like the Queen Mum, I can understand, but bloody old footballers, bloody roll on. I whispered as much to the girl beside me, but I don't think she heard, with all the table banging.

Then the chairman called for silence. After the all-time greats, he would now like to introduce one of our younger stars, hmm, could be me, who is still only twenty-one, yes sounds familiar, who is already established in the England team, well that's not me, so I leaned over to make some sarcastic comment to Dez, forgetting I wasn't talking to him.

'So ladies and gentlemen, a big hand for Joe Swift – but don't throw any Cadbury's Flakes!'

For a moment, I saw myself standing up, dropping my trousers, and flashing my bum. It was a near thing. Then I heard myself saying don't clap, ladies and gentlemen, just rattle your dentures, an improvement on that John Lennon remark. Both thoughts went through my head, but I did neither of course. I stood up, looked suitably shy and modest, accepted the applause nicely, as my mother would have wished, thought what a load of shits you are, then sat down again. I did, however, put my tongue out, at least my tongue crept out of its own accord, didn't like what it saw, and slid back in again.

Sonia burst out laughing, leaned over and gave me a huge hug. Dez cheered, too wildly. Hugo banged the table with his fat hands. Flatman eased his bum, relocating a few tons of hardened hairy shit while he thought no one was watching. Tracy put on fresh lipstick. The girl beside me played with a spoon, looking demurely bored.

'Goodness, I don't think I introduced you properly to Zoe, my daughter,' said Sonia.

'We've met,' said Zoe.

I had never guessed for one moment. Sonia was dark-haired and vivacious, her hair pulled back in the Spanish style, with a red ribbon at the back, while Zoe was so fair and still.

I wanted to know more about her, but Hugo dominated most of the meal, egged on by Dez, who kept on asking him stupid questions about one of his new projects.

'It's tapes for kids,' said Hugo, 'telling them how to score goals, plus booklets and diagrams.'

'Sounds fantastic,' said Dez.

'Sounds boring to me,' I said. 'Who wants to sit and listen to records.'

'It's not records, Joe,' said Hugo. 'Records are passé, I'm talking about tapes.'

'What's the difference,' I said. 'You can't learn anything by sitting listening to tapes on your tape recorder.'

'I don't seem to have made myself clear,' said Hugo. 'These are videotapes. The technology has been developed, and very soon they'll go mass market, as these things always do. I plan to be in on it. It's all very exciting.'

'Yeh, sounds really great,' said Dez.

'What we need though are players who are good talkers, who can explain things well, who understand the game . . .'

'Go no further,' said Dez. 'That's my boy. Joe's a fucking natural.'

'That's what I think,' said Hugo.

'Players don't know how they score goals,' I said. 'It can't be explained in words. Look at the shit reporters come out with, trying to describe it in newspapers.'

'Bloody true,' said Dez.

'And even if you could describe it in words,' I continued, 'then so what? It won't make people score goals.'

'You're forgetting the pictures, Joe,' explained Hugo. 'We would string together your greatest goals, and you could talk us through them, or study great goals and moves from the past. People love watching goals, but they also like to think they are being instructed, learning secrets . . .'

'Just sounds like a money-making con to me,' I said.

'You've got it!' said Hugo banging on the table. Dez was slapping his back.

'Seriously,' continued Hugo, calming down. 'Football has not wakened up yet to the enormous commercial possibilities which now exist. There are millions of people out there, all round the world, who are fascinated by famous footballers. They will buy and watch anything about them – if it's attractively packaged and presented, which is where I come in.'

'And you and me Joe,' said Dez. 'We've gotta be in on this.'

'Jolly good,' said Hugo. 'This is my card. Give me a buzz next week. We're about to start work on a demo tape.'

I couldn't wait for the meal to be over. I hadn't really understood what Hugo was on about and had no intention of seeing him again. Buying a sweetshop I could understand, and I'd just done that, well, allowed my name to be used, but the word video had not reached me yet.

There was a bit of milling about afterwards, people changing tables, going round, drinking brandies. I tried to chat to Zoe but she was up the minute the meal was over, saying she had to go home with her father, see he was all right. Sonia seemed to have disappeared. Dez had his arm round Tracy, giving her his home number, and his office number. I had a couple of brandies forced upon me, then finished off the second bottle of Beaujolais which Sonia had ordered for our table. I'd drunk most of it, as Sonia and Zoe drank only mineral water. I hate non-drinkers when I'm drinking.

Dez then went off to phone. It sounded like a taxi firm, asking about some car, and I thought he was chickening out of driving me home, which would have been sensible, as he'd been on the champagne all night, but then he reappeared.

'Let's go,' I said to Dez, making for the exit.

In the car on the way home, Dez wanted to talk about Hugo, saying I shouldn't be so nasty to him, he could put a lot of new business our way.

'I hate him,' I said. 'He's a shite hawk.'

I wanted to ask about Zoe, how old she was, how come Sonia and her braindead husband came to have such a stunning daughter.

'She's a bait,' said Dez.

I thought he meant sandwiches, as taken by Northern workmen to work, not that Dez would know that expression, being a cockney bastard.

'Sonia brought her along,' said Dez, 'knowing you'd fancy her.'

He might not be up on general knowledge, but this time Dez had been ahead of me on general understanding.

He then announced that he'd got us fixed up, but I was hardly listening. I'd drunk too much, and eaten too much, and was starting to fall asleep.

'Wake up, you cunt,' said Dez. 'Two lovely ladies will be arriving soon at your place . . .'

'My place?' I said.

'Well they can't come to my place, can they, be sensible. They'd wake the wife and kids, do me a favour.'

'Count me out,' I said. 'I'm knackered.'

Outside my place was a Jaguar, half on the pavement, the lights full on. Inside my apartment, lying down on my new sofa, already half undressed, was Tracy.

'Oh fucking hell,' I said, turning to Dez, who was all smirks. 'Just don't wake me up, you cunt.'

I threw off my jacket and my shoes, and staggered into my bedroom. On the bed was Sonia.

'Oh no,' I said.

'You must be exhausted,' said Sonia. 'Don't worry. I've just come to give you a goodnight kiss.'

'I'd rather have cocoa,' I said.

She started to undress me, pulling off my socks first, then my underpants. I could feel her kissing my legs, feeling my thighs, sliding her hands up and down, oohing and ahhing, making silly noises. Not that it was doing much for me, I was half asleep. Then she started asking idiot questions about bruises and scars, kissing them better, before eventually moving up to the main attraction, caressing it, talking to it, not that it was showing much interest.

'Hello old friend, old sport, how you feeling, hmm, a bit better for seeing me I hope, I've missed you, where have you been, no don't tell me, I don't think I'd like to know . . .'

I smiled and at last began to feel something stirring, deep in the basement, then a buzzing in my head, then a louder buzzing from next door, in the living room. It was the front-door intercom. Oh fuck. Must be one of the snotty neighbours, complaining about the Jag on the pavement.

'Shush,' said Sonia, putting her finger to my lips. 'Let Dez handle it. I'll handle this.'

I could hear a car outside, then lots of banging and shouting, Dez going downstairs, a car being driven away, then Dez coming back into the flat with someone.

'Where's our Joe then?' said a Geordie voice.

'He's gone to bed early, getting ready for tomorrow,' said Dez. 'This is my wife Cindy, Mr Swift. We're just going. But I'll show you to your bedroom first. You must be exhausted, after that long journey. Joe doesn't know I arranged that car for you. Just a little surprise. Wait till he sees your face in the morning . . .'

I groaned, rolled over, and went to sleep.

Dear Joe,
It is a diabolical liberty to call me a strip-club owner, you
know that Joe, believe me, and you have really used me,
after all we done for you, I don't have to spell it out, and I
resent that stuff about hairy shit, what is this, *Viz* or *Comic
Cuts* or what, and about being fat, that is so untrue, I have
just been to Champneys health farm for the weekend and lost
£300, in one weekend, worth every penny, but no, this is
serious, Joe, I won't have this shit about stripping, I am a
company director and if you repeat that shit, the boys will
be round, believe me.

Yours,
SIDNEY (FLATMAN)

16

I blame my Dad. He should never have come. He should have stuck to his belief that he would only bring me bad luck. I blame Dez, the stupid bastard. Oh yeh, great idea, arranging transport for my Dad behind my back, but he might have warned me he was coming. And I also blame that Romanian thug Constanescu, the one built like an outside shithouse. I think that covers everyone. Except the real culprit, the real idiot, the one who really suffered.

I can't bear to talk about it even now, so let's get it over with. 1987, and my fourth England game, yeh, not on the trot, as I said, because there were six in that period, and I was omitted from two. My three games so far had been games with no pattern, no point, and each time I felt like an uninvited guest, put in by the press and the public against the manager's better judgment, least that's how it seemed to me.

At Spurs, once it was agreed the midfield revolved round me, that the object was to get the ball to Swifty, let him be the clever bugger, let him take responsibility, then I always felt on top of my game. I didn't always play well, come on, I am human, though mostly I did, but I was always totally confident, knew what I was doing, why I was there, and so did everyone around me. In the England games, I was given a new role almost every time, usually peripheral, meant to stay back, or play wide, or give cover, never to dominate, because that role either did not exist, because of the team tactics, or was to be assumed by someone else. I like being a leader, not one of the led. I can take it when things go wrong, as they always do. I don't hide. I don't fade from the game. I try harder. That was the problem.

In the seventh minute I got the ball in midfield, won it from their centre-forward when he should have passed, as we were all falling back, caught on the hop, and he had men on either wing. I held the ball, swivelling round, waiting for support. It was too far to dash for goal, and too early in the game for anything flash, and anyway I had instructions to feed other people, get movements going down the wing. I'm usually pretty good at holding off tackles, thanks to my big arse, awkward elbows, powerful ego, and I enjoy working sideways, taking my time, even when I know it annoys the crowd, who don't realise that other players are supposed to be taking up positions.

While I farted around, the centre-forward I'd taken the ball from crept up on me and hooked the ball away. I thought he was miles away upfield, so I screamed at the ref, claiming a tackle from behind, then I dashed like hell after the player and did a sliding tackle at about a hundred miles an hour. I was supposed to have stopped doing that, two seasons previously, after the coaches had drummed it into me that it's no use winning the ball that way, as you end up on the ground. There was no real danger anyway, as it was only just in our half, and our defence was ready for him, so I shouldn't have attempted such a wild and desperate tackle. We both went down in a heap. Their players came storming at me as if I'd tried to kill him, but he was up in seconds, while I just lay there, unable to move. The stretcher came on, I was carried off, they got a free kick for my foul, and they scored, oh fuck, that's enough of this, I can't stand it any more.

Where was I? Where am I? It's bad enough being stuck here, in this dump, without having to think back to other occasions when I felt stuck, and dumped, and sick, and gutted.

I remember being dragged slowly round the edge of the Wembley pitch with photographers hovering above me like vultures, mixed up with this helicopter which was in the sky right above me, then an ambulance man put a blanket over my head so I could see nothing, except the same scene, only cloudier. I heard a sudden roar, and I thought for a moment we'd scored, direct from the free kick I'd won, what a hero, then it turned to boos and jeers and I passed out with the pain.

For weeks I denied it was my fault. I maintained the bloke had jumped on my leg deliberately, after I'd tackled him, okay, I should not have tried a sliding tackle in the first place, but he had done it, no question, the cunt, listen, I felt him kick me. I even thumped a reporter who got into the private hospital and asked if I regretted my own recklessness.

It was caused by disappointment – with myself. That was all it was. I was so furious at having lost the ball, through my own stupidity, and I was so desperate to get it back, that I just lashed out. The sort of thing I did as a kid, and thought I'd outgrown.

I was in hospital four weeks in all, and had three operations, as the first two didn't work. They denied that of course. They said the knee joint was worse than they had expected, and in the end had to be taken apart, then remade. It was the knee, my right one, where I'd had a cartilage out at nineteen, when I was in the Reserves. I'd always been pleased how quickly it healed, back to full fitness in three weeks, and I'd convinced myself I was a quick healer. There are such players, just as there are those with low pain thresholds, who can carry on with broken bones, while others are off at the first knock. Up till then I'd had my share of injuries, but never missed more than two games at a time, even with my cartilage, which was at the end of the season, so that helped.

I didn't fucking do it deliberately. Okay, I know I said I won't go over it again, I know it's all history, but as I lay there, those four weeks, I had to read all this shit about how I'd deliberately caused it, because I'd been stupid and bad-tempered. Columnists not on the sports pages got in on the act by saying it was typical of our times, another self-inflicted wound for the country. What shit. But what hurt me most was the suggestion that I did not deserve sympathy – because it was all my own fucking fault.

Of course it wasn't *all* my own fault. Do you think I would have charged in, knowing what was going to happen? Piss off. Was I planning to have my knee shattered? Get stuffed. I tried to argue this, when a slightly more intelligent reporter from the Sunday papers came to see me, but I could never make myself clear. I said the cause of the injury was very simple – bad luck. That's all. Whether the tackle was silly or sensible, nasty or nice, is making a value judgment after the event, and is irrelevant. You charge in a hundred times, legitimately or otherwise, and come out ninety-nine times with nobody injured. That time, my luck turned. Next question.

Joe Public loved being self-righteous, blaming me, tut-tutting, even enjoying my disaster, and I suppose in a way I had given them ammunition. I'd been a big mouth, always shooting off, anything for a laugh or to annoy, which to me was not being a big mouth, just being myself. Then of course the nightclubs, bashing up cars, getting fined, getting banned, showing my bum in the papers, oh all those stupid incidents, which have nothing at all to do with how I play on the park.

There were people who saw it as a judgment. I deserved a broken knee, for screwing around, being too clever by half, being too successful, getting too much money, being too young, being on the planet, living and breathing. There is this trait in the British character that enjoys people being down, after they have been up.

It was about two months before I was up and hobbling on crutches, coming into the club for treatment and simple exercises. By this time, most papers had forgotten about me, which was a relief. So had the club.

That's the hardest thing of all to bear. Any injured player will tell you this. 'Fault' doesn't come into it, as it's soon forgotten if you chopped someone down, or if they chopped you down. It's the fact of having an injury that matters. It means that you don't matter. You go out of their mind, out of their reckoning. It's as if you've never played for the first team, never been part of their success. They see you in the corridor, look at you, then move on, as if trying to remember who you are, as if you might contaminate them with your injury.

You are still allowed to be there in the flesh, hanging around when they're getting ready, sitting on the bench, or limping into the dressing room after a match, but you're not there in spirit. There are jokes and rows you've missed, tensions you are unaware of. It was then that I first realised that playing for a team, any team, but especially one at the top, is like being in a secret society. Outsiders can't know the references, what has gone before, what is now going on.

So I tried to keep away on match days, hanging around as little as possible, refusing to be sympathised with, refusing to appear pathetic, going in and out for treatment only. It meant that as the weeks went on, there were people appearing in the team I hardly knew. Young players coming through. New players being bought.

There was a story that I would never play again. I wanted Arnold to sue when that appeared. I don't know why. It didn't damage my value, as you have no value when you are seriously injured, but it damaged my spirit. And my income. My name was not worth as much to shops who wanted me to open their new premises, or manufacturers who wanted me to endorse their products, but I did get more radio and TV work. I had time for that, which I hadn't in the past, going on the radio and giving little half-time commentaries or pithy post-match comments. I enjoyed it. I would not have gone to matches otherwise. Perhaps I half believed my career might end, so I had to try other things.

Dez began to fade, after he had sold a few ghosted columns on my injury, the same one several times, almost word for word. I negotiated my tv and radio stuff myself, doing it for nothing really, just for the experience, as I had time on my hands.

Sonia didn't fade. She was the only one from the beginning who understood that I was not to blame. She knew it was sheer bad luck. She chauffeured me, took me to physio, back and forward to specialists, brought me meals, changed the tv channels, drove me everywhere I wanted to go. She played cards and Scrabble with me, when I was feeling mentally alert, and massaged the old cock when I hadn't the strength or agility for a wank.

We tried to have it off once, when I was still in hospital, the Wellington, standing up in my private lav, me in my pyjamas, still on crutches, what a larf that was. Afterwards, I leaned back against the wall, and set off three emergency bells. Before she'd got her knickers back on, they were rushing in with life-support machines and blood drips.

She did a fair job, old Sonia. There's nothing more lonely than being injured. Another reason for having a wife. They're handy to kick around, moan at, complain to, blame for everything. Yup, wives do have their uses. I could do with one now.

Once the plaster was off and I'd given up the crutches, I was soon able to drive myself. So I gave Sonia the chuck. Cruel? Typical rotten sod behaviour? Probably. But I don't care what you think.

Like all relationships, the inside is never as it seems from the outside. Yes, she'd been a great help. Okay, so she acted like an unpaid nurse. Of course, I would have been lost without her. She even got herself interviewed as the Florence Nightingale of White Hart Lane, North London's Mother Teresa, Sister of Mercy mothering poor old Joe. With her posh voice, respectable husband, wealthy background, it did look as if she was doing charity work, helping a poor young person. Nobody could have believed what she was really after. I don't think I've met a randier woman in my life. Though, sitting here now, one does hope there are more sitting outside.

Sex wasn't the problem. Either way. During all those weeks, moping and miserable, she'd begun to drive me mad. She didn't expect me to give her anything in return, except the occasional fuck. She genuinely liked to give, not to receive. But she did like thanks. She liked me to be grateful, acknowledge what she'd done, say thank you thank you thank you for every present or thoughtful idea. I hate all that slop. I grew to detest being dependent on her. She was too kind, piling it on, making me feel guilty. So one morning, before she had arrived to see how I was, making her morning call, doubtless bringing something thoughtful for me, I left a note saying I was going away for a while, but thanks for everything, see you.

'Dad, I'm home,' I said.

The back door was open. I'd just walked in, sat myself on the sofa and turned on the telly, out of habit, not because I wanted to watch anything. Then I got up again, went to the car, brought in my bag and a bottle of champagne for my Dad, given to me by Sonia, plus some chocolates and fruit for Colin, also from Sonia. Who says I'm not thoughtful?

'Dad, it's me.'

I presumed he must be at home, as it was Saturday, and the door was open. I should have rung or written, but it was a spur-of-the-moment decision. Anyway, I don't ring people, or write. I got up and looked round the room. There were the same miniature bottles of cognac and whisky in the cocktail cabinet, collected by my Mum, and three brass monkeys, which had belonged to my Gran, which no one had polished since my Mum died. Above the mantelpiece was the same view of Durham Cathedral, seen from the river, a real watercolour, not a print, which my mother had been so proud of. My Dad had given it to her when they were courting.

On the mantelpiece were some of the cups I'd won at school, but they'd been shoved in a corner, making way for a new photo of Fanny, in her graduation gown and funny hat, and a photo I hadn't seen before of Colin in a stupid costume, wearing a joke beard. Lined up, on a shelf, standing back to back as if about to be inspected, were photos of us as babies and children, all very familiar, plus their wedding photo. I could see no modern photo of me.

There was an envelope behind the clock, addressed to Dad, already opened, so I sat down to read it. A five-pound note fell out as I unfolded the letter. It was from Fanny, four neat pages in her immaculate handwriting. All the girls in her year at Cockermouth Grammar wrote like that. They failed on the boys. One of the reasons I never write by hand is that I can't form the words without my wrist stiffening up.

It was all about this new school she was teaching at in Sunderland, how hard it was, how undisciplined the kids, but the staff were nice and she was settling into her room and hoped to find a flat soon. There was no mention of the fiver, or why she was sending it.

'Oh it's you,' said Fanny, coming down the stairs and into the living room. 'I thought it was Colin coming back.'

'Where's Dad?'

'Working of course. Making the most of it, while it lasts.'

'How do you mean?' I said, folding the letter back in the envelope.

'Haven't you heard?' said Fanny. 'They're closing the school.'

'So what will happen?'

'Nobody knows,' said Fanny. 'He could be on the dole, unless they offer him something elsewhere. And homeless. There's a petition to save it, which is rich. They all complained when the school opened, as they didn't want borstal boys on their doorstep. Now they don't want it closed.'

'He never told me,' I said.

'Perhaps you never asked.'

She gave me a cold smile, which I ignored. Fanny was always good at getting in sly digs.

'So how's the injury, superstar? Have you written that book yet?'

'Don't ask me,' I said, groaning.

'So how else will we find out? You've told us not to believe anything in the papers.'

She didn't add that if I wrote or rang home, they would know the truth, or know something. But I got the message.

'I should be back in full training in a month.'

'That's good. What is it now, six months since, er, the accident happened?'

I was watching for any trace of a smirk, any suggestion that it was my fault, but she was bending down, picking up the fiver which I had let fall on the carpet.

'What's that for?' I asked.

'For? For him. I've sent him something ever since I started work. Two quid at first, then a fiver now I've got this scale job. I just slip it in my weekly letter. Amazing really, in two years, it's never gone missing, not once.'

'Bloody well done,' I said. 'Good for you. Three cheers. Where's Colin then? At work? Doing some overtime?'

My Dad had written, about four weeks previously, boasting about Colin's great success in being taken on as apprentice electrician. How hard it had been, how fierce the competition. Colin hadn't wanted it to be known he was Joe Swift's brother. He had got the job on his own.

'He's rehearsing for his play. It's the first night tonight. You must come and see it. I've come through specially for it.'

'Play?'

'Yeh, it's only a little part, but he's really quite good.'

'How's the electricianing?'

'He hates it,' said Fanny. 'But who wouldn't. As an apprentice, you get all the dirty jobs to do. Didn't you, as an apprentice?'

'No, it's not the same thing.'

'It's good that at last he's found something he really enjoys. Such a shame amateur acting doesn't lead anywhere.'

'Oh you never know,' I said, picking up a paper.

'You were the lucky one,' continued Fanny. 'You always knew you wanted to be be footballer . . .'

'Did I?' I started, sarcastically. I was about to say I was beginning to regret it, now I was injured, hanging around, getting depressed, miserable, fed up, hoping perhaps for a bit of sympathy.

'And I was lucky as well,' said Fanny. 'I always wanted to go to university, but poor old Colin had no ambitions, and wasn't good at anything at all, quite frankly. Remember those awful school reports he got . . .'

'Not really,' I said, getting up.

'But everyone always liked him, that's the nice thing. He's always had such a nice personality.'

Oh Gawd, give me strength. Now I remember why I hardly ever came home. All they ever talked about was bloody Colin and his bloody problems. I thought at first this was to keep me in my place, show that I might be famous outside, but we were all equal inside the family. I was now coming to the conclusion that basically they had turned against me. They didn't like me any more, if they ever did. Bugger them.

'God, I feel stiff,' I said, getting up and walking round the room. 'It's the longest drive I've done since my injury. I hope I haven't overdone it. Ohh.'

'Good of you to come anyway,' said Fanny. 'Dad will be pleased. He's feeling pretty depressed at the moment.'

'I'm sure,' I said, abstractedly. 'Any tea?'

'You know where the kettle is. Nothing has changed. Especially you.'

'What does that mean?'

'You're just as selfish as ever.'

'Oh fuck, don't start that. That's all I need.'

'Worse if anything, since you've had people rushing around doing things for you all the time. Who is this woman Sonia?'

'She's nobody.'

'Yes, they're all nobodies to you, Joe. You just take take take, then discard.'

'You don't know anything.'

'I know you haven't written to Dad in a year, and rung him only once.'

'I brought him down to that England match, didn't I. That was only six months ago, bloody hell, cost a bloody fortune, that taxi.'

'I've heard about that evening, and what really happened. He felt like a package which nobody had ordered and nobody wanted . . .'

'I can't help how he feels.'

'Precisely. You don't care for anyone's feelings, just your own.'

'I didn't mean that.'

'You don't do anything for anyone.'

'What about that car? Oh yeh, soon forget about that, don't you.'

Two years ago, I bought Dad a new Rover. I'd just got the first contract with the garage, and they did me a special deal. It was in the *Cumberland News*, me handing it over to him, which I thought he would like, but he hated it, saying it was embarrassing, why hadn't I kept it a secret. You can never win.

'He won't be able to afford to run it soon, if he's out of work,' said Fanny.

'I'm out of work,' I said.

'Don't be stupid.'

'I am. you don't get any win bonuses, when you're not playing. Nobody wants you to open any pizza parlours, not when you're injured.'

'My heart weeps.'

I was in fact feeling a bit hard-up. The lease of the stupid flat had cost a fortune, then I had to do it up to a certain standard, which was in the contract, and at the same time my income had gone down in the last six months. Not that I knew how much I was earning. Haven't done, since I was seventeen, but I did know I had no capital, nothing stashed away for a rainy day.

'You haven't asked me what it's been like, being injured,' I said.

'I don't have to,' said Fanny. 'I know you'll tell us. All you're interested in is yourself.'

'Piss off,' I said, going to the back door. 'I'm off to see Tom.'

'Oh yes, Tom, your best friend,' said Fanny. 'Pity you never write to him either, then you might know he's in America, doing a Ph.D . . .'

HOTEL
INTER·CONTINENTAL
BUCHAREST

Dear Joe Swift,

With reference to your aforementioned reference to me, please to say that I am not a thug. I have a degree in botany from University of Bucharest and a Masters from U.C. Davis in wine culture and soccer theory. I majored in the principle and practice of falling backwards on the opponent's leg when tackled from behind, *viz* a sliding tackle, thereby rendering him impotent and/or how you say, knackered.

As the home of hooligans, it seems to me that English peoples can not call the kettle black.

Yours,
CUCY CONSTANESCU

17

It was 1988 and five o'clock, almost getting dark, and we were still training, the second training session of the day, but then that's the system in Germany. We were deep in the countryside, surrounded by fields, but I could see the lights of Hamburg, some ten miles away. It was supposed to be a secret training ground, not listed in any phonebooks, but on the day I arrived over five thousand turned out to welcome me.

That day, only about a hundred were watching, mostly kids straight from school in their funny school shorts and a few old men with nothing better to do. We were practising a new free kick and Serge, the trainer, was doing his nut, screaming and shouting, blowing his whistle. Then he screamed at his interpreter, as if he was causing the trouble.

I stood on the halfway line, watching, trying to look interested, my mind wandering. I was not involved, or he would probably be blaming me. If I was involved, if it was me taking the free kick, which I should have been, which would have been the sensible thing, I'd soon sort them out, even in my pidgin German, no problem.

Ah well, he's bound to pack up soon, I thought. Even Yugoslavs have got to rest, or else he'll have a heart attack. That would be interesting. I've never seen anyone actually do that on a training pitch before. Knackered, yes. Dead, not quite.

He'd been here three years, this Serge, whereas I'd been here only three months, but I now spoke more German than he did. I mean literally. I spoke it more, meaning more often, even though I still knew fuck all. Serge could speak German and English, so we were told, only he never did. Once training was over, he retreated to his own little world, speaking to no one, sharing a flat with his interpreter, also a Yugo, also an uptight, grim-faced silent bastard.

Thanks to Karin's help, I was now prepared to chunter on, have a go, making it up, adding bits of English, making faces, slapping them on the back, wink, wink, say no more, eh Fritzy baby. Having been silent and tongue-tied for almost two months, I realised that people like you to at least attempt their language. At school, I'd put myself down as bad at languages, as a dummy, cos I failed that O-level French mock. So much for formal education. Learning anything is a matter of time, place and motivation. And that doesn't always happen when you're at school.

If only I hadn't arrived in such a hurry, I might have taken some lessons beforehand. I didn't know any grammar, couldn't write a word, but I could talk in football. That's an international language. Even the Germans use the same words.

'*Machtig Maus, Machtig Maus.*'

I could hear the kids mouthing my name behind me as we trooped down the lane to the dressing rooms. I didn't like this nickname at first. I've never considered myself small, or mousy. Stocky, perhaps, definitely chunky, and very hunky. I would have preferred to have been known as the Kaiser, as a born leader, but some other Kraut has that name, and will have it for always. I liked the Mighty bit, though, that's very me.

The dressing room was hellish at first, not understanding what was going on, not knowing the personalities, and so bloody quiet. I was used to noisy dressing rooms, with me being the noisiest, leading all the chat, orchestrating the stupid tricks. I couldn't understand it. Was it Germany? Was it just Eintracht Hamburg? Was it me?

I felt so frustrated those first two months, sitting silently, having things to say in my head, observations to make, but not being able to get my tongue round any words. I'd look at the faces, the expressions, the smiles, the shouts, the moans and know without knowing it that *he*'d be the leading moaner, *he*'d be the joker, him over there, he was obviously the one who got picked upon. All dressing rooms have the same personalities. Just like life, tra la. There's always someone who's slow and stupid, the one thought to be brainy, or flash, or a hick, or mean, or Jack the Lad. Now what's the German for Jack the Lad? God, I've forgotten. Joe Swift, probably.

What happened was that I was approached out of the blue by this German agent and went secretly to Glasgow, don't ask me why, to meet Horst, the manager of Eintracht Hamburg. He was dead smooth, very charming, good English, knew all about me, with a massive dossier, and especially my medical dossier. Don't know how he got that. But it proved I had recovered perfectly from my knee trouble. In just one month back in the Spurs team, I was playing out of my skin, having my best games ever, stronger, more determined than before, as if to make up for lost time, as if determined to prove everyone wrong, to show that I now could control my temper.

I'd never thought of going abroad, but at once it seemed obvious. Spurs didn't seem the same. There were constant changes, new manager, new directors, new directions, and I didn't like the way things were going. Being out had showed me that it wasn't so marvellous after all, being in.

I got a hundred grand in my hand, capital at last, half of which went straight on a luxury bungalow for my Dad, so bugger you, Fanny. I bought Sonia a pearl necklace, not cheap, and said thanks for everything, but I'm orf.

Horst promised me £500,000 over three years, if I stayed that long. Half would be my salary and the other half from business deals, which he was already fixing up for me. That was about four times what I was earning in England – plus cash up front.

It took me about three minutes to decide, though I let Arnold argue the toss for about three days before I signed the forms.

Then I thought, what have I done? Have I been too hasty? It all happened so suddenly that I had made no preparations. Horst said I shouldn't worry about that. It would make it more exciting, more fun. What about the language, I said. Don't worry, he said. He spoke English. The Trainer also spoke English. There was a Swede and a Dutchman in the team, each with good English, and most of the Germans spoke some English. *Nicht* problem. As a single man, with no ties, I could move quickly, easily. So I did.

'Joe Swift?' said an English voice as I was coming out of the gates of the training ground. 'I'm the journalist who's been pestering you, sorry about that, but you said you might spare me some time after training, if that's okay . . .'

'Non sprecken zee Eenglish,' I grunted, looking round, trying to see if the white Porsches had arrived yet. I didn't remember making any arrangements with any reporter, but then I never do.

'Would this be a suitable time?'

'No,' I said, 'so you'd better piss off.'

I was in a bad temper after the training, and various other things.

'On the phone yesterday, from London, I rang you. You kindly agreed to an interview, after training.'

'Did I? Doesn't fucking sound like me.'

I walked towards the car park, with him following me, plus a few dozen German kids and families.

'Do you always get all these people following you?'

'This is bugger all. First day I turned up, there were five thousand of them. Then it went down to fuck all, when they decided I was shit . . .'

He started to write something in a little notebook and I grabbed his pen.

'That was a joke, you cunt. I've had enough problems with my jokes.'

'Such as?'

'I told jokes about my salary, when I first arrived, what a bloody mistake that was.'

'How do you mean?'

'The German press picked it up, and never let me forget it.'

'What sort of joke?'

'Oh Christ, don't fucking go on about it, you arsehole . . .'

'I've got a taxi waiting,' said the reporter. 'Can I give you a lift into town?'

'No, so just piss off.'

'Joe, Joe, calm down,' said a female voice behind me. 'No need to be so rude, my sweetest.'

It was Karin, getting out off her white Porsche. I hadn't seen her arrive and park almost behind where we were standing. She gave me a huge kiss, practically sweeping me off my feet. That's when I looked like a mighty mouse, beside Karin. She was six foot tall, all legs, but then all international models are like that. She was wearing huge padded shoulders, which I'd never seen before, and her blonde hair was cut short on top, like a crewcut, and shaved up the back. She looked amazing, like an Amazon. An Amazing Amazon.

'And such language, Joe,' smiled Karin. 'I've never heard you swear so much.'

'I'm enjoying it,' I said. 'I've just fucking realised I haven't fucking sworn for three months.'

'Is that because you have to speak German?' asked the reporter.

'That's it,' I said. 'In an English dressing room, every second word is fuck, but there's no point in swearing in English here, is there? I've come to Germany, to speak better English.'

'That's fascinating,' said the reporter, getting out his little book again. I groaned.

'Put that away, for Christ's sake.'

'Joe, don't be so rude,' said Karin.

'I am sorry to bother you,' said the reporter, apologetically, 'but could you possibly give me some time?'

'What for?'

'The *Sunday Times Magazine*. My name is Edward Hunter. It's a sort of colour piece, not a football article, so I promise I won't get involved in any football politics or rows . . .'

'What rows? There aren't any.'

'Sorry, I mean it's the culture shock which interests me, you coming here, picking up the language, integrating into the dressing room, and into German life. I think it's absolutely fascinating.'

'Oh yeh, who says so?'

I'd refused all interviews so far with the English press, since I got stitched up. In that first week, some fucker from the *Sun* rang me up and said was it true I was getting half a million for three years. 'And the rest,' I said, without even thinking.

It didn't get much attention in the English press, but then the Germans picked it up, and I had to deny, say it was a joke. God, the scenes it caused, outside and inside the dressing room.

'Okay, then later,' I said. 'Come to my flat about nine.'

'Can I bring a photographer?'

'No,' I said.

'What's the address?'

'Dunno.'

'Or phone number?'

'No idea,' I said, getting into the Porsche beside Karin.

She leaned out and scribbled my address on his notebook, then we roared out of the car park, heading towards Hamburg.

We went first to a tv station where I was to give my first-ever interview in German. So far I'd spoken in English and they had translated it, but I'd just won the German Goal of the Month competition, which is judged by the viewers, not by so-called bloody experts, as they do in England, so I'd decided I'd talk it through. I'd prepared the words in my head, with Karin's help. It was a brilliant goal, but in the game we had been rubbish and got stuffed 4-1. Karin said stick to describing the goal. Don't get into any arguments or explanations or show off in any way. You need to keep a low profile from now on. You've done enough damage. To yourself.

It was lucky meeting Karin. And not just for the obvious reasons. I'd had this old bloke at first, a retired teacher, who was supposed to give me German lessons three times a week, but I never turned up. He was such an idiot, wanting me to learn grammar, write things down, sit at a desk and concentrate. Once I met Karin, it was learning on the job. Such as in bed.

She looked sensational. I always like that in a teacher. Thirdly, she was as famous as me. She was a Countess in her own right, brought up with an English nanny, school in Switzerland, college in the States. She was well known in German society before she became a model, but now everyone knew her, for her face, her legs, her hair, and most of all for her style. You don't get a lot of that in Germany.

She was also rich, which helped, and she'd earned it. Sonia had been rich, but only through her husband. Karin was an equal, that was the best thing of all. It was the first time I'd ever gone out with anyone with her own career, her own life, her own mind.

Right, the obvious thing. What was she like to fuck. Hmm. I did find her exciting and stimulating, and I liked the way she was so cool, but don't repeat this, she wasn't really all that sexy. I never really knew where her mind was, apart from looking in the mirror, no that's not true. She wasn't vain. It was all a game, being a model, dressing up, looking sexy. Deep down she thought she was ugly. Deeper down, she didn't give a bugger how she looked, what she did, what she took. That's what I found really exciting.

Karin waited in hospitality while I did the TV interview, and so she didn't see the interviewer give me her home number. She was small and blonde with enormous tits, not my sort at all, I like a bit of elegance or exoticism, but naturally I put her number away, for another day, another delight.

Then we went to a sales conference in a large hotel, given by Adidas, one of the club's sponsors. It was a club commitment, so I had to turn up, but I managed to avoid being photographed with any of their stuff. Arnold had got me £50,000 from a rival company, Socca, just for letting them use my name on their new boots, Socca Swift. You must have seen them.

After that we walked a few streets to the Hamburg Business Centre, which was a mistake, walking I mean. I got recognized by some supporters of Hamburg SV, the other Hamburg club. (Okay, there's St Pauli as well, but no one follows them.) So I had to put up with a few jeers. Harmless really. About the worst they said was Shit on Eintracht Hamburg. They are somehow old-fashioned, all German supporters, still wearing scarves and badges.

I noticed one badge, worn by two of our supporters, directed at Werder Bremen, one of our traditional rivals. Karin made me stand still till I'd translated it. '*Was ist grün und stinkt nach fisch.*' Easy, huh? Come on. You can guess it, which is what I did. What is green and stinks of fish. Also harmless. The real abuse was kept for Bayern Munich, at the far end of Germany, which everyone in Hamburg hates, for being so rich and successful.

At the Hamburg Business Centre it was the launch of a new range of toiletry for men. I was going to promote their aftershave in tv advertising, so I had to stand around like a wanker, posing for the trade press. They tried to photograph me with Karin, but she was too smart for that. She was avoiding any shots because under her contact with German *Vogue* she couldn't be seen in any rival mags. She buggered off to a private room till I was finished, making long-distance calls at their expense to America. The richer you are, the more fun it is ripping richer people off.

Herr Dr Wolfgang grabbed me afterwards, my so-called German agent, arranged by Horst, and insisted me and Karin joined him for dinner at a little place he'd booked, very new, very quiet, he said, which was a lie. It turned out to be the opening of the latest trendy place and was chokka with creeps wanting autographs, including the waiters, having obviously been told I was coming. I suspect Wolfgang had shares in it, or was getting a backhander. Terrible how you come to think everyone is on some fiddle. Once you are on the fiddle yourself.

I insisted we ate in a corner, on our own, or I was leaving. Over the meal, Wolfgang told me that a sausage manufacturer wanted to name a sausage after me, which amused Karin, typecasting, she said, I had just the body for it. So I grabbed her arm and we did some armwrestling, till we'd knocked everything off the table. I let her win. The young waitress, who had a tattoo on her arm, the first I'd seen on a woman, took photographs, till I told her to get lost.

Forget the sausages, I told Wolfgang, I'll only promote Cumberland sausages, the best in the world. Vat is that, he asked. Can I have their marketing manager, please. I agreed to donate a single hair of my head for a charity auction and agreed to give a quote, in my pidgin German, to advertise a new beer for £50,000.

At ten-thirty I remembered the English reporter, waiting at my place since nine. Karin was by now enjoying herself, posing for the waitress, but I said let's go. I told Wolfgang I'd sign his various forms another day, or not, as the case may be. I was beginning to think that he was just a German Dez, but with a doctorate. Every conman in Germany is a Herr Doctor.

Edward Hunter was waiting in the front reception area of my luxury apartment block, being watched by the security guard.

'Sorry I'm late,' I said as I got into the lift with Karin, followed by the reporter.

'Get the kettle on pet,' I said to Karin when we got into my flat. 'Make yourself useful. Life's not all cash and cunt you know. Don't forget the third C in life. No, not kettle, petal. Cup of char, Ma.'

Karin disappeared and I looked to see if he was writing all this rubbish down, but he just smiled, looking round the room, taking things in. I'd had a few drinks, in fact quite a few, having been to all those places.

'Splendid view you've got,' he said, going to the window and looking out. 'Where's the Reeperbahn?'

'You're not a fucking peeping tom are you?' I said. 'Come on, sit down and cut the fancy chat. I know you bastards. Soften them up with shit about the furniture, get in the arselicking, kid on you're a human being, then wham, in for the kill. It's the first thing they teach you at journalism school.'

'You're so right,' said Edward, sitting down. 'And the surprising thing is, it so often works.'

'Where's the bloody tea, woman?' I shouted. 'These bloody working women don't know their arse from their fanny. She'll be in the bedroom already, knickers off, so make it snappy.'

Why was I showing off? That was partly it. I also thought it would be amusing to see if he would describe me as typical English male chauvinist pig, like all footballers, treating women as slaves. I knew that Karin would not be making me any tea. She didn't know what a kettle looked like and had never made a meal in her life. She would be lying on my bed, reading a fashion mag with one hand, probably playing with herself with the other, while talking to New York on my bloody phone, so bloody hurry up, mate.

'Why did you come to Germany?'

'The money,' I said. 'Next question.'

'How much?'

'You cheeky sod.'

So I told him. What the hell. I said it was £500,000, but not to quote me directly. It was out already, so the damage had been done.

'What damage?'

'I fucking told you.'

'I don't quite think you did,' he said, looking back through his little notebook. So I told him the whole story. Well, almost.

'I thought nobody was talking to me in the dressing room those first few weeks, cos I was a fucking foreigner, not speaking the language. That wasn't the reason.'

'What was it?'

'It was cos they hated me. They were jealous of all the attention I'd got when I arrived, that huge crowd at the training ground, all the publicity. Then when the money came out, twice what they were getting, bloody hell, that really did it, they went spare.'

'How do you mean?'

'The buggers wouldn't even pass to me on the pitch. I'd go for a Doppel Pass, that's a one-two in German, and I wouldn't get the fucking thing back.'

'Anything else?'

'Oh yeh, fucking lots of little things, on the pitch, and in training, buggering me around. I don't want to remember them.'

'How is it now?'

'Oh fine, great, we all get on fine. Good set of lads. Just like footballers anywhere. Good atmosphere.'

'Even though you are so near the bottom of the league . . .?'

'I thought this wasn't going to be all fucking football? You said it was going to be culture, or some shit.'

He then asked me some questions about Germany, the language, the people, how I met Karin, how she had helped me, all harmless stuff, but then he got back to football again, trying to stir things up, get the inside dope on the club. He was a sly, pushy sod, and I was wishing I'd not been so open with him. You can't trust any journalist. Live radio and tv is best, then you can control it.

'Listen, it's early days. I've only been here three months. It takes time for me to adjust to their style, and them to adjust to me. They play with a libero here, which is new to me. But it's getting better all the time.'

'And do you enjoy it?'

'Course I fucking do. I love playing football. Always have done. Always will.'

'Any regrets?'

'Best thing I ever did.'

'And will you stay?'

'Wouldn't you, for half a million quid? Now fuck off. I'm told they do a good cup of tea at Heathrow.'

When he'd gone, I opened the bedroom door, but there was no sign of Karin. I hadn't even heard her leaving.

Then the bedside phone rang. It was Arnold, ringing me from London.

'Your Dad's house is going through okay,' he said. 'But I now think we should put it in your name, not your Dad's. That way it won't go into his estate when he dies, which means you won't have to share the proceeds with Fanny and Colin. Do you understand?'

'Ugh,' I grunted.

'There will be no capital gains to pay, as we can say he was a dependent relative. I think that will be best. Don't you agree, Joe?'

'You what?' I said, not concentrating, picking up a note Karin had left.

'I know you wanted it to be in his name, for his pride, but I think this way is better. What do you think, Joe?'

'I think you should get me out of my contract. I've made a big fucking mistake . . .'

THE TIMES

1 Pennington Street, London E1 9XN
Telephone: 071-782 5000 Fax: 071-782 5046

Dear Joe,

I object to being described as sly and untrustworthy, which is probably libellous, I should think. Not one nasty word appeared about you – in fact not one word appeared. Full stop. The *Sunday Times* didn't like the interview, you might remember, and it was never used. A shame really, especially for the photographer. While you kept me waiting hours at your flat, the photographer followed you around. He got a good shot of you arm-wrestling with Karin at that restaurant, and also later when she returned and was locked in an interesting situation with that tattooed waitress. Should you want to buy the snaps, do let me know. They won't be cheap.

Yours slily,
EDWARD HUNTER

18

Then what happened? Oh yes. Lots. I'll take it in order. I got sent off. For fighting. It was against Bayern Munich, away in 1989, and there was this seven-foot-high Bavarian giant who had obviously been given orders to stop me playing. He thought it meant stop me, full stop, so he lashed out every time I tried to move, breathe, have my being, kicking me so hard for so long that I lost my temper. Yes, I know I was a reformed character, but there are limits.

I nutted him, or gave him the Glasgow nod as the jocks call it, a form of greeting unknown in Europe, so you can usually get away with it, if you're quick, but this goon went down as if I'd knifed him. Gawd knows why he hadn't been booked earlier. I think the ref was bent, or blind, anyway, he was a real homer, the sort you get everywhere, repeat, homer, short for lover of the home team, who gets conned or intimidated by the home crowd and the home club, nothing to do with his sex life, though you never know. When things get out of hand, and they lose control, they always pick on any away player first. So I got a red card, pronto, straight off, straight into the headlines. The German FA then suspended me for four weeks. Turned out to be the best move I'd made since I arrived in Germany, though I didn't know it at the time.

Karin went away, modelling in Barbados, part of her contract, so she said. I thought of going with her, to carry her shoulderpads, help with the rum punches, till the club said that under my contract I still had to train every day, even though I couldn't play. I got on to Arnold but he agreed that was the case. He also pointed out that

I could not leave in under a year, or I'd lose all the upfront money, the signing-on fee, which I'd already spent.

When Karin came back she was off to Paris for the spring shows, so each day after training, I just hung around the flat, doing nothing. I even asked that sausage firm, the one I'd turned down, if they still wanted me for any advertising, even for a tiny sausage, a frankfurter, tinned would do, I'm not proud, but they said no, they now wanted to get a ballet dancer. The image was better, and less controversial.

Until that sending-off, I'd had two real problems. The first problem, as I'd told that slimy, sorry, smart reporter, was that the team hated me. They still did. I'd lied when I said we were now all friends.

The day he came, after I'd finished training, I'd found a dead rat in my locker. That was why I was in such a temper. I think I know who put it there. They still hadn't forgiven me for being a flash outsider who'd had too much publicity, too many commercial contracts, too many freebies, and for getting that jammy Goal of the Month and being invited on the telly. I can't help having charisma. They were so grey, so boring, you wouldn't have offered them a column in a parish magazine.

I also happened to replace someone they and the crowd had all liked, a longtime servant of the club, as if there can ever be such a thing, we're all servants of ourselves. He'd been booted out to make way for me. Not that I could be blamed for that. We all take someone else's place. Ask God. That's the way He made us.

All the same, if I had been playing like hot shit, being an unpopular sod would not have mattered. Success brings friends. Failure finds enemies. Gawd, full of good stuff today. Must be the bloody chapel bells, making me contemplative.

What I didn't tell the reporter was my other and bigger problem. That was with the management, not the players. I hadn't realised the German system when I signed, which was my fault, though I blamed Arnold. He said conveyancing was his speciality, not European football. If I had asked him to check out Hamburg, he would have done, but I hadn't. However, if I now wanted another lawyer to handle my affairs, fine, he'd wish me good day. I liked that. Catch Dez, or Wolfgang, agreeing to go quietly.

In Germany, they have a manager, which was Horst, who seemed a good bloke, at least he liked me, was desperate to have me, promised me the earth, kisses and cuddles, can I lick your arse, dear boy, nothing too much trouble, Joe my old friend. And all in English. A shame I never saw him again. He had seemed a decent sort.

My daily dealings turned out to be with the trainer, the deadly Serge, who was in sole charge of the team – training, tactics, picking the team. The manager did his managing somewhere out of sight, finance, administration, PR, sponsorship, managing the club but not managing the players, except for money and transfers. In my case, Horst had initiated and supervised all details of my transfer. Without telling Serge.

I slowly discovered that Horst was on the skids. That had been his last throw, buying me, his last claim to work miracles, show off his contacts and influence, give the club a boost, improve publicity, increase gate receipts, and get us up the league.

Serge was also on the skids, but he had his own plans to rescue the club, and they didn't include me, in fact they didn't include any suggestions or ideas Horst might have. He therefore stuck to his libero system, which in this case meant his Rudi, number five, coming forward, like Beckenbauer in the old days, to start attacks. I was told to support him, help him go forward, but be ready to fill in behind, should he get caught, which he did all the time. He'd once been a good midfield player for Holland, but now he was just a crock.

Oh Gawd. I'd never experienced power politics before. I didn't know they existed in football, but now I was caught right in the middle. It gives me a headache, just to think about it. As if I haven't got enough headaches.

I learned a lot of lessons, such as not to be too hasty in criticising players who appear not to be playing well after they have played well at their previous club. It doesn't mean to say that overnight they have turned rubbish. I supposed it happens in all walks of life. If the new environment is not right, the atmosphere not conducive, the internal organisation not quite the same as before, then the external results can be disastrous. Are you with me? Okay, let's move on.

So that was the position when I got myself suspended. Nobody cried for me. No letters of sympathy from fans. No one predicted on the sports pages that the team would now do even worse, which was what I hoped for. I began to think I would be on my way, allowed to go. A club can always find a way to break a player's contract, which a player can rarely do.

First game, which I didn't see, as I refused to travel, was a boring draw, away in the UEFA cup to an Icelandic amateur team of deep-sea sealshaggers whom they should have stuffed. Next, they got hammered in the Bundesliga by Werder Bremen, of all people, and at home. Next two games they also got thrashed. By this time they had zoomed right down the league till they were second from bottom.

Come back, Joe Swift, all is forgiven. Now is the time for Mighty Mouse. That was what I expected. Instead the reaction from the press and from fans was one of resignation, then despair, followed by desperation.

Then at last there was sudden action. Horst and Serge had been fighting like mad behind the scenes, blaming each other, maintaining the other was the real cause of all the problems. They were both sacked on the same day.

I came back from my suspension to an even quieter dressing room than when I first arrived. It wasn't antagonism this time, but resignation. There was no point in hating me any more. I was their only hope, which was what the new Coach, Mick McNutter, decided.

Yes, the same Mick McNutter who had been at Spurs when I was sixteen. These coincidences happen all the time in football. The team you leave is always the next one you get drawn against in the cup. You always play a blinder against the team who chucked you out. The manager you hate always arrives at your next club. Actually, it's not really coincidence. It's a small world, football, with only two thousand professionals in England, plus ninety-two managers, hardly bigger than a large comprehensive school. The swings are bound to come round, the same ugly mugs keep reappearing.

Mick had gone from Spurs to Bergen in Norway and taken them, god knows how, to the final of the UEFA cup the year before. He was the new miracle worker, for half an hour anyway. And he was cheap. He jumped at the chance of coaching a first-division German club.

The new manager was German, and didn't speak any English, but he stuck totally to his own domain, leaving everything to do with the team to Mick, who didn't speak English either, being a scouser, har har, sorry Mick, just a joke. Mick did speak the same football language as me, i.e. play four-square at the back, four in the middle and two up front, you know it makes sense, if you happen to have run-of-the-mill players who are never going to manage Total Football. Make sure every fucker knows his function, works his balls off, and you won't often get stuffed. On the other hand, you won't make much progress or set the North Sea on fire. For that you need at least one creative player, someone licensed to kill the opposition with the unexpected. Step forward Joe Swift. Your time has come. Arise, Mighty Mouse.

Mick said I was to move up and be the midfield playmaker. The team had to work to me and my strengths. He also made me captain. Those were the new orders. The old order had failed. It was their last chance, otherwise it would be second division football next season, and second division wages.

The rest is history, German football history. I don't expect people in Britain to remember it. English teams were still out of Europe, so Europe might as well have been on another planet. Today things are better, so I'm told, and most British papers now have a regular rundown of the major European leagues. Do they have a regular rundown on me, or am I forgotten for the moment?

We won the next six matches on the trot and zoomed up the league, getting into the top four, though it was too late in the season to have a chance of the league. In the UEFA cup, after struggling against the so-called poor teams, like that Iceland club and then Fenerbahçe of Turkey, we turned it on against the good teams, beating Glasgow Celtic, Atletico Madrid and Lazio.

We eventually got to the final against Nantes of France. Everyone was thrilled and amazed, though it was a good year for Germany all round, with several teams doing well. The UEFA final was two-legged in those days, home and away. We won the first at home, 2–0, and should have hammered them, so we felt optimistic about the second leg.

None of the lads had played in France before, or spoke any French, and moaned on about the food, said to be funny, and the women, said to very peculiar, i.e. unwilling to open their legs for Germans. Don't worry, lads, I said. As captain, I will lead you, do not fear. I do speak the language, and have an O-level (F for fantastic) to prove it.

'The froggy women hate the English just as much as the bloody Germans,' said Rudi, our centre-half. His English, now he was speaking it, was very good. And so was his achilles tendon, the longtime injury which had been slowing him down. If only he'd let on when I first arrived that he could speak such good English. He could even do a scouse accent, which made Mick smile, though now he was a Trainer, he'd taken a vow of non-smiling.

'I'll be the one to score,' continued Rudi. 'Not you Joe, yah bugger. You'll see.'

So we put a thousand marks on it, for the first to get it away in France. Photographs would help, or first-hand observation. Failing that, Scout's honour to tell the truth. Rudi had been a Boy Scout as well, so that was lucky.

At Nantes airport we were met by a large group of French press. The local paper, *Nantes Ocean*, interviewed me under the assumption that I was the Trainer. I told them our plan was to play 7-2-1, with five centre-halves, that our win bonus was a new Mercedes each and a prison sentence if we lost, or hanging, depending on the goals against. I still have the cutting somewhere.

About twenty reporters from *L'Équipe* were also there, and they could not be fooled. They knew my whole life story, once a forward with Cockermouth *Garçons*, ran away from Spurs when *jeune*, famous for his *derrière* at White Hart Lane. They had the facts and figures, goals and assists, every detail of our revival in the Bundesliga, and how I'd become Germany's Player of the Month.

Mick had booked us into a hotel in the middle of the town which was pretty boring and basic, no TV or minibar or anything, not what we were used to in Germany. Mick had chosen it mainly for convenience, rather than putting us out in the country, because of possible traffic problems. He'd done a recce, in the rush-hour. He'd also vetted every Nantes player and his grandmother. No wonder the Germans loved him. He was more efficient than they were.

'I've got only one colour TV in my room,' I announced, coming down to the little private lounge which had been set aside for us. 'And the bar's useless. Only half full.'

'I've complained about the swimming pool,' said Rudi. 'I want the water changed at once. The last person must have been pissing in it.'

'Heh, I haven't got a TV or a bar in my room,' said Hans, our goalkeeper, looking worried. 'Or seen the swimming pool.'

'Oh no, Hans, they haven't missed you out again,' I said, picking up the phone and speaking in my pretend French.

'Right, that's sorted out,' I said, putting down the phone. 'The hotel manager wants to see you at reception. Take your swimming costume.'

Hans staggered out, all six foot five of him, while I hid, not wanting to be thumped when he got back. Everyone else was pissing themselves.

There is no correlation between fun and success in football. You can feel relaxed before a match, having good times, a few laughs, all friends together, great spirit, then go out and get slaughtered. Or you can all hate each other, be split into cliques who never talk to each other, feel miserable and want to leave the club, then you go out and play inspired football. So it goes. Or doesn't.

We got invited to a dinner by the Nantes club in some restaurant, with posh little invitations pushed under our door. I was quite looking forward to it, but Mick said no chance. The directors would go, along with the German press who had come with us on our charter plane, but he wanted all players to have an early night. We could go out now, have some fresh air before supper, then it was an early bed.

Most of us went out for a walk around the town. Half went shopping, including me, while the other half went into anything that looked like a nightclub or disco or bar, led by Rudi, hoping to talk some dopy girl into coming back to the hotel. It was too early, and they all failed. Their faces and names were not known, not in a foreign provincial town, so what chance had they without paying, and footballers don't pay, unlike the football press.

The shoppers came back staggering under parcels of stupid French dolls and Eiffel Towers in snowstorms or frilly knickers. I was the only one who bought wine, six bottles of Muscatel, gift wrapped, awfully tasteful.

Our supper was in a special dining room, and the menu had been vetted by Mick. It was veal or steak, which sounded safe, but they came with little dabs of garlic butter on top which I thought was great but most people pushed it away, going yuck, awful, scheissen, can't we have ketchup. Carafes of wine came without asking, and everyone moaned at that as well, demanding beer. Ah, just like footballers everywhere.

There was dried toast wrapped in plastic, which I'd never had before. It looked like baby like rusks and disintegrated when you tried to eat it, so everyone threw it around the room, mainly at Hans, shouting catch, here's an easy one.

'Just what I was looking for,' said Rudi, gathering up some of the packets and putting them in his pocket. 'That's the wife's present sorted out.'

Curfew was ten o'clock. Mick positioned himself at the front door to check everyone in and not let them out again, while his two assistants patrolled the hotel, one in the corridors and one in the bar, where three local scrubbers had arrived and were sitting on high stools, practically showing their fannies. They looked so rough not even Rudi would have been tempted. Anyway, that would have been cheating. No paying.

I went straight to my room and rang the hotel shop. When we'd arrived, I'd gone there for a paper, and discovered the girl running it was English. I'd bought a *Guardian*, just to impress her, boasted I was a famous player, superstar in Germany. She'd never heard of me, but she was very friendly, and said yes, she'd have a drink with me in the evening. I thought six bottles of Muscatel would be enough for us.

There was no answer from the shop, bugger it. I rang reception and chatted up the reception manager, saying I was a friend of the shopgirl from England. He said that's funny, she comes from Edinburgh, a teaching assistant from the university, working part-time to make some money, and I said England, Edinburgh, it's all the same. He didn't have her home number, but said she would be on duty tomorrow afternoon.

The next day went very slowly, as it always does on match days, but worst away from home. We had the afternoon free, so I was looking forward to limbering up with my Edinburgh friend, getting myself match fit, but there was no sign of her. The shop remained closed all afternoon.

It might seem strange, that I should remember so much about the hotel, and this girl, when we were about to play a vital European final. That's nothing. I've seen players, in Europe and England, play cards, up to and immediately after a big game, as if the match was a minor interruption to their routine. They can forget who scored, yet tell you who had the aces and kings and how many pounds they lost.

We got on our coach at seven, two hours before kick-off, which was just as well as the streets were chokka, not with fans, but with food. There were rows and rows of stalls selling nougat, that horrible French sort, hot dogs, sweets, drinks, pastries, ham rolls, doughnuts. Unlike a British or German match, there seemed to be no stalls selling football scarves and mementoes.

As we got nearer we came across the fans, all well-behaved, older than in Germany or England, a lot of them wearing tartan berets. Once at the ground, the noise increased and they were soon cheering and blowing trumpets and chanting.

The dressing room, like the stadium, was spartan and seemed to be made entirely of concrete. New bars of soap and blue towels were laid out on the benches for each player, still in their wrapping paper.

'More presents,' said Rudi, putting them in his bag. 'I don't know why I spoil her so much.'

Hans was going round clutching his stomach and complaining of diarrhoea, so our doc gave him some pills. He complained of stomach pains before most matches. I wandered round not getting changed in my usual way, messing about till everyone else was ready. In a corner I found a large cardboard box, addressed to Les Hamburgers. I was about to open it, when Mick took it from me.

'It'll be the presents,' said Mick. 'They asked me for a list of stuff you'd like. I don't know what they've chosen. If it had been up to me it would have been alarm clocks for all of you. Or a comb and scissors.'

Good one, Mick. In just five years he was word-perfect at managerspeak, making the corny dressing-room jokes all managers make.

The presents had been wrapped individually in green tissue paper, with a bow, and we all tore into them, dead excited. Inside was a posh-looking box – containing a Waterman's propelling pencil.

'Not much bloody use for this lot,' said Rudi. 'None of them can write.'

We all settled down after that as the coaches went round, massaging limbs, oiling muscles. I couldn't find any programmes, which annoyed me. I was looking forward to reading out choice bits in pretend Frog-Deutsch.

The dressing room was getting hotter and hotter. There was no light or ventilation and it was like being stuck in a concrete bunker. Mick went out, to complain, so I thought, and came back swearing and frothing.

'They've changed their bloody strip,' shouted Mick, kicking the table so hard a bottle of embrocation fell off and spilled on the floor.

The Germans looked confused, thinking something really serious had happened, till Mick's interpreter explained.

'They told me last week they'd play in yellow. They always play in yellow. That's why they're called the bloody Canaries. Fucking frogs.'

We all looked suitably upset on his behalf, grateful to have some outside body to moan about.

'What's the reason, boss?' asked Rudi.

'Bloody French TV,' said Mick. 'They want Nantes to play in green.'

We all enjoyed moaning even more. Every player everywhere hates being messed around by the TV.

Hans had to change his shirt, as he was wearing green, so there was a hunt through our skip for another goalkeeper's jersey. At least it took Hans's mind off his stupid stomach.

We were terrible in the first half. They ran rings round us, doing neat one-twos, slicing through our midfield and putting our defence under constant pressure. Rudi was falling around, getting caught out of position, made to look a right idiot. They got two goals in the first twenty minutes and it didn't look as if we had a chance.

At half-time Mick actually threw a glass of water at Rudi, the first time I'd seen that happen. Punches, yes, but nothing that might break and endanger everyone.

In the second half we tightened up, but were still not playing well. But for Hans in goal we would have conceded another two. It went to extra time, with the score 2-2 on aggregate, by which time Nantes were growing tired and nervous. After all their great work, they realised one goal from us would ruin it for them, as an away goal from us would count as double in the event of a draw.

I was knackered, having screamed and shouted at them throughout the second half, urging them to concentrate, hold the ball, play it sensibly, do nothing silly, till we had a chance. European two-leg matches are all about tactics, alas, which is not my natural game.

With five minutes to go, I moved through from the halfway line, getting past two men, leaving one on the ground complaining to the ref that I'd elbowed him. Their defence expected I would now wait for help, but I dashed into the penalty box, my old trick, and their right-back lunged at me and down I went.

I took the penalty. Their goalie got a hand to it and it rebounded off the post, but the ref said he'd moved. I took it again, with the crowd going demented, and tapped it slowly into the other corner this time, leaving him stranded. A sharp, short ending to a long-haul story, if not a very glorious one. But we had won. A European final medal to add to my South Eastern Counties Youth Cup medal.

Mick was so pleased he said we could all go to the Mayor's reception in some château. We didn't actually want to, whereas the night before we'd have liked anything to break up the monotony. Now we just wanted to get pissed, not have to be polite and appear in public. On the lads' behalf I said we were all tired, and could we just stay half an hour. It was an amazing castle, right in the middle of the city, with a drawbridge and moat, powdered flunkeys handing out drinks and a magnificent-looking buffet. When you play these European matches it's all bloody *entente cordiale*. The officials and councillors get their snouts in the trough, while the poor fucking footballers have to do all the work.

Back in the hotel most of us sat in a private bar getting smashed. Rudi had disappeared, presumably looking for talent. Every ten minutes I rang the Scottish girl's home number, which I'd finally got from reception, but there was no answer.

I staggered to bed about one o'clock, to find my room locked. Bloody hell, had I locked myself out? Then I heard a noise inside. Someone was there. The Scottish girl, waiting for me? I could hear the door being unlocked.

'Congratulations, Joe. I didn't know you could be so cool.'

It was Karin, looking fantastic. She'd seen the match on TV in Paris and driven down to offer her personal congratulations. Which she did, in the best possible way. So I'd scored, but that bugger Rudi never paid up.

Next morning, Karin told me she'd been appointed house model for Ralph Lauren at some huge salary for only twelve days' work a year. She'd rented a penthouse in New York and was going to live there, sharing with a girlfriend. She'd really come to say farewell.

Goodbye Karin. Nice knowing you. Also *auf wiedersehen* Hamburg. The season ended in triumph, with no one ever knowing what I had had to put up with during that year, but I'd vowed to leave, determined never to get caught in that sort of situation ever again.

Radio Nederland

Dear Joe, you old fat bugger person,

That you have written brought back happy memories. What a great night we had in Nantes, och aye the noo. My wife often talks about Old Lang Syne. I can now do Scottish better than scouser as you know, she comes from bonny Edinburgh. That was our first night together and we got married six months later, after my divorce came through. You already knew Countess Karin, so that did not count. You owe me 1,000 marks.

Yours the noo,
RUDI

19

It was that England match against Brazil in 1989 that did it. You will see my goal repeated on TV as long as there *is* TV, probably till the last syllable of recorded time. That's from Shakespeare, Kevin Shakespeare, used to be in the Reserves at Spurs, great bloke, a graduate in Latin or something, always coming out with quotations, but so thick he hadn't an ounce of football brain or common sense. If clever people could play football then Brian Glanville would be captain of England.

I could sense it was going to be a great game when we all arrived that Sunday afternoon at the Burnham Beeches hotel. Bobby Robson smiled at me. Wow. I'd flown from Hamburg, only three days after the Nantes match, and I staggered through the door, hardly able to walk. He was standing there with his clipboard as he always did, checking us in, not as names but as bodies, wanting to know who the walking wounded were, who was carrying what injury, which clubs and which players he'd have to send panic messages to, bringing in last-minute replacements. A manager's lot is not a happy one, least not in England, with so many league games, unquote. That's what they all say. Have you ever heard of a happy England manager?

This was a friendly, to be held the next day at Wembley, so some clubs were being economical with the truth, reporting mysterious ailments, which just as suddenly cleared up one day later for last-moment relegation battles. It was of course utterly vital for Bobby Robson to have his chosen team available, with the World Cup getting near.

Some of the World Cup preparations were already under way, the really vital, important ones, such as modelling suits, sun specs, shoes, tracksuits, jockstraps, all the new tat that we were promoting in order to make ourselves even more money. It was estimated by the lads that the England pool, in which I hoped to have a stake, would bring in one million pounds. Worth poncing around for.

'Shazam,' I shouted. I let my new tracksuit fall to the ground and stood there in my union-jack underpants with two medals round my plastic hairy chest, a swastika and my UEFA cup medal. Then I did twenty press-ups on the ground, just to show how fit I was. That was when he smiled, ticking me on his clipboard.

'Daft as a brush,' he said.

Yes, he said that about me long before he said it about Gazza. Mind you, in my case it wasn't really true. In Gazza's case, well, let's call it an understatement.

They'd all heard about our UEFA success, and seen highlights on the telly, but naturally it was the win bonus the lads wanted to hear about, was it really true I would make half a million in three years, and who was this model bird the *Sun* was linking me with, and was she a cunt or a cuntess, har har? It was good to hear sophisticated English humour again.

It was also good to see the lads again. Butcher was still into heavy metal, with his Walkman permanently round his earholes. Pop Robson was into crosswords, being a hintellectual. Gazza was on to his bookie, pouring money down the telephone. The rest played cards, read thrillers, phoned home, hung around, chatted to hangers-on, the usual stuff.

I talked to Lineker about his time in Spain, which he loved. Even after two years he was going to Spanish lessons three times a week. Hmm. Very wise. Then I talked football with Waddle and Barnes. Usual moans, but I suppose it must be hell being a winger. You can't win. The Boss wants you to cover back when they attack, so you're knackered by the time you get the ball. If their fullback comes forward, you're supposed to go with him, so you're not there when we attack. And if you argue back and say you want a free role, as you get with your club, he thinks you want a free role to skive. You know your best contribution is to create and attack, so you should be allowed to stay up, but he says ah, it's a team game, everyone has to do their bit. In midfield, you don't have those arguments. You just run your balls off, every game.

Next morning we did some light training, then some light modelling, standing around being photographed like a load of wallies, then a few interviews. Gary Lineker was doing an anti-drug advertisement for some foreign television which we all tried to ruin, making stupid noises in the background.

Gazza was refusing any interviews, as he was under contract with the *Sun*, but spent his time throwing grapes at people who were giving interviews.

I felt a lump going down Wembley Way, no not my modelling fee, but inside, the old heart fluttering. Those German stadiums always seemed so brutal, and quite small really. Wembley, for a player, is vast, in every way. The twin towers seem to reach the sky, and at the same time back into our past. It's part of heritage, innit.

On the way there it's always like one big friendly party, as every supporter, from either side, is in a mood to enjoy himself, happy just to be there. You get a bit more nervous when those huge doors open, ready to gobble you up, and the coach drives straight through, as if you're about to enter an aircraft hanger. The dressing rooms are enormous, more like museums than work-rooms, which they are during the week, and about as ancient. I don't mind that. You just think of all the stars who have gone before.

In the dressing room Butcher was his usual self, shouting and bellowing, stomping around, geeing everyone up. Barnesy retired for a bath, taking the programme with him. I did my usual jack-the-lad bit, mucking around, making jokes, waiting till the last minute to get ready.

There was a good crowd, over sixty thousand for a Monday evening friendly, but Brazil always brings them in. I also like to think I was part of the attraction. Okay, when you go abroad the English crowds usually go off you, you go out of their mind, out of their daily papers, and your old fans believe you have been a greedy selfish bastard for going off at all.

I could hear a few boos from Spurs fans when I came on the pitch, plus a few Arsenal jeers, which I expected. Supporters can change jobs, change towns, change countries, but will never forgive you if you move down the road to a rival club. I couldn't see why they held going to Germany against me. Spurs had paid nothing for me, and made a million quid, which was good at the time, though now seems decidedly modest.

Fans forget we're professionals, it's our job, we do it for money, for Christ's sake, so that always has to be our number one concern. Not the only concern. Just number one. A fan takes a self-imposed vow of blind loyalty, and good luck to him, but he can't expect us to do the same. His connection with his club is a one-sided, very soppy, amateur affair, based on no logic but pure accident – of birth, residence or family tradition. The club doesn't give a bugger for any fans, and will never put them first.

So it upset me, hearing those Spurs fans booing. Opposition boos I can take, because it makes sense, if only hooligan sense, and I thrive on it, but this was to register dislike of me as a person, not as a player. The sods. It probably did gee me up, not that it was necessary.

Bryan Robson didn't play in the end, poor lad. He buggered something in the so-called light training. For the first time for England I was being allowed to play my game, and the others had to fit in, get the ball to me, see what I could do. I'd shown new leadership qualities against Nantes, inspiring and organising the team, which I did again, but this time I didn't have to go back as much. I was able to stay forward and create. Platty was the one to stay back, cover for me, so I didn't have to worry about that. Thanks, Dave.

Lineker got the first goal, thanks to moi. Remember it? I beat three people, went for the byeline, made as if to turn it back to Platty steaming in, then chipped it over, ever so gently, as soft as a zephyr, is that a car Kevin, you're bound to know, and it landed right on Gary's noodle. I think he blew it in. Saved him upsetting his hair or his smile.

They got two goals back, both from free kicks, both amazing, then I decided to turn it on. Now, which was the best goal of my hat trick? Hmm. I have watched the video a few times, about three hundred times a week, till I ended up here, videoless. The last goal, of course, as it was so Brazilian. It began deep in our half, started by me with a couple of one-twos, then I dribbled on my own from the halfway line, first to one wing, then the other, leaving six players on their arses, drew the goalie, then walked it in, waving the while to the whole crowd who were already on their feet. Including the Spurs fans.

196

Did I have an orgasm? Some people do, you know. I've heard Gazza describe it in those terms. There is the most amazing burst of pure joy, of excitement, of relief. You are on a high, walking on the water, unable to explain what happened, where you are, how you did it, or why you ended up sliding twenty feet across the turf on your arse with your hands in the air. Then afterwards there is a moment of tiredness, feeling drained. Yes, there are similarities. Personally, I think scoring goals is the better sensation.

'Let's go,' said Arnold, as I came out of the players' entrance after I'd sunk a few bevvies.

'I've promised to go up West with some of the lads,' I said. 'We're going to this black club.'

He took my arm and propelled me through the usual gang of hangers-on and creeps, many of whom I recognized but did not acknowledge, till we came to the car park where his Rolls was waiting. We got in and he handed me a beard and a moustache.

'Bloody hell, it's not party time is it?'

'Just put it on and shut up,' said Arnold, pressing the button for the electric windows. There was a yell from outside. A fat finger had been caught in the window on my side.

'Fucking hell,' screamed Dez, jumping up and down, sucking his fingers. He was wearing a pinstriped suit, with the pins as wide as a zebra crossing, trying to make himself look like a professional gent. He looked dodgier than ever. He was also fatter and more bloated, panting and wheezing from running after us.

I let the window down again and looked out, which meant my beard slipped. Arnold swore and leaned across and fixed it, warning me I had to put it on properly, otherwise I'd have to lie down on the back seat with a blanket over my head.

'I've got great tickets for Rod Stewart tonight,' wheezed Dez. 'You gotta come. Gonna be mega. Then there's a great party at Tramps.'

I felt very old, very world-weary. Dez was in a timewarp. I now preferred Pavarotti, thanks to Karin, or classic Bob Marley, thanks to Rudi, rather than any chewing-gum pop shit, and as for a night out with Dez, I'd done that, been there, got the t-shirt, and the parking fines.

'You've made a mistake,' I said, pressing the window button. 'I'm not Paul Gascoigne.'

'Heh, Joe, that was fucking marvellous about the plastic hairy chest,' said Dez, sticking his fat arm through the window and trying to stop it going up. 'And the swastika! Wow! Make a fantastic photo. I've got this picture agency who could flog it round the world, so what we could do is . . .'

How could he have learned about that? That was a joke between me and Bobby Robson. There were no photographers around, but some reporter must have spotted it. Who cares? A hero can do no wrong, till he's no longer a hero, which in football, at best, all things being equal, lasts a maximum of six days, till the next match.

We drove east along the North Circular, then cut up and joined the M1 at junction two. Arnold said there might have been people looking out for us at Junction One.

'What goes, Arnold?'

'You'll see,' he said.

'Are you scared your motor's bugged? Come on, talk, tell me, don't be so mysterious. You're not bloody John le Carré.'

'All in good time,' he said. He pressed a button and a tray came out of a compartment behind my back, laden with smoked salmon sandwiches and a bottle of champagne.

'You know I hate champagne,' I said.

'Sorry, that's not for you,' he said. He pressed another button and some beer appeared, beautifully cooled. He then told me to open a compartment in front. Inside was a miniature colour TV.

Arnold had obviously been doing well, since he took over my affairs, though he screamed if I ever suggested it. He maintained he was already doing well, long before I chanced to use his firm to secure that flat.

It was a great arrangement all round, far better than having an agent taking twenty per cent. That's their share, if not more, on everything you do outside football, and sometimes inside football, as they always take a hefty slice of any transfer fee, or other personal inducements or sweeteners to change clubs. Even if you remain at the same club, they will now negotiate a staying-on fee, usually kept secret, but it can easily be a hundred grand, just for going nowhere, doing nothing. Yes, there's a lot of money to be made.

The agents who usually attach themselves to footballers are either chancers like Dez, ex-barrowboys with no experience of football, or ex-players or ex-football journalists, who are usually idiots with little experience of the business world. In either case, it is in their interest to milk you dry, encourage you to do everything, change clubs, change products, going on about it being a short life so you've got to make it while they can. Which means while they can.

With Arnold, I paid him for his professional advice, in the normal way one does with a lawyer, whether I used his advice or not. Normal of course means two hundred quid an hour. Gulp. Yes, it seemed a lot to me as well, when I first went to his office in New Cavendish Street to discuss some complications on the lease on my flat. There was an hourglass on his desk and I thought fucking hell, every time he farts or goes to the lav, I'll be paying for that as well.

It was expensive, in relation to the flat, but it has worked out cheap ever since I've been in the big money. When a hundred grand offer comes in from a clothing company wanting my name and physog on some new bit of rubbish to rip off the kids and their mums, he goes through the contract line by line, checks the firm out, as these sort of firms can go bust without ever paying, evaluates the possibility of rival firms offering more, considers it in relation to my whole portfolio, and tells me what he thinks. Then it's up to me. There's nothing extra in it for him, whether I say yes or no. He still gets his two hundred. Someone like Dez would expect twenty thousand. Greedy bastard.

Gradually Arnold had taken over all my affairs. Once I went to Germany he handled all my letters, bills, commercial offers. He'd taken on an assistant just to screen my post, not at two hundred an hour, do you mind, more like two quid an hour, as a trainee lawyer. She paid the boring bills, fielded enquiries and offers from the media, wrote bums-rush letters, then passed the important things on to Arnold to make a final sifting before presenting me with the good stuff.

He also arranged my accounts and made regular visits to the Bahamas, to my offshore company, to make sure no bugger had run off with the loot. I wasn't so happy about that. With my business deals I felt in direct control, in that me and Arnold together knew the people concerned. With the Bahamas there were two other layers of agents and banks creaming off their share. It still saved tax, that's if your income was big enough, but I felt a bit uneasy about it, being a socialist. Oh, didn't I tell you? I'm about the only Labour-voting footballer in captivity.

Arnold is also a socialist. He went to a grammar school and then Oxford, and won a Blue for football, lives in a posh house in Hampstead, has a villa in Portugal, a Rolls and a Porsche, and why not, there's nothing in the Labour party manifesto that says you can't have possessions, so Arnold always tells me. But he does send his kids to comprehensive. Bully for Arnold.

My Dad of course has always been a socialist. So that's something I picked up from him. There must be others. Only the other morning, while shaving, I looked in the mirror and thought bloody hell, it's him. That has been a recurring worry, this last year, now I'm getting near the age he had his mental breakdown, or whatever it was. Let's not think about it. Let's get back to the story. Tom was right. Writing a book is great therapy.

'You're not taking me to see my Dad,' I said to Arnold. I'd recognized Spaghetti Junction and realised we were on the M6.

'Would you like that?'

I hesitated. Out of guilt. I hadn't seen him for almost a year, since I went to Hamburg, though I did send him a postcard recently. Dear Dad. I am in Hamburg. Hope he got it.

'Yeh, why not, the miserable old sod,' I said. 'I always like to see his smiling face. Oh fuck, I should have invited him down for today.'

'He was there,' said Arnold, smiling. 'And he didn't bring you bad luck, after all, did he.'

'Thanks, Arnold.'

We passed through Birmingham and I thought, thank God I don't live in Birmingham. Imagine playing for Villa. Or West Brom or Birmingham City, if they're still playing. Then Birmingham came back. I'd forgotten that the Dunlop castle thing is the sign to look for. There seemed much more of it this time, more spewing chimneys and concrete towerblocks and I thought, it's everywhere. Birmingham has taken over England.

At least the Lake District will look the same. And Cockermouth never changes. It will be quite good having Arnold with me. He can drive me back tomorrow. One night with my Dad will be more than enough.

I was just beginning to wonder how my Dad was getting home, if he was at the game (why hadn't Arnold given him a lift?), when we suddenly pulled up at a motorway service station, Hilton Park, south of Lancaster. I thought at first we were stopping for petrol, but Arnold drove to the far end of the car park, near the motel, and stopped the car facing some trees. He told me to put on my moustache and beard again.

'Get stuffed. This is just daft. Come on, we can be home in an hour and a half. Stop messing around.'

'Someone is meeting us here,' said Arnold, looking at his watch. 'With a very interesting proposition. He wants to put it to you personally, starting from the beginning. I think you'll be interested.'

'I'm not modelling beards, whatever the fucking money.'

'It has to be secret because they don't want an auction. No one else knows you're unhappy at Hamburg.'

'So you told them?'

'Let's say I dropped a few clues,' said Arnold, opening the car door, looking round carefully.

'Why aren't you in a beard, Arnold, now that you're so fucking famous?'

Arnold had been profiled in *You* magazine only the other week. Since looking after me his profile had soared, appearing on TV and radio, giving his views on the state of football, whither a superleague, whither the freedom of contract. It had also brought him in some other footballers as clients, plus a couple of pop stars.

He got out and started doing some exercises, bending and stretching, then jogging on the spot. He was in loose baggy trousers and a shortsleeve shirt with his initials on the pocket, A.C. He always dressed neat, but casual, a mark of a true modern professional, as Dez will never understand. For a bloke of thirty-seven he was in pretty good shape, thin and wiry, though I didn't like his Graeme Souness moustache which he had recently acquired, special offer by the look of it.

'I was knackered yesterday,' he said, getting into the car again. 'I spent the whole of last evening with the heat pads on. I thought I wouldn't make it today.'

'That would have been good,' I said. 'I could have gone straight back to Hamburg.'

'I got a hat trick, though, so it was worth it, not that my wife thinks so. She's threatening to divorce me if I carry on much longer. I do seem to be getting so many injuries these days, and it takes me ages to recover.'

'You're too old, Arnold. Stick to wanking.'

'Oh, I do that as well,' he said. 'The thing is I'm fit enough to play football, but not fit enough to recover from playing football . . .'

Arnold could be very boring when he started yattering on about his Sunday-morning football team on Hampstead Heath, Dartmouth Park United, which he had helped to start. Amateurs often think it gives then an insight into the real game, licensed to comment, able to share, just because they too can kick a ball around. They have as much understanding as Boy Scouts on their annual camp know what it's like to fight in Vietnam.

A large Dormobile pulled in beside us, with bikes at the back, bunks for about ten, water and gas bottles attached, plus a TV aerial, the sort I fantasised about as a kid when I contemplated running away in style, not with a bundle but with a luxury mobile home. I might get one. Me and Karin could tour the Black Forest, if she ever came back from New York.

A fat man with a handkerchief knotted on his head peeped out from the back door, looked around, then jumped out, carrying a kettle. He came to our car and knocked on the window.

'Have you got any sugar, mate?' he asked.

Arnold immediately opened the door and let him in. This was obviously the codeword.

'So it *is* John le Carré,' I said. 'I was right after all.' The man took off his handkerchief, produced a sheaf of papers from his kettle and started consulting them.

He was representing Manchester United, so he whispered, and went straight into his spiel. They were offering three million pounds for me, the biggest fee ever paid between British clubs, for a three-year contract. My salary would be £150,000 a year, plus bonuses to be discussed, and a signing-on fee, also to be discussed, which could be arranged to my advantage, paid as and where I wanted it, but it would be dependent on any compensation to be paid to Hamburg. Arnold then discussed the possibility of that happening, quoting sections from my contract, quoting previous cases.

A Range Rover pulling a caravan arrived on our other side, parking with difficulty, just a few feet away. The driver got out carrying a camera and started taking photographs.

'Oh my God,' said the Man. U. man. 'It's the *Sun*.'

I looked round and he had fallen to the floor, cowering. Arnold had put his hands over his face. The bloke with the camera then went round to the back of his Range Rover and climbed on top, taking more photographs, all of the caravan, from different angles, totally ignoring us. Then he got back into the car and drove off.

'As I was saying,' said the Man. U. man, getting up and dusting himself. 'If we can agree the basic terms now, we can get on to the finer details later. At the moment, speed and secrecy are of the essence . . .'

'Were you at the match?' asked Arnold, softly. 'Joe was amazing, absolutely amazing. There's going to be a lot of interest in the next few days, from all over Britain, and Europe, a lot of interest indeed . . .'

'Well, I'm not interested,' I said, flatly.

The man at first did not seem to hear. He was looking at his files again and giving some sort of signal to the Dormobile.

'Alex is waiting to meet you,' he said, smiling. 'I'll tell him to put the real kettle on . . .'

He leaned over between us, smirking, clapping me on the back, trying to shake Arnold by the hand. Arnold was fiddling with some switch on his radio.

I will say this for Arnold. He is quick. He had understood my reaction at once, and did not attempt to persuade me or take the matter further, not at that stage.

'Well I think we know enough for the time being,' he said, opening the door and switching on the car engine. 'Jolly good of you to spare the time. We'll be in touch. Enjoy the tea.'

We didn't speak on the way home, not till we had passed Birmingham.

'I followed Man U as a boy,' mused Arnold. 'Denis Law was my hero, not George Best, which was funny. Best could be pushed out of the game. But Denis was smarter.'

'I hated them,' I said. 'My team was Newcastle.'

'They still are the wealthiest club in England, you know. They're desperate for you. A shame, really.'

'Why didn't you tell me?'

'You might have refused to go. I needed to get the details of their terms. They wouldn't discuss money until we all met. Now I have all the details. We can take it from there. And we can take it anywhere we like. I've got what I wanted. The first deal is on the table. Now it's up to you to decide where you want to go . . .'

He turned on his radio-cassette, on which he had recorded the whole conversation. He played it back on the way home, several times, especially the bit where he and the other bloke dived on the floor.

'Now I know why he was wearing that stupid handkerchief on his head,' said Arnold.

'Why?' I said.

'Just in case the *Sun* caught him. Boom boom.'

I was glad Arnold felt amused, but I didn't feel very cheerful. Nervous, if anything.

I was about to make a big decision. I knew I couldn't go back, either to London, or Manchester. I'd done that. There was no challenge in repeating the English experience, even if it did lead this time to more money and more pots than I'd ever won at Spurs. English football is English football.

I'd had a taste of foreign fields, not a successful one, but enough to want more. And I wanted to do it properly next time.

PHILIPS

Frederiklaan 10a
5616 NH Eindhoven
telefoon (040) 51 19 17
telex nr. 35000 NL UTFDA
fax nr. 040-(7)55194

Rabobank Eindhoven Noord
rekening nr. 15 01 38 083
gironr. van de bank
1197467

Dear Joe,
    What I said, jokingly, was, 'I wish we had Rush.' You are not daft. You don't even look like a brush. But if you're a socialist, then I'm a Dutchman.

Yours,

BOBBY ROBSON

20

I was driving back from the Rituro in 1990, singing the while, clapping in time to my Bob Marley CD, a leaving present from Karin, in my brand new Ferrari, a welcome present from the President, grateful to be released, pleased that the ordeal was over, now normal life could resume. But of course the Rituro is normal life, if you happen to have lived all your working life as an Italian footballer. Poor sods.

I had made such good preparations this time, taking Italian lessons even before I had signed, and had spent most of the summer listening to tapes and videos. I wasn't going to get caught in the dressing room, having to sit like a dummy.

Secondly, I'd got Arnold to check out Marinello, the President, to make sure he was worth all those billions, that he did own all those newspapers, TV stations and factories, that his passion in life really was football, that he personally owned the club, was not about to sell or be taken over, and that he made all the decisions. I'd had enough of committees farting around and power struggles between impotents.

I'd also insisted that I was not to be the only big, expensive new star. I'd be the main star, no question, and I had no worries about that, in fact if I hadn't been made captain and midfield general I wouldn't have come, but I wanted him to prove his ambitions for the club by lashing out on other new players, not just me. The team might have done well last season, running away with Serie B, but doing well in Serie A was another matter.

Yes, that had been a worry, deciding to join what had traditionally

206

been a second division team. They'd been in Serie A for about half an hour, twenty years ago, but had languished in B ever since, until Marinello came along. He'd failed to buy Torino, where his main factory was, and been treated like an upstart, dismissed as a hick from the south, so he'd bought all the shares in AC Sporting Venice, and was determined to prove everyone wrong.

When it came to business he was obviously a shit, no question, how do you get all that money from scratch, and he looked repulsive, a little fat ugly, bloated bastard, but I liked him. He made me laugh, just the look of him, an ugly shit pretending to be no other than an ugly shit. What you saw was what there was, and he made no attempt to be smooth and charming, the way Horst had been in Hamburg.

The cleverclogs in the Sunday heavies all said I'd regret it. They flashed their knowledge of Italian football and said Venice would never break through, the city and the region could not support a top team, they would be another Empoli, a one-season wonder. Marinello would get fed up and disappear as quickly as he'd come, or go bust. The fans would crucify me as an Englishman, once things went wrong, which they were bound to.

I spoke to Graeme Souness and Trevor Francis about Italy. They both loved it, but they confirmed that when things went wrong at a big club your life could be hell. I reckoned that at a smaller club, with smaller expectations, they might have more patience.

I'd come to Italy for lots of reasons. The clothes. Well you gorra think about these things. Stay too long in Hamburg and I could end up dressing like a German. The culture, my darlings, of course. Nice class of person, nice class of building, nice class of wine in Italy. Then the sun, *naturellement*. Oh, and the money. Yes, we're getting hot, getting near the real reasons, though not the main one. The football.

Italian football has to be the best in the world. They don't produce the best players. At this moment in time, sitting where I'm sitting, though what do I know, stuck here, the best players in the world are German – and they're all playing in Italy. That's got to prove something. The best Dutch players are also here, and the South Americans. Italy has the best, the most modern stadiums and the biggest crowds. Strange that in Germany, a much richer country, the crowds should be comparatively small, the stadiums poor, the wages modest.

In Italy football is a national passion, not just a pastime, a madness, which has little logic in it, especially when it comes to financial logic. There is a breed of larger-than-life multi-millionaires who see it as their duty to buy success at any price. That doesn't happen in Germany, or England, though you see it in Spain, and a bit now in France. It must be the Mediterranean sun, addling all their tiny Latin brains.

Germany had been a mistake for me, but I like to think I learned from it and salvaged something. Was I daft to try a second foreign country? Go through the culture shock all again? I can't think of many British footballers who have done that. The Yugos, they move around all the time, but where else have they got to go, and Maradona, he was in Spain and Italy.

If I'm going to consider myself a top footballer, then I have to have been in Italy. That was my thinking. Otherwise, I'd look back and regret it. (And do I? Oh shurrup. This could have happened to me anywhere.) I wanted the challenge. To see if I could improve my skills and expand my experience. To see if I could survive.

I stopped the car and looked at some road signs and thought, bloody hell, where am I. I'd driven down from the hills for about an hour, as instructed, all on my own. I wanted to test the new motor, as I hadn't used it on the Rituro, being too knackered to even start it. They had offered a chauffeur-driven car, or someone to go with me, thinking that being English I'd have no idea what to do and be lost from the moment I landed. Fuck off, I said. I'm not Rushy.

They'd paid £4.7 million for me, just beating Chris Waddle's fee from Marseilles, making me the highest-priced British player. Maradona of course had cost Naples £5 million, almost five years earlier, while AC Milan had paid £5.5 million for Ruud Gullit, which was then the world's record transfer.

Hamburg were well pleased, having paid only a million for me, while Spurs were well sick, realising they had sold me too cheaply. Man. U. had offered a reasonable price, around the British market value, which had encouraged the foreign clubs to come in. It's all of course a nonsense, a fantasy world of inflated values, how can anyone be worth that much for kicking a ball around when you think what nurses and teachers and social workers get, right, I think that establishes my socialist credentials.

No British club could of course compete with Venice's personal offer. Would you believe half a million a year? But don't repeat it. It's still coming in there, somewhere, spread out amongst the various companies and overseas holdings. Think what a panic I'd be in now, stuck here, while imagining Dez being in sole charge of my finances. Can I trust Arnold? Hmm. I wish that thought hadn't struck me.

Venezia, said the signpost, where the fuck's that? I got out my maps and plans and addresses, as provided by the club in their highly efficient way. Oh Christ, what an idiot, how could I be so stupid? I bet even Rushy didn't make that mistake.

I'd only been there once, in the dark and mist, after me and Arnold had taken a quick look at the ground, which was several miles out of Venice anyway, on the mainland, then I'd gone straight to the Rituro. That was where I'd been for the last four weeks, don't talk about it, it was a hell I'd like to forget.

It means retreat, like a monastic retreat, but is more like prison, or what at the time I imagined a prison would be like, total captivity, in a camp in the hills, miles away from civilisation. All Italians teams do this for their pre-season training. It makes all British clubs seem like a doddle, mornings only, then home to relax.

We were up at seven in the morning for light exercises, then it was breakfast, so-called, and first day I thought great, I'll have a good tuck in, a fry-up, the full works, having been up so early, but all we got was a cappucino and a dry roll. Bloody hell. In the morning we had intensive training then we broke for a short lunch, salad and pasta, ugh. After that we went to bed, compulsory bed, stripped off under the bed clothes, no cheating. I couldn't believe it. That was followed by more training, from five until seven. Dinner was eight till nine.

The only free time we had, in the whole four weeks, was from nine till ten, between dinner and lights out. That first night I rushed to the bar, just a little one, but I'd noticed it at lunchtime, thinking I'll get in first, before the crush. I ordered a Peroni, and waited, and waited. No bugger turned up. I ordered another one and noticed that the barman was writing it down on a little pad under the counter. It was all free, supplied by the club, so what the fuck was he doing, spying on me?

Then I began to wonder where *was* everyone. Don't say it was going to be like Hamburg, no socialising just because I was a foreign star on a big wage. I'd gone to great lengths this time to keep it secret, though I need not have worried. I discovered later that four players were getting more than me, including half-witted Hans, yes, the same, our goalie from Hamburg.

Did I smell? Had I said something? Perhaps I'd misunderstood the arrangements and they were now all in someone's bedroom, watching a blue video or shafting some waitress.

I got the barman to ring Gino, our centre-forward, with whom I was rooming, and he said he was in bed, just finishing a letter to his wife. That was when I made my first and probably worst discovery about Italian footballers. They do not drink.

British footballers, and Germans are much the same, live to drink, play to drink, it's what keeps you going during training, thinking of all the lagers you'll sink afterwards. Whether you win or lose on a Saturday, the object is to get smashed afterwards. It's called enjoying yourself. Then you try to drive home, which of course you rarely can, not in a straight line.

I wonder if that's why English players, on the whole, are more musclebound than Italians? I could have a new theory coming on here. I now know that English players don't train any harder, far less if anything, so it's not the physical training which builds up the muscles, but the bar-room training. The alcohol increases their body weight and mass.

Italian players do take a glass or two of wine with their dinner, so they're not teetotal, and a glass of that horrible fizzy water at lunch, but that's all. They don't drink, as such, I mean they don't go out and drink, touring various bars, just to drink. Foony people.

As I was standing there, draining my second Peroni, thinking this is no fun, I can't drink on my own, I need the lads around, sinking the pints together, Tito, one of the younger coaches, came in and pulled up a stool beside the bar. 'Sit down, Joe, if you please.'

I thought hurrah, I'm going to have a drinking companion, then I saw his stern, serious face and thought, oh no, I'm going to get a bloody lecture about drinking on my own, which I've always hated anyway, pathetic. Or perhaps he was going to ask me if I was homesick, depressed, emotionally disturbed. Well, at least it would help my Italian, having a non-football conversation. So I sat down on the stool he was offering me.

'Thank you, Joe,' he said, walking out.

That was it. He never said another thing. Next day I told this story to Gino and he explained it to me. I think.

Italian coaches know English players drink a lot, so that was not the real worry, because I'd soon change my ways and pick up Italian social habits. Oh yeh, I said. What Tito was worried about was me standing, you know, on my legs. That was why we were sent to bed in the afternoon. Italian coaches believe that professional footballers must always take care to rest their most precious assets, their legs. Standing on them after training, or even worse, after a match, for hour after hour at a bar in the English manner, is a very silly thing to do. They're right, you know. I now never stand up when I can sit down. And if I'm really sensible, I get someone else to carry the pints to my gob and pour them in.

My next discovery about Italian football life was *sex*. The players are all for it, like players everywhere, lying down of course, saving their energy, none of the gymnastic stuff. It's the training staff who are against it. They've got it into their thick heads that it is bad for you before a match, even several days before a match. That morning, before I'd left the Rituro, there was a final pep-talk on plans and routines for the season ahead. We were reminded that sex was okay on Mondays, *bueno*, no *problema*, or Tuesdays, even Wednesdays. But on Thursday, with the weekend approaching, we should be sensible. On Saturday, the eve of the match, we should refrain completely, no sex please, we're Italian. Now I do think that is rubbish, though it's a view which is prevalent throughout the Italian league. They think sex saps your strength. What cobblers.

I can see that a bunk-up during half-time, however pleasant, however relaxing, might be a distraction in the dressing room, and having it off during a throw-in or a penalty kick could lead to a loss of concentration, but stroll on, a fuck the night before, or even the morning of the match, is as good as a tonic. Better than fizzy water any time.

I parked my car at Venice railway station, as instructed, in an underground car park, where Marinello had booked me a permanent parking place. All the lads had said I was stupid to want to live in Venice. It was dead, but dead, like living in a museum. I wouldn't be able to have a car, it was all canals. It was full of tourists.

Worst of all, there would be no talent, just foreigners, passing through.

In Hamburg I'd lived in this new modern block, all concrete and functional. I thought this time, being in an historic place, I should live in an historic part, have the whole experience. As for talent, I can pull them anywhere. Always have done.

The moment I parked, a bloke in that stupid outfit the gondoliers wear took my bag out of the car. He also insisted on carrying my papers, club details, the map of Venice, address of my pad, all my bits and pieces. I had the name somewhere of the Italian teacher the club had organised for me, who was to meet me that evening.

We then zoomed down the Grand Canal in one of Marinello's private *vaporetti*, also at my disposal whenever I needed it, and I was dumped near the Academia Bridge. I then set off towards the Salute Church, following my map. The address called it a Palazzo, but when I found the right street it seemed very modest, and the front entrance was simply a black door in a wall. I pulled a rope bell and a uniformed butler appeared, ushering me into an internal courtyard, with orange and lemon trees. Beyond were marble steps leading up to the front door proper, very grand, with a large hall filled with statues. He then led me into a large sitting-room with its own gallery and asked if I would like a drink. A bit big for one person, I thought, looking round, but great for parties. I'll have a live group playing up there on the gallery.

I could have brought a friend, all expenses paid, to live with me for the first year, help me settle in, as I hadn't got a wife. The club was very keen on this, presumably to keep me out of bad company, or from feeling lonely. I couldn't think of anyone I wanted to live with, and anyway I don't mind living alone, not that I expected to, not all the time.

'Mr Swift? Come up and see your bedroom, honey.'

It was an American voice, singsongy, rather sexy. I went up to the balcony, looking for my bedroom, and perhaps my bedroom honey.

'In here, Mr Swift, or can I call you Joe? I feel I know so much about you already.'

A small dumpy woman in a ridiculous frilly skirt, very short, far too flouncy for a woman of her age, whatever it was, perhaps forty, was standing on the bed in her bare feet, trying to take down a

212

painting from the wall. I could see her frilly silk underwear, very expensive, as she strained to reach the painting. Naturally, I tried to avert my eyes.

'Can you help me?' she purred. 'Though I should be helping you, for goodness' sake. That's what I'm here for.'

I got the painting down and handed it to her. She then sat on the bed, beckoning me to sit beside her, patting a place for me.

'Welcome to AC Venice,' she said, beaming, leaning back and staring at me, then leaning forward again to give me a little kiss. 'Please call me Tickles.'

'Why?' I said flatly.

'That's my name, you silly boy. My husband is sorry he can't be here today, but I've organised a little welcome pack for you, downstairs in the kitchen.'

I got up to go, but she grabbed my hand and held on to it, telling me that if ever I wanted anything, I just had to contact her. Her husband was so busy that often he could not do all the things he promised. This was their private Palazzo, she explained, well, one of their Palazzos, now at my complete disposal. Karl the butler would cook for me and provide anything else I wanted. It was so nice that I'd requested an old house. Most footballers hated such things, but then most footballers have no soul, didn't I agree. I agreed, looking round the room, wondering how I could get out, without offending her.

'Whereabouts in England are you from?'

'You won't know it,' I said. 'Cockermouth, up in the North.'

'Is it near Newcastle?'

'Other side,' I said.

'Goddammit, I was sure you were a Geordie boy. Marinello told me you were. Wait till I see him. Anyway, I know you are going to be very happy here. You do know it is an English club?'

'How do you mean, like?'

'It was founded by you English, which is why it's called AC Sporting Venice. Sporting for sporting, which I'm sure you are. AC for Athletic Club and Venice, for Venice, in English. It's like AC Milan. They should be called AC Milano, but it never has been, except for a few years during the war when that fool Mussolini said it should be AC Milano. Once they'd hung him up by his ankles from a lamppost, they changed it back to AC Milan.'

'I didn't know that,' I said, getting up. 'I must unpack.'

'Do you like the painting?' she said, following me out of the bedroom, carrying the painting. 'It's a Renoir. I'm putting it in a safe, just in case anyone gets too boisterous in the bedroom. I know what footballers are like . . .'

She linked my arm as we came down the stairs. At the bottom stood Karl, the butler.

'Mr Graham to see you sir,' said Karl.

'Well I must be going,' said Tickles, giving me another kiss, then she swept out, carrying the painting.

Into the room came Tom Graham. From Cockermouth. My oldest friend.

'Bloody hell,' I said, standing up. 'Look what the fucking cat's brought in. What are you doing here?'

I gave him a hug, not exactly Cumbrian style, but when in Italy, one begins to act like an Italian, even after four weeks.

'I'm your tutor. *Parla Italiano* and all that.'

'I thought you were in America?'

'Was in America. I'm now here, teaching English.'

'I can speak fucking English.'

'Then we can learn Italian together.'

I ordered Karl to bring drinks, lots of them, and Tom explained how he came to be in Venice. After he got a First at Cambridge, he thought he'd do research in America, but he hated it. He then did a TEFL course – teaching English as a foreign language – and had been wandering round Italy ever since, ending up in a language school in Venice.

'So all your bloody cleverness got you nowhere,' I said when he'd finished his story.

'Oh, I wouldn't say that,' said Tom. 'I can speak Italian. I've got a room of my own. I've got a suntan. What else is there?'

'Money.'

'Oh no, I've no money, but on the other hand I have no commitments or responsibilities. I can move round the world as I like, as long as I don't mind living on fuck all.'

'I've got commitments,' I said. 'If this fucking club doesn't win the league in two years, the Italian press will crucify me. Come on, let's go out and get pissed.'

'Actually, they're not too bad,' said Tom, getting up. 'It's blanket coverage they go in for here, rather than sensation. They have acres of space to fill every day. There's one daily paper, just devoted to football. You'll be driven mad by them, but they need you more than you need them. It's the fans that'll crucify you, not the press.'

'Thanks a lot,' I said.

'Oh Christ,' said Tom, looking at this watch. 'I should have been at the Gritti five minutes ago.'

'What's that,' I said, 'a breakfast cereal?'

'Big posh hotel. Madame Largo, who runs our school, is giving a farewell drink for somebody, and I promised to be there.'

'You can miss it. Sounds boring.'

'Can't really. She got me the job. Someone from your club approached her for a tutor for you, and she suggested me.'

'Come on, then. I'll go with you.'

We walked along the Grand Canal to the Gritti Palace, which did look like a palace, outside and inside, with magnificent terraces, marble halls, huge chandeliers, etc.

The party was in a private room, not very big, just thirty or so people, standing around drinking white wine. I asked Tom to get me a beer, which led to a refusal at first, till two waiters spotted me.

'Meester Sweeft, certainly Meester Sweeft,' they shouted, falling over themselves to get it first.

We stood in a corner while Tom told me which teachers were piss-artists, which fancied little boys, which were loonies and misfits and would be on their way soon, as Madame Largo would be sorting them out. She was in the driving seat, able to pick and choose from a never-ending supply of arts graduates.

'You'll have to meet her,' said Tom.

'I don't want to meet some old bag. Met one already. Who's that bewer?'

That's a Cumbrian expression, one I hadn't used for years. Oh, it was good to have someone from the old country to talk to, after being locked up with Italian sadists for the last four weeks.

'Tom, I'm so glad you managed it,' said a tall, elegant woman in a cream suit, coming over to talk to us. 'This is Mr Swift, I presume.'

'Joe, this is Linda Largo, my boss. Say hello nicely.'

215

'Hello nicely,' I said, shaking hands.

She smiled, and moved on to another group.

'Stuck-up bitch,' I said. 'You never told me she was English.'

'From Scunthorpe,' said Tom.

'I could tell she was Fourth Division.'

'Was Fourth. She's now definitely First.'

Tom explained how she'd married an Italian in London, after a whirlwind romance. He'd brought her back to Venice, where he died of a heart attack, leaving her with two kids and no money. She got a job in a language school, one of the dodgy ones, who then sacked her, so she began her own little school, for her own kids and kids of friends. It went so well that she now had three schools and employed a hundred teachers.

'Yeh, she's not bad,' I said, watching her across the room. 'Quite classy.'

'And clever,' said Tom.

'I could give her one.'

'No chance.'

'You've tried, have you? Or are you a poofter, since you went to that Cambridge?'

'Yeh, I just fancy Gondoliers.'

'Jest one Cornetto,' I sang, rather loudly, in a pretend Italian accent. 'Geev eet to 'er . . .'

The waiters all smiled. The teachers looked over their shoulders, wondering who the yob was, about to complain, then saw it was me and also smiled, indulgently. They'd seen it was me from the moment I'd arrived, but pretended not to, trying to be superior. You can always tell, just by the way people look, then look away, nudging each other, telling them not to look, which they do of course.

'So how are you enjoying Venice, Mr Swift?'

It was Madame Largo, floating back again, doing her hostess bit.

'Looks not bad,' I said. 'Pity about the flooding.'

'We're working on it.'

'I could do with someone to show me round,' I said, meaningfully.

'You've got Tom.'

'He's no good. He's an uncultured bastard from Cockermouth, just like me. I need someone classy, sophisticated, just like you, to show me the real Venice.'

'How kind. What exactly are you interested in, hmm?'

'You,' I said. She gave a wintery smile. 'I mean you showing me round, telling me the best things to see in Venice.'

'Oh, that's easy. There are only two painters to see in Venice, and just two places to see them. Have you got a pen and paper Tom, so you can write them down for Mr Swift? Right, forget the Canalettos, the Queen of England has more and better Canalettos. Same for Titian. I recommend you look out for Tintoretto . . .'

'He's Juventus's new hard man, is he?'

'And the best place to see him is the San Rocco. Secondly, Carpaccio, can you spell that, Tom, and the best place for that is San Giorgio degli Schiavoni . . .'

'I've seen a Renoir so far,' I said. 'In private hands of course. Not a patch on Lowry, if you ask me. I've got two of them at home.'

'How interesting. Originals?'

'Bloody hell, what do you think I am. It was my lawyer suggested I invested in them. I also got a couple of Mrs Bradleys, but you won't have heard of her.'

'Of course I have,' said Madame Largo. 'Miss Carter Wore Pink. I'd like to see them some time.'

'They're not here,' I said. 'They're on my Dad's wall, in his new bungalow in the Lake District. He doesn't know how much I paid for them, or he'd shit himself. I could arrange a private showing for you, some time . . .'

'That would be kind,' said Madame Largo, smiling. She moved on to another group, but turned now and again to gesture in my direction, obviously telling people about me. That showed her. Thought she was dealing with a right dickhead.

Tom and I then went for dinner, just the two of us. I did ask Madame Largo, but she had a meeting to go to. I was pretty tired by then anyway, so it was enough just to sit and chat to Tom about ye olden days, about his family, about school, about old Botty, about what happened to the people we'd grown up with.

I got home about one in the morning. Karl was still up and opened the door for me, still in his uniform. I went to the kitchen, looking for a beer, and on the table was a hamper, my welcome to Venice hamper. Inside was a York ham, a Stilton Cheese, Dundee Marmalade, Marmite, and six bottles of Newcastle Brown Ale. I've always hated Newcastle Brown, but it was a nice thought, from that stupid woman.

'Sorry about the wrong beer, honey,' said a voice as I went up the stairs to my bedroom. 'But I've also got some Scotch.'

She was lying on the bed, and looked as if she had been drinking hard. There was a bottle of malt whisky beside her. Above her head was the Renoir, back on the wall.

'Let me *really* welcome you to Italy.'

'That would be nice,' I said. 'But I'm not allowed to break training. We've got a cup match tomorrow. Italian rules . . .'

'Oh, just a little one. I won't tell . . .'

Keswick, Cumbria

Dear Joe,

I am sorry to be so long in replying, but you know what retirement's like – there is even more to do! I retired as Head of English at Cockermouth School in 1979 – before it went completely comprehensive, thank goodness. We now live in Keswick and I'm very active in Keswick literary life, lecturing and writing. I do remember that you had a flair for expressing yourself, though your essays did verge on the colloquial. However, I don't remember saying you would get into Oxford. Could you alter that? A happy thought, none the less.

The reason I am writing to you direct, and not to your London lawyer, Mr Cross, as instructed, is to say that I would like to see the completed book. I am not promising, but I should be able to review it for the Keswick *Reminder*. (Very influential in the Keswick area, and in parts of Borrowdale.)

I have got the address of your Venice club from a very good book I recently reviewed, on Football Grounds of Europe, so I hope this reaches you. All old Cockermouthians were horrified by the Drama which befell you. There has not been much about it recently, not in the Keswick *Reminder* anyway, so I hope you have recovered from your dreadful experience.

Yours aye,
GEORGE BOTT

21

About a mile from the San Siro stadium all the roads were completely blocked, despite the efforts of the police car and police motor bikes guiding our coach. All seventy thousand supporters going to the match in 1991 seemed to be travelling by car, each with his horn wailing.

We came to a halt and hundreds of AC Milan supporters banged on our windows, screaming and spitting. They were the ultras, the more fanatical Italian hooligans, who usually made a special effort to barrack me, being a foreigner and captain. English teams were still banned from Europe, because of the hooligans, but what was happening on the terraces in Italy was far worse and far nastier than anything I'd seen in England.

Nobody on our coach gave any sign that we could see the ultras. Footballers the world over know when to turn the other cheek, as long as you are safe inside. Gino, who was sitting behind me, said that when he played here once, for Juventus against Inter Milan – who share the San Siro stadium with AC Milan – they had to be locked in the dressing room for two hours after the match, for their own safety. And they'd been beaten, one–nil. Think what would have happened if they'd won.

From a distance, the San Siro looked a bit like a concrete and glass Coliseum. Oh yes, I know what that looks like. After a season in Italy, I'd been to all the major cities, and made a point of visiting all the major sites. For my own sake, and also to impress Madame Largo. As we got nearer the stadium, I could see thousands of supporters marching up the outside staircases, up and up and round and up, like ants on a treadmill, carrying their red and black banners and flags, screaming and chanting. Building work was almost completed, ready for the World Cup, but they'd organised it so the capacity had hardly been affected. I remember at Spurs, when the West Stand was being built, it was like playing in a morgue for most of one season.

Ah, the World Cup. That was really, deep down, why I'd come. I reckoned it was bound to improve my chances of staying in the England team, knowing all about Italy. If only as interpreter to the England team. Joke. But I was getting pretty fluent. Thanks to Tom's teaching, and my own endeavours. You don't have to understand the grammar, but you do have to make an effort, keep trying, bashing on regardless, and people will always respond. It helps if the other person is intelligent, and knows what you must be trying to say. It also helps if you are famous, and people want to listen to what you're trying to say.

It's noticeable that the footballers who didn't learn the language, like Jimmy Greaves, Ian Rush and Luther Blisset, did poorly in Italy. Or did one cause the other? Hmm. I'll ask Lovely Largo that one. While people like Liam Brady, Trevor Francis, Ray Wilkins learned the language and played well. On the whole though, British players have not really succeeded in Italy, none of them becoming mega, not since John Charles, and I don't want to hear about him again, thank you very much. Three Italian championships, two Italian cups, a hundred goals, *grazie*, I know, I get reminded of that, everywhere I go. It depressed me at first, then I took it as a compliment. It showed how well I was succeeding. Every Italian commentator expected me not just to be in the England team but to be the player Italy should fear most, because of what I was achieving at Venice.

We had the element of surprise, coming from Serie B and having three foreign players in the team, new to Italy. We had the element of excitement, carried on by the impetus of the previous season. And we had me, a true Brit, combining Italian skills with British determination.

I remember before our first league match, away to Genoa, whom we should not have feared, as they too had recently come up from Serie B, the lads on the coach talking about 'hoping for a result', the usual football cliché. Then it came out they were hoping for a draw.

I practically screamed at them. I couldn't speak much Italian, so Tom had to translate, but I screamed all the same. What an attitude. What defeatism.

I explained that in England, no team went into a match hoping for a draw. Afterwards, well, you might be satisfied with it, but beforehand, even playing Liverpool away, you went on the field convinced you could win, determined to thump them. They all laughed, saying that was cheap psychology, empty bravado. I said no, it was genuine. When that whistle blew, you rolled up your sleeves and said get stuck in lads, this is our day, we're gonna show the fuckers. That's the English attitude. Never mind the skills, just count the spirit.

So that was the first thing I did – encourage the whole team to believe we would win every game, inspiring them by my confidence, leading by example. The result of this was that we gave away a lot of goals, and we did get stuffed a few times, in those early games, which led to words with Roco. Well, silence more than words. All he did was smoke more furiously and look at me sadly afterwards, with his baggy eyes, his lank greasy hair, shaking his head. I'd gone through life with managers and coaches who were screamers and shouters, so it was strange to have someone who said nothing, bottling it all up. I'd have preferred a bollocking. It gives you something to react against. With silence, you go silent, and get more depressed.

But we kept on scoring goals, thanks to me urging the midfield forward all the time. Roco tightened up at the back. He was brilliant as a coach, working one to one, for ever whispering in ears, gently cajoling and encouraging, devising simple plans for almost every situation, especially dead balls, without confusing everyone, which is what usually happens with so-called master tacticians. He bought Jovi from the Cameroon, a country no one had heard of at the time, but he'd done well for Bordeaux in the French league. We thought he was a midget when he first arrived, so small and fragile looking, but he moved forward like a dart, and could get back just as quickly. He roomed with Hans, twice his size, who became his best friend. In turn, his form was transformed. We still gave away a lot of goals, a lot in Italian terms, but we began to win by scoring a lot more, winning matches 3-2 and even 4-3 which was unheard of.

We were now level on points with AC Milan, but needed to beat them to win the League. I felt they would be more scared of us, playing at home. And I knew they would be out to needle me, spitting and shirt-tugging from the beginning, threatening and intimidating. That was when being English was a help. Most of the intimidations meant nothing, as I didn't understand their regional accents.

Many of the best Italian players come from Lombardy, just as so many English players come from the Northeast, and have their own regional accent, but in Italy, all regional accents are stronger than in England, and even to Italians they can sound like a foreign language. So Tom says. He's the know-all.

'Fucking hell, look at that lot,' I said, pointing to a huge banner just outside the stadium. 'Can you read what it says?'

Tom was sitting beside me, making notes. It was his first visit to the San Siro and he'd been commissioned to write an article about it for the *Independent*. He'd just given up teaching at the language school and was now working full-time for me. Not just as my tutor, but my secretary, helper and drinking companion, especially drinking companion. No chance of having one of those in Italy. Eating companion, yes. Druggy companion, easy. Whoring companion, definitely. But someone to go out and get pissed with, who would protect me from the press, the public and the police, was a definite advantage. Tom has a socio-cultural explanation as to why Italians don't go boozing. They're scared of getting their clothes dirty.

Tom also had another function to fulfil, now he'd joined my fulltime staff, but he hadn't quite become aware of it. I was going to tell him when he moved his stuff into my place.

He'd been allowed on the team coach, and in the dressing room, from the beginning of the season, officially to translate for me. That wasn't necessary any more, as I could manage most situations, but he had stayed on as my friend. I could demand and be given anything, as long as I was the star of a successful team. I could probably have got Tom in the side if I'd wanted. I quite fancied that, just to be one up on Maradona. His brother had arrived in the Naples team.

'Which banner?' asked Tom.

The big one I'd spotted was now being waved in the other direction so I couldn't quite make out all the words. It had my name and '*Figlio di Putana*'.

'It means your mother was a whore,' said Tom. 'Not very rude

223

really. You should see what it's like when they play Naples. They range from "Welcome to Civilisation" to "What Hitler did to the Jews should be done to all Neapolitans".'

I thought about my mother. Was that why I fancied Linda, as a substitute mother? I did seem to go for the older woman, such as Karin and Sonia. When it was a matter of a one-night stand, then any age would do, though under seventeen was my first preference.

'There's the Motor Head Boys,' said Tom, pointing to another banner as we entered the stadium. 'And that looks like the Red Bad Devils and the Panzer Korps. No sign of the Crazy Skins tonight. They're my favourite.'

He was compiling a list of Italian football gangs who had taken English names, usually with the words slightly wrong, or out of date. He was also noting how many Italian fans were wearing British football shirts, such as Liverpool or Celtic, for their fame, or Aston Villa, for their pretty colours. That would give him another five hundred words for the *Independent*.

It's funny how I seem to have such a good effect on my friends. I not only make them famous and more successful, I help them change careers. Arnold was now a regular Radio 4 presenter, with his own interview programme – 'Cross-Examine'. Tom was becoming a journalist. Now what could I do for Linda? Hmm. We shall see.

I went out on to the pitch to inspect it with some of the lads, and immediately ducked for cover. I'd got used to the firecrackers and smoke bombs since I arrived in Italy, but this was like gunfire. I was sure they were lobbing real explosives over the wire fences. I stood for a while, smiling, trying to look unperturbed, watching the flags. I love the sight of them. They are like sails unfurling, so huge they could cover a small village.

In England, the singing and the chanting is better, funnier and louder, in fact you hear the English chants now being copied all round Europe, such as Here We Go, but in Italy, the overall spectacle is greater, more magnificent, with those colours and sounds. I can hear and see and smell them now, as I sit here, wishing I was there.

There was talk in the dressing room about all the famous managers who had turned up from overseas teams, and from other Italian clubs. I heard someone say Graeme Souness was there, carrying a large chequebook, hoping to tempt back an exile. Now who could that be?

I was last to strip off, as usual, and I spent a long time being massaged, which did little good, but I liked the attention and sense of well-being. It wasn't the sort of muscle pain which responded to massage, or to heat or ultrasonic treatment. It was a pain I'd had for some weeks, which came and went, but never really moved away. I asked the doc for a painkiller, which he immediately gave, and at once I felt better.

I caught Tom making a face at me. He thought I should avoid the painkillers, maintaining I was storing up problems for the future. Bugger the future, I said. My future is going to be arthritic, I know that, I'll be a bloody cripple by the time I'm forty, unable to walk, wank, lift a pint to my face, no need to tell me squire, that's the future all footballers have to look forward to. It's the present I want treated, not the future.

Tom believed I should rest for a couple of weeks, which was mad, how could I, when we were so near the title, or see a specialist and have it properly diagnosed, but I couldn't face being told some depressing news. I knew the pain was deep, probably inside the groin, a dull, leaden, heavy sort of ache. Age, probably, that was all. I could live with the problems of age, as we all have to, with the help of the painkillers.

In a way, modern treatment is all cosmetic, aimed at hiding and disguising, preparing you for the public, making you presentable in the quickest possible time. Or like battery farming. Footballers are the Christmas turkeys, fattened and fittened up, ready for the opening of the festive season, which just happens to come round once a week, not once a year. Lucky turkeys.

But the human body can't be cheated, and gets its own back eventually. With turkeys, it's the taste which goes. With footballers, it's longevity. I think modern training methods, pounding you into the ground, and medical methods, picking you up again when you're not ready, will reduce not prolong a playing career. I predict that in the future all footballers will retire at twenty-seven.

If they've had any success at all, they'll have a million quidlets in the bank, which is good, but they'll be physically and mentally knackered, which is bad, too incapable of spending their loot. Some will retire even earlier, like Bjorn Borg, then they'll regret it, feeling lost and stranded, with no reason for living or being. Luckily, all footballers die young.

Why am I going on like this? When I've got this big match to tell you about? Christ knows. Because I'm now twenty-seven and fear my football career could soon be over? Or being stuck in this place, fearing *everything* is now over?

So back to the San Siro dressing room, with its blue tiles half-way up the walls, long and rectangular, like a municipal indoor swimming pool, and there's Roco, going round, whispering sweet fuck-all in every deaf ear. You never listen at that stage, just as you can't hear anything from the touchline, however hard they shout. I was more bothered about lav paper. They'd run out. Imagine, state-of-the-art stadium, and you can't even have a crap in comfort. So much for Italian efficiency.

As it happens, Roco had something useful to say before that match. It now comes back to me. Are you concentrating?

He and the ten million scouts had been watching AC Milan for yonks and decided that their back four, who were working without a sweeper, were over-trained, over-drilled, over-disciplined. They man-marked, as most Italian teams did that season, and did it brilliantly, hence the few goals against, but they could be upset.

Roco told me and Gino, who shared most corners with me, to knock them over to the far post, as per normal, for the first twenty minutes, so that the Milan defenders would fall into their normal positions for corners. Then to switch to short corners. You can work out the theory for yourself, you're clever, having read this far you must be. I feel rather tired this evening. God, I hope they haven't drugged me.

The noise and tumult was incredible when we came out on to the pitch, guns and fireworks, artillery and mortar, joy and ecstasy. That was Milan. I think our supporters were hiding, suffocating under their puny banners, hidden by their modest flags. The stadium was awash with red and black. It was like D-Day, or what my Dad said D-Day was like, a mammoth Victory parade, only the battle had not even begun.

We got a goal in the seventh minute, can you think of a better time, okay then one minute before half time, but the thing about the seventh minute is that the opposition feel they have found their feet, think they are into their game. A first-minute goal is a fluke, and good teams know this and ignore it. But a seventh-minute goal is usually worked for, and knocks the confidence out of the other side.

It was one of our typical moves, prepared in training, which they should have been ready for, if they'd done their scouting, or perhaps they had been too arrogant and ignored their scouting reports. I set Jovi away on an overlap from deep in our half, the sort of run he loved, which looked suicidal in the Italian league, where fullbacks rarely go on mad solo runs. But against a man-marking system no one is quite sure who should be taking out a fullback who suddenly appears on the edge of your penalty area. Jovi kept going, almost unimpeded, to their goal-line, then he pulled the ball back for me to shoot, storming in on the run. I hit the sort of ball that could have gone anywhere, out of the stadium, out of the planet, or into the net. It didn't reach the net but hit the bar, making it shake for about three minutes, then rebounded apparently harmlessly into space. Usually, after such a run, Jovi gets back, whatever happens, but this time he had waited – and the ball trickled out to him while their defence stood mesmerised, still wondering how the bar had survived. He gave it even more welly, and this time in it flew. Yes, I call that a planned goal, though it should have been me who had scored, according to the best-laid plans on Roco's drawing board.

There was silence at half-time. We were one–nil up, but we knew it meant nothing. My groin was beginning to ache slightly, so I had another injection.

They scored in the seventh minute of the second half. Jammy, of course, as goals against you always are. You can always point to what went wrong from your point of view. It was Jovi at fault this time. He passed back to Hans, it missed him, God knows how, hit the post, and went in off their centre-forward, who naturally claimed it as a brilliant reflex goal. Perhaps it was.

It became a game of two, not halves, ha ha, you thought you knew what was coming, but two corners. Amazing, really, that we got so few. I can't remember any in the first half, but the minute we got one in the second we started taking short corners, as instructed. The first one immediately confused them. Our second came with only ten minutes to go, out on the left, so I took it.

I passed it short, back no more than five metres, to Gino, who had come in close, for another short corner. Crowds hate short corners, they think you are pissing around. Even in Italy, they prefer a high ball and a bit of quick excitement in the goal-mouth.

The short-corner theory depends on them having to send a defender out, which means one less in the penalty area. You are two against one, so you can always keep the ball. At this moment, Jovi came up, making three against one, so they sent out another attacker to help the one already there. Now what does the defence do? That is always the big weakness in a man-to-man marking system. Unless they have planned for every eventuality, and have one or two players who are supposed to mark zonally at set pieces, there is a moment of hesitation while they readjust, deciding who will mark whom. It doesn't necessarily let you in, but for a moment it unhinges them, making them vulnerable.

Jovi then shoved the ball square to me and I lined up as if to belt it, as I'd done earlier, but instead I dashed through, elbows flying. You guessed it, but they didn't. Two players went for me at once in their confusion and I was brought down. The crowd went hysterical. No argument. Clear penalty. I didn't even have to writhe in agony or put on the usual Italian theatricals.

Now, this is the bit you can't guess, unless you were there. I wasn't worried by the pandemonium as I lined up to take the penalty. I knew that by making it 2–1 we must win, with only a few minutes to go, and would take the Italian league, which would be incredible, for a team just promoted.

I went forward slowly, deliberately, taking my time, knowing exactly where I was going to put it. With my left foot, of course, mid-height, hard into the right-hand corner. No problem.

I reached the ball, God I can hardly believe it now – and fell over. The ball trickled harmlessly wide. Now this is even more amazing. As I lay on the ground, already seeing the action replays in my head, all in endless slow motion, my first reaction was to laugh. It's only a game, I was saying to myself, and a funny old game.

I managed to wipe the smile from the inside and banged the ground with my fists, as one does. I got up slowly and kicked the turf, then bent over, clutching my head in my hands, the usual sick-as-a-parrot stuff. The crowd were silent at first, unbelieving, thinking they had missed something, that the ref would make the penalty be taken again, there must have been some infringement. Then they exploded.

It was my groin, a sudden darting pain which distracted me, but I did not admit it at the time, even to myself. The press asked if it was the turf, had I hit a divot, and I said possibly, or it might have been cramp. I took the blame anyway, saying it was stupid of me to have taken the penalty when I was feeling knackered. It was all my fault.

Milan won the title, on goal difference, and the celebrations went on for weeks – but I was the hero. Now that *is* funny. Their crowd loved me, said I was by far the best player, I deserved my penalty, which I had won, and I should have scored, and it would have served their own team right. Our club got the satisfaction of having done so well, in their first time in the top division, and considered the moral victory was theirs.

After the match, two things happened. I became the most desired player in Italy, which of course means the world as we know it, folks. So I was over the *luna*. Secondly, the cramp did not go away. I had to face the inevitable. I went in for a groin operation. And missed the World Cup. Sick, you must be choking. It was the worst thing that ever happened to me. Until now.

Manager
GRAEME SOUNESS

Chief Executive/General Secretary
PETER ROBINSON

LIVERPOOL
FOOTBALL CLUB
& ATHLETIC GROUNDS plc
Company Registration Number 35668, England

ANFIELD ROAD, LIVERPOOL L4 0TH.

Dear Joe,

Yes, I was interested in you, as I'm interested in all good players, so it was a shame we never got the pennies right. You did play well that evening, considering. If you ever change your mind, let me know now. We might find a place for you at Liverpool. But not taking penalties.

Best wishes
Yours sincerely

GRAEME SOUNESS

22

So now I'm here, wherever here is. To get here, to the beginning of here, to put you in the picture, herewise, I'll have to go back two months, when I was coming back from an England game early in 1992.

The World Cup was long since over and we were getting towards the end of another Italian season. The stars of the World Cup had been dropped or lost form, like Schillaci, or were injured and out of the headlines, like Gazza. I was still doing the business, showing that Venice were not one-season wonders, up amongst the leaders all season, and I was soon back in the England team. How could Graham Taylor, working towards the European nations finals, not pick me?

It was for a friendly, yawn yawn, but it was against Northern Ireland, kick kick, the same game we have been playing since the beginning of time, thump thump, kicking ass, taking bodies, leaving the dead to look after themselves, the usual stuff, the usual stiffs.

Some people didn't expect me to turn up. Not after the news which had broken the day before. My head would be quote too big to get through the security gate at Heathrow, unquote, said the *Sun*. A potty little friendly will be beneath me, assumed the *Mirror*. A spot of diplomatic flu would seem imminent, opined the *Times*. Look out for a recurrence of his groin strain which he might need to rest at the end of the season, suggested the *Independent*, working on information from a normally reliable source, well done, Tom, that must mean fifty pee in the post for the tip-off.

My favourite pre-match comment was in the *Mail*. They too agreed

I would not turn up, but for a very simple reason: what had I now got to prove. Ah, how true, how very true.

Could Graham Taylor not pick me, after Juventus had announced they were paying ten million for me, repeat, ten million quid, the biggest sum ever paid for a bloke who kicks a football around for a living? Not to mention European Footballer of the Year and heartthrob of two nations. Yup. And I have letters to prove it, mostly proposing marriage, or similar.

We won the Italian Cup, as you know, which doesn't mean as much as it does in England, but we were also lying second in the league. Arnold had opened a branch office in Italy to deal with the media attention and the commercial offers. There was one amazing offer from the Gulf, once the war was over, from a sheik who wanted me to fly out in his private jet, play football for half an hour on his lawn with his kids, then fly back again. He would get out of it a private video, for home consumption only, Arnold stipulated that, and I would get one million quid. Nah, I said, rather stay in bed on my day off.

Then Arnold let it out that my contract with Venice was for two years only. It was now almost up. Well, chaos, pandemonium, and for three days I went into hiding.

Juventus and Torino enquired first, followed by five other Italian clubs, then came Marseilles, Real Madrid and Barcelona. Not far behind, in speed, if not in money, were Tranmere Rovers and Blackburn Rovers, with Carlisle United limping along in the rear. Cheeky sods. They thought that at the age of twenty-seven I might fancy returning to my roots in the North. On your bikes.

There was a week of messing around, rumours and lies, reports and denials. I told Arnold to say first to ten million and I'm yours. Let's not fuck around, I ain't got time to haggle, show us the colour of your dosh. It was then done in five days. Juventus agreed to ten million, the biggest transfer fee in the history of football. The timing was pretty smart, part Arnold, part luck, part injuries or loss of form by other star players. Juventus, champions twenty-two times, were getting desperate. They were out of Europe for the first time in twenty-eight years, and decided a Brit could be their savour once again. So watch it, John Charles.

I'm sworn to secrecy on how it gets paid, to whom and when, and what my sweetener has been, and my salary and private share options, not to mention my bonuses depending on our gates, position in the league, matches televised and number of ice-creams sold by half-time. Arnold thought of everything that might happen. Except this.

I turned up for the Northern Ireland game because I wanted to. I like playing at Wembley. I also wanted to get away from Italy for a few days, once the deal had been signed and sealed. Life in Venice was not too, let us say, jolly, not a load of larfs any more. The club had made an absolute fortune on me, and Marinello was well chuffed, far more than I expected. He had been willing to take five million from Ascoli, of all places, who were first to put up real money, trying to keep up with boring old Bari. Then Udinese said six million, trying to show they were as flush as Lazio. They soon disappeared when the big boys began to talk turkey.

I also needed to be in London to sign some legal papers as the new squire of a rather large, rather choice shooting and hunting and fishing estate in Cumbria, don't you know. I'd bought Rigg Hall, formerly a stately hall, now a disused borstal, soon to be a health spa and leisure complex, the most luxurious, best-equipped in all Britain, look out for mega-announcements. I own the site freehold, isn't that sweet. (There's a clue as to how I paid for it.) I've already gone into partnership with the people who will develop and equip it, on the understanding that Joseph Swift, Senior, will be Consultant Manager, for his lifetime, or longer. Oh yes, and I also bought a house for Fanny and for Colin. What a good lad.

I had to meet the health spa people in London, so it all worked in very nicely, very sweetly, especially as Marinello said he would come to the match too, in his private jet, that was the good news, to save me from the media, till Tickles said she would come as well, which was bad news. Luckily, Tom came with me. Tickles was his business.

Keeping her at bay was part of his job. Oh yes, sorry son, did I forget to tell you? I can't tell her to fuck off, can I Tom, she's the boss's wife, so it's up to you to distract her, how do I know, do anything, tell her any old lies, I'm a poofter, I'm secretly married, I'm impotent, and if all else fails, fuck her yourself, look, you've got a bloody big salary. Now get in that bedroom and earn it.

Linda had been complaining about the awful Tickles, but I said it was all in Tickles's half-witted mind, she must know what it's like in my position, dopy women throwing themselves at you all the time, so what do you expect dopy blokes to do but take advantage. Linda hates those sort of conversations. She doesn't seem to believe them. You'd think she was my bloody mother.

After the match, a boring draw, we went by helicopter from Wembley, which was well smart, sorry, I'm probably two years behind with well smart language, straight to Heathrow and into Marinello's jet, that's the way to do it, folks. If I wasn't so poor, I'd have my own private plane. Linda hates these sort of conversations. She was on the plane as well, one of my personal guests, but she didn't see the match, going shopping instead, I dunno, so much for moral support.

I gave England a wave as we left, wondering when I'd be back next, trying to work out what things I missed. Fresh milk, yeh, and the bread. English newspapers, only some. English telly, only the comedies, the sport is much better in Italy and there's much more of it, from all over Europe. Chocolate digestives, certainly, but I have them sent. Eggs and bacon for breakfast, marmalade, steak and kidney pie, yes all losses, but I'm coping. Ice-cream vans, I could do with more of them. Sarcasm, I miss that. So hard to use it in a foreign language.

I flopped on to a couch that had been provided for me and ordered a bottle of Fleurie, but there was only champagne on board, what a rubbish plane, but a useful one all the same.

'Yes, I think I'll have one of these,' I said, as I sat drinking champagne somewhere over the Alps. Marinello was on his phone, ringing the world, spending some of the millions he'd made out of me. Tickles was on her exercise bike. Tom was reading some new novel, set in Cumbria, about some lass called Christabel. 'Bagsy after you,' I said to him. 'Is it by Jilly Cooper? I really fancy her.' He looked up and smiled.

There was also a couple of Italian journalists, tame hacks who normally follow me around but know their place, which is to keep well out of the way, speak when spoken to, and one word out of order and bingo, no more free trips.

'Are you listening, cloff ears?' I said.

Linda was also reading, at least turning the pages of a pile of English and American fashion magazines she'd just bought in London.

'I am trying to read,' she said. 'I thought you were resting.'

I was flat out on a couch, nursing my wounds, oh just the usual ones, both legs black and blue, ankles bleeding, minor stuff which you pick up in every match, but I was worried about the dull groin ache, which had returned, luckily not while the Juventus medical was being done.

'I am going to buy my own plane,' I said. 'What do you think?'

'Lovely,' she said, going back to her magazines. 'Just don't do it in purple.'

That was Tickles's handiwork. She decided the interior decor of Marinello's plane should be done in the club's colour, which is a royal shade of purple, not too bad on a shirt, but hideoso in a confined space. Even her exercise bike was purple. *And* her veins. Why did she do it? Did she think we all got off at the sight of the wrinkled cheeks on her wrinkled bum, crinkling and creaking up and down? No wonder Tom was so deep in his book. No wonder Marinello lives on the phone.

'Or perhaps I'll have to make do with a helicopter,' I sighed. 'As I'm so poor.'

'How can you make such disgusting remarks when you're earning a million a year?' said Linda, throwing down her book. 'I know you do it just to annoy, but you're doing it more often since that ridiculous ten million contract.'

'It isn't ridiculous,' I said. 'It was cheap.'

'Oh, shut up,' she said, throwing a magazine at me.

'That hurt,' I said. 'You don't want me out of action, do you?'

She ignored that. I liked her when she got angry with me. I never seemed to have arguments with people any more, not with people I knew. They all kept in with me. Strangers, yes, there's always some loony who wants to pick a fight, who decides he hates you, who is twisted and jealous. That's why famous people stick with famous people. They understand what it's like.

'There are people dying in the streets of Yugoslavia, starving in Africa, and you go on and on about your gross salary being too small. It's obscene.'

'Have you got *Forbes* magazine there?' I asked, knowing she hadn't.

'You're so greedy as well, just like all rich people. It's take take take, and you feel cheated if you don't get enough. Call yourself a socialist. What shit.'

'If you look in *Forbes* magazine you'll see a list of the ten richest sports stars in the world. Guess how many footballers are in the top ten.'

'I don't know and I don't care.'

'Come on, then. Which sports people do best? I think it's jolly interesting. Tom, can you guess?'

'Darts players,' said Tom, without looking up.

'Piss off,' I said. 'Right I'll tell you, as you're all rotten and won't play. *There is not one footballer in the top ten.*'

I looked around. Tom and Linda were both pretending to read again, but I knew I'd got their attention. I could also tell that Marinello had one of his fat ears cocked in my direction.

'Two boxers are top, one you've probably not even heard of – Evander Holyfield, who earned £35 million last year. Mike Tyson was second, on a measly £17 million. Then comes a basketball player whose name I've forgotten on £9 million, followed by another boxer, George Foreman, on £8 million. Then we've got the motor-racing drivers, such as Ayrton Senna on £7 million and Alain Prost on £6 million, plus Nigel Mansell, who's ninth on the list, and the only Brit, on just over £5 million. There's also two golfers, Arnold Palmer on £6 million and Jack Nicklaus who's last with only £5 million. Not one bloody footballer anywhere near that lot.'

'My heart bleeds,' said Linda.

'So it should,' I said. 'Footballers are getting bloody short-changed, if you ask me. We're the world's number one spectator sport. How many watch us compared with a boxing match, or a basketball game, eh, answer me that? We're getting conned.'

'It is irrelevant, people getting more than you,' said Linda. 'And disgusting. Rich people are so greedy, always complaining that someone somewhere is getting more. So what?'

'So we have to put up with endless shit in the press, especially the crappy British press, saying we are overpaid selfish greedy bastards. I'm pig sick of all that. Look at the stick I've had from the London tabloids in the last week. You'd have thought they'd be proud of me, being the world's most expensive footballer, but are they buggery.'

'I'm proud of you, darling,' said Tickles, pausing for breath.

'The comparisons are not valid,' said Tom, quietly. 'You are playing in a team sport, unlike all those other sportsmen.'

'What about the basketball player?' I said.

'Okay, but nine out of the ten are solo performers – the four boxers, three racing drivers and the two golfers. They are on their own, keeping their own money. That's the first point. Secondly, they happen to be in sports where there are individual prize purses for every event, which isn't the same as in football where people are on salaries.'

Trust Tom to be logical, and not emotional like Linda. He'd also memorised the list I'd given him, which had taken me hours to remember, knowing I'd use it some time with Linda.

'Yes, but the top people in football should now be making the same as the top people in other sports,' I said. 'Football is getting the sort of commercial deals which tennis and motor-racing has always had. I think the sponsors are getting us cheap, when you think what they get out it, and we're being ripped off by the TV companies who show our games to millions at a cost of bugger-all. Gawd knows where it all goes, though I have my suspicions . . .'

I nodded meaningfully in the direction of Marinello.

'Don't looka at me,' he said, puffing at his cigar, and dialling another number. 'I'm skin broke.'

'God I hate conversations like this,' said Linda. 'It really does sicken me when rich people moan about money.'

'And I hate this shit,' I said, pouring myself out some more champagne, which of course I hate, but I had to drink something, hadn't I, post-match, you always need something, it's what playing is all about, etc, though at least I was lying down, taking the weight off my wallet.

Linda also hates me saying I hate things, then accepting them – whether champagne, presents or girls. She maintains it proves I have no standards, that it diminishes any good tastes, any fine experiences, I might have. I say on the contrary. I appreciate the fine things when they come along, having sampled the rubbish. Oh, we have this sort of philosophical chat all the time, don't you worry. But I could sense this time she was annoyed with me.

It never struck me of course that our conversation about money would turn out to be both relevant and obscene.

At Venice airport Linda got a taxi to her school while the Marinellos were picked up by their chauffeur. Tom was going back to the Palazzo, on his own, to pack up our stuff for the move to Turin. I'd decided to stay somewhere else, for my last few nights in Venice. Too many people now knew where I was living. Too much aggravation. Too many threatening letters from lunatics.

I was getting a boat to a secret destination, okay, I might as well tell you, it doesn't matter now. Tom had booked a suite at the Cipriani, and was to join me later that night. Their private boat was waiting to take me all the way there, the best way to arrive in Venice, don't miss it if you ever have the choice, if you are ever unlucky enough to be rich.

There was a gang of photographers and reporters waiting at the airport, but not as many as I'd feared. I'd had the worst of it the week before when the contract was signed. I went into a V.I.P. lounge and gave them fifteen minutes, the usual crap, then said that's it, I'm knackered, give us a break lads, I've got to rest, I've had a brutal game, I'm exhausted, you lot are more terrifying than the I.R.A. What a stupid remark, I don't know why I said it. Thinking of the Irish match, I suppose.

When they'd all gone, I went to find my boat. Tom was still with me to see me off, as he knew the Cipriani departure point and what their uniformed lackeys looked like.

As I came through the arrivals hall, I could see a bloke waving at me from one of the telephone booths, so I waved back, but kept walking. I didn't want to talk to any fans.

'Meester Sweeft, Meester Sweeft,' a voice called after me. 'My leetle girl is hospital. Please, you speak to her, no?'

I looked round. He was a grey-haired, middle-aged bloke in a blue denim shirt and baggy trousers, a bit old to have a little girl, so I remember thinking. He had his hand over the phone and had stepped out to call after me, imploring me, one hand fingering a cross round his neck.

It often happens. People on the phone to their girlfriends suddenly see me and say, heh, you won't believe this, but Joe Swift has just passed me, oh yeh, the girlfriend says, I don't believe you. It used to amuse me in Germany to blurt out a few words in German. Now it was just a bore. Italians had become increasingly rude and aggressive, as if it was my duty to speak to their stupid girlfriends. But this bloke looked nice, polite, and his little girl was ill.

So I went back, stepped inside the phone booth, took the phone from him. And that's the last thing I remember.

H.M. Prison, Pentonville

Dear Joe, you old wanker, welcome to the gang. I hope this finds you as it leaves me, now you know what it feels like, har har, but at least I can watch telly and smoke a few joints, if I had the money, which is why I'm writing to you. I'm told you are writing a book and if I'm in it, I'll want paid right, no messing. I know you can't send anything at present but tell your lawyer fucker, who I'm still suing for loss of trade, that unless I get ten grand at once, I'm coming to sort you out, when I get out of here, when you get out of there, okay.

Yours
DEZ

23

I woke up in darkness, feeling terrible. I often wake up and think, where am I, whose bed is this, how did I get here, which hotel is it, what was I drinking, have we got a match today, what day is it, I know, I'll just go back to sleep. Then it turns out to be my own bed. But I never had a headache like that one, even after a night on the piss-awful Italian beer. I felt I had no body, no flesh and bones, only a very battered, very small brain-cell.

I lay for a while, doing nothing, thinking nothing, then slowly I forced my eyes to focus properly. It wasn't dark. There was a blanket over my head. Then I made my fingers investigate my surroundings. I was lying on a sort of stretcher. Had I been injured, carried off the pitch, like that Wembley game against Romania. Perhaps I was concussed, no, the only time I've been concussed, seriously concussed, was when I was knocked out cold in a reserve match at Spurs after I collided with the West Ham goalie and I ended up in hospital with two of his front teeth buried in my knee. That time I didn't know I was concussed. You don't, till it's over.

I was in some sort of van or lorry, rattling along a country track, what the fuck was going on? Even Cockermouth School's minibus wasn't as bad as this. I pulled down part of the blanket, enough to let me see over the edges. It was an ambulance. So I was injured. There were two blokes in white coats sitting beside me, each carrying a gun. Hold on. Ambulancemen don't carry guns, not even in Italy.

One of them realised I was awake. He leaned over me, stuck the gun in my ribs, and said, keep quiet, you, or else, speaking in English, with a heavy accent, then he gave me a kick and pulled the blanket back over my head. I must have fallen asleep again.

Next time I woke I was in a cell with my head shaved and wearing a long, dark brown robe. I could hear church bells outside and then people singing. Well that's it, then, I thought. I'm in heaven.

Those first few days were the worst. The bastard who kicked me kept on kicking me, every hour, when he came into my cell, just to warn me in case I made any noise, shouted out, gave any trouble or tried to escape.

I never thought of escaping. There had obviously been some mistake which would be cleared up very soon. That's what I thought, in my fuddled state – the drugs were still making me dopy. There must have been some on that phone when the bloke handed it to me, a chloroform pad or something. Then when I collapsed the 'ambulancemen' appeared and took me away. What the hell was Tom doing, letting them get away with it?

I measured my cell, six feet by seven feet eight inches, measuring it with my body, which is five foot nine at the last count. Locked up in a cell, there wasn't a lot else to do, not for that first week. Perhaps I'll have a recount, see if I've shrunk, or the cell has grown.

I have a wooden bed, mattress, one rough blanket, a mat beside it over a lino floor, a radiator, a small plywood desk, a bible and a sink which stinks as if the previous occupants had all been pissing in it, which of course I've been doing, though I have a slop pail which I'm supposed to use.

There's one window, high up, impossible to see out of. Above my bed, on the whitewashed stone wall, is a cheap and nasty plastic statue of Christ on the cross. On the inside of the wooden door, which faces me as I lie on my bed, is a list of events, starting at 4.30 with *matines*, whatever they are, then *messe*, which sounds awful, *sexte* which sounds good, *none* which sounds boring. The day ends at 20h 30 with *complin*. I always thought complin was breakfast pap for old folks and invalids, so at first I thought it was mealtimes, not religious services. Till the bloody bells started.

Food is brought in either by the bastard or the other bloke, who is nicer, three times a day, all horrible. A bowl of coffee in the morning, with stale bread floating in it. Soup at lunchtime. Shitty rissoles in the evening. It's improved a bit recently, and I sometimes get fruit. Strangely enough, they've always brought wine with supper. As monasteries go, I suppose that makes it luxurious.

It took me three days to work out it was some sort of monastery, listening to the monks shuffling on the gravel outside, the older ones coughing and spluttering, but never talking. I hear their feet going up some steps into the chapel next door, then the same old singing and chanting, seven times a day, at the same time, all male voices, some of them very croaky and feeble. I thought it was Italian at first, or French, now I realise it must be Latin.

I'm in some sort of guest wing, which the monks, if they *are* monks, never use, and never enter. The bastard, who is dressed like a monk, but clearly isn't, lives in some sort of office two doors down the corridor, because I can hear him opening his door when he comes to visit me. I think the nice guy could be on the other side.

On the fourth day here I was trying to stand on the radiator, to see out of the window, when I heard this rattling noise coming from the pipes. The radiator wasn't on, but it's obviously connected to some central heating system. In the winter it must get very cold, which makes me think we are high up, in some hilly region.

'Dan Dan, Dan-Dan-Dan, Dan-Dan-DAN DAN!'

That was the radiator talking, or at least sending out signals. It took me a while to work out the rhythm. When it was repeated again, I banged on my radiator and whispered loudly against the wall, just one word.

'*Inga-land!*'

Okay, they make it into two words when the lads on the terraces shout it out. From the other side of the wall, I could hear the same whisper. I smiled at once. Tom had been taken as well.

I met him two days later, when I was suddenly taken out of the cell for the first time, early in the morning, and allowed to exercise in an internal courtyard. The singing from the chapel was very loud, indicating that all the monks were inside.

The bastard guarded us, letting us see he had his gun under his robe, warning us not to talk to each other or make any noise. We didn't talk the first day, but after that we were allowed to have a cold shower in an outside lavatory, and with the water running and the pipes vibrating, we have managed to talk every day.

Tom's cell is next to the office, and he told me he could hear the occasional whine and bleeb bleeb of a fax machine. Then he heard the bastard talking to the nice guy, in French. Unless they got what they wanted, whatever that was, they would start sending parts of my anatomy through the post. So that's when I knew I'd been kidnapped. Thanks Tom. That really cheered me up.

But who are they? Terrorists, thought Tom at first, Red Brigade extremists, right wing or left wing, who knows, probably demanding political amnesty, or freedom for one of their gang who'd been captured.

Their conversation became more intellectual and Tom then got it into his head they were students. There had been a recent group of French students at his school, learning Italian, who had become activists in the Save Venice movement, you know, from falling into the sea. Perhaps that's all they are, said Tom, just half-witted students, trying to publicise their cause, harmless lads, we'll be out soon. Oh yeh, I said, so why does that bastard keep kicking me?

At last he heard money being mentioned, ten million wanted, or else. That made me think they could be football fans, true ultras, who were trying to raise the same amount I had been sold for in order to keep me in Venice. Bloody stupid, but totally possible, knowing the fanaticism of Italian fans. I've had shopkeepers rushing out into the street shoving shirts into my hand, even offering their daughters, if we've had a good game. A bad defeat, and your car gets set on fire. By your own supporters.

I thought about that argument with Linda, and all the moans I've had over the years about money. And the boasts. I should have kept my big mouth shut about the Juventus transfer fee. And the rest. It caused enough damage in Germany. I've always felt players should reveal their salaries and bonus details, at least to other players. People in the same team rarely know what everyone is getting. It's a trick by the management. They swear you to secrecy, con you into thinking you are on the best deal, so keep it quiet, Joe, don't let the others know, or we'll have to pay you less. I hate all that.

My salary had been all over the papers, not just the transfer fee. I should have denied it. Every half-witted, unbalanced jealous bastard in the whole of Europe must have looked at it and thought, why should he have all that? I know. Let's have him. If he's so valuable, we could make ourselves a fortune.

Who were they trying to get it from, Juventus or Marinello? The deal was complicated, with part payments, some now, some later, some in the post, and I didn't know what stage it had reached, or who would lose most if they kept me locked up for months. Perhaps for ever. I began to worry I'd miss the European finals. England needs me.

During those first two weeks, they were very nervous, arguing with each other, then the bastard would come in and kick me. We decided neither Juventus or Marinello was offering money, that was the problem. They'd stolen a valuable property but no one was willing to buy it back. They might soon be forced to cut off my fingers or toes or goolies.

Then Tom suggested they sent a fax to Arnold, at his home, he knew his number, explaining he was my agent, he would get some ransom money together, he'd want me back safe and sound, it was in his interest. If they didn't include their own fax number, how could anyone trace a single fax message? They were very suspicious, but Tom was sure they were considering it.

One morning he heard them reading aloud from the *Herald Tribune*, that boring American paper you see all over Europe. It was a classified ad, in code, and they were immediately much more relaxed. Arnold had apparently replied and promised them money, on certain conditions, such as our safety, but a million was impossible. They seemed happy to wait. They even let us read the *Herald Tribune* every day, but there were no more messages.

That was when Tom started talking to them properly, in French, saying Arnold was a very eminent lawyer, he wouldn't let them down, he could be trusted, a lawyer's brief was to work only for his client, and anyway he loved Joe too much to want him harmed. Then he asked the nice guy to let him have a pencil and a pad, to send a fax to Arnold, telling him in his own words that we were both fit and well, saying that the money should be paid up at once. Under their supervision, of course. I signed the letter as well. Then they faxed it, swearing Arnold to secrecy, or I'd be killed at once.

Tom was getting on so well with the nice guy that he was allowed to keep the pencil and paper. Tom explained he wanted to keep a diary, which of course they could read, a philosophical diary, recounting his feelings, the sensations about being locked up, the religious impulses he was experiencing, listening to their wonderful music.

He had noticed that it was always the bastard who brought us food during services, and took us for exercise during services, which indicated the nice guy was elsewhere, i.e. in the chapel. He did appear to be more like a real monk, perhaps a lay helper, whose real job it was to run the guest wing. Perhaps they were both religious nuts, who wanted the money for God. Or to save the monastery. It did look very rundown, from what we could see. I climbed a wall once, in the internal courtyard, and saw some dirty old vats, stinking of stale wine, inside a dilapidated warehouse. Tom said they probably had their own winery. That must be their little business, like other monasteries make incense, or soap, or cheeses. It would explain why they had the fax.

We were still waiting for Arnold to do something, so Tom then suggested I should be allowed to write as well. I could do my memoirs. We'd get them to fax Arnold, saying I was working on my life story, at long last, and send a little synopsis. He could hold an auction, get some money up front, and it would help pay our ransom.

I didn't think they would agree. I was sure they would want to use the fax as little as possible, in case it was traced. Tom said they wouldn't be traced, Arnold didn't know their fax number. It was going to him privately at his home and he would pass the manuscript personally to the publisher without saying how he got it. He could be trusted not to inform the police. He knew we were alive and well, that was the main thing. This was Arnold's only hope of getting us out. And don't forget, he stood to make ten per cent of the book. That made them smile. Yes, he's the clever one, old Tom. He didn't get his First for nothing.

Tom offered to help me do the writing and I said get lost. I'll do it my way, etc, it's my story, etc. As you know.

So, I've nearly finished. Taken me two months, working every day, and my fingers are knackered. The chapters have gone out, one by one, to Arnold, by fax. This last one is going this evening, when I finish this bit. Safer than posting, when you think about it, as the postal marks could be a clue.

Arnold says he's got £100,000 for the book. Their demands have come down all the time, and we think they might now accept that, and let us go. If I'd known that in the first place, I could have given them a cheque at the airport and not needed to go through all this.

On the other hand, I've written my book, which Fanny has been on at me to do for years. I've also lost a stone in weight, so that's good. And guess what, my groin is brilliant. Not a twinge for two months. Much better than any mad quack with his modern medicines. I'll be in a better state to turn out for Juventus, if I ever get out of here. I could even make Sweden.

They are now our friends, sort of, though the bastard with the gun is still a bastard, and believes that all capitalist pigs should be destroyed, which means me. Only the nice one is a religious maniac. They are both unbalanced, and could do something stupid at any time, but their motivation is money. No question. The bastard wants it for himself, though he says it is to fight capitalism. The religious one keeps on saying he's going to save the monastery, when he gets his share.

I've left Arnold to clean up any libels, get permissions from various folks. Once the publisher has got this chapter, he has to pay all the money into a Swiss bank account. I like the idea that I have bought myself out, earning my own freedom, rather than relying on those multi-millionaire conmen, such as Marinello. A lot of fucking good he's been. He's done bugger-all to find us, or pay up the money. Heh, perhaps were are *in* Switzerland. I never thought of that before.

Once they have confirmation that the money has gone through to the Swiss bank, Tom is sure they'll let us go. Do I believe it? Do you believe it? By the time you read this, you'll know what happened. If I got out. Or not.

What the hell's that noise? That's not a bloody gun is it, oh God. I can hear noises outside . . .

VENEZIA

Dear Reader,

I found Joe under the bed, hiding. What a scaredy-cat. It was just the local police, come on a routine investigation. The monastery wine is *appellation contrôlée*, but they had heard rumours that the monks had been watering it with cheap plonk from Morocco, full of chemicals. Which was true. But the two kidnappers didn't know that. They thought it was a real raid, and that they'd been found, so they shot themselves. And we have been released.

And Dear Joe, I just want to say two final things before I fax this. Stop going on about it being all your own work. Could you have written such a brilliant book all on your own, without my help? Oh yes, you soon forget. Who stayed up all night, knocking every chapter into shape, before it was sent? Secondly, Linda and I hope you will be very happy in the rest of your career. Either football or writing. Ta-ra.

TOM

A NOTE ON THE AUTHOR

Hunter Davies is author of the classic book on football, *The Glory Game*, plus thirty other books, including biographies of the Beatles, Wordsworth, George Stephenson, Columbus, as well as novels, travel books and children's fiction. He is also a broadcaster, presenting programmes on BBC Radio 4, and a journalist, known for his profiles in *YOU* magazine and his football column in the *Independent*. He is married to the novelist and biographer Margaret Forster, and they divide their life between London and the Lake District.